RECKLESSLY ROGUE

ROYALS GONE ROGUE

ERIN NICHOLAS

ROYALS GONE ROGUE

The Series

Reluctantly Royal (Torin & Abigail)

Reluctantly Rogue (Jonah & Linnea)

Rags to Royals (Cian & Scarlett)

Recklessly Rogue (Henry & Ruby)

About the Book

I have a hot British bodyguard in my guest room.

Could be worse, I guess. Like...bats in the attic?
Though bats don't rip your panties and ruin you for all
other men.

How did *this* happen?

My sister married the prince he protects, so I now have an
extra room and insisted my friend stay with me when she
left her husband.

Her husband is being a *real* a-hole about that.

**Which made the bodyguard all growly and he moved in
to protect us.**

That sounds nice, I know.

But he's my ex.

And when his best friend married my sister, we agreed to do the mature adult thing: avoid each other for the rest of our lives.

Now he's sleeping down the hall, walking around looking delicious, talking with that panty-melting accent, just... taking care of me.

And giving my friend pep talks, making her little boy airplane-shaped pancakes, and making her jerk ex sorry.

So, I really can't be blamed for what happens in the shower—he should have been quieter if he didn't want company—or against the wall in the kitchen.

But here's the problem: the royals have become the family he never had growing up. He'll never quit. And I've spent the past sixteen years helping my sister raise her daughter. Now's my chance to finally go to law school—which can't happen here in my tiny hometown.

So, we need to help my friend and *nothing more*.

We can't be reckless. Not with where we take our clothes off. Not with our words. And certainly not with our hearts.

Author Note and Content Advisory

I know you have lots and lots and lots of books to choose from and that time is one of your most valuable resources. That you've chosen to spend some of that time on this book means so much to me!

Here's what you can expect besides a heart-warming, fun romance about a wounded, cinnamon roll bodyguard who falls first and hard for a sassy, small-town bartender with big dreams and an even bigger heart:

- Steamy, on-page, open-door sex scenes
- Graphic language
- Discussion of verbal, emotional, and physical abuse by a domestic partner of a secondary character—off page.
- Heroine with some religious trauma.
- A couple of estranged, neglectful, pretty terrible fathers.
- A traumatic parental death—in the past, off page.

If any of that is something you do not want to read, close the book now and return it. No worries! I want you to be happy while reading this book and to have a smile on your face when you close it at The End!

I hope you love Henry and Ruby's love story and the time you spend in this fictional world!

xo

Erin

A Brief History of Cara & the Royal Family

In 1848 Tadhg O'Grady was an Irish sailor accompanying King Frederick VII, of Denmark to the Faroe Islands. Their ship was attacked by pirates, and the ships were sunk. Fifty people perished, but Tadhg rescued three men, including King Frederick.

The King was so grateful that he gave Tadhg the southernmost island where they were pulled to shore.

Tadhg named the island Cara, the Irish word for friend.

The O'Gradys have ruled the small island, that is just a bit bigger than Rhode Island, in the North Atlantic ever since.

The Modern Royal Family

King Diarmuid took the throne when he was 39 and his father died suddenly of a heart attack.

He has ruled for 43 years. But he has now had three heart attacks and is 82 years old.

His son was in line and ready to ascend to the throne but was tragically killed in a car accident 21 years ago, leaving Diarmuid's eldest grandson, Declan, next in line.

But at age 18, Declan abdicated, moved to the US, and cut ties with the family. He has not returned to Cara since. He has built up a multi-billion-dollar company and become a playboy billionaire celebrity of sorts. Americans celebrate the rich as if they're royalty, so he's getting a taste of what he could have had in Cara, but with *far* fewer rules.

At least he's charitable with his money.

Next in line then, is the second grandson, Torin. At age 19, Torin approached the king with a plan to transition the monarchy to a representative government over a 10-year period.

Diarmuid refused.

So Torin followed in his older brother's footsteps, abdicating and leaving Cara for the US. He traveled, studied, and generally enjoyed his life of a royal-in-hiding very much. Eventually, though, his conscience got the better of him and he returned to Cara to take his place on the throne.

Then he learned that the arranged marriage between him and Lady Linnea Olsen the family had always joked about, was not a joke.

So, he got himself another princess. One he was madly in love with.

Which left Linnea free to marry Torin's bodyguard and best

friend, Jonah. Which, obviously, left her unavailable to marry the next prince in line.

Princess Fiona, third in line, and the youngest, their brother Cian, both abdicated as well. They went to the US with Torin and found life as royals-in-hiding to be fun and pressure-free.

Fiona became an animal advocate, rescuing, rehabilitating, and rehoming abused, neglected, and displaced animals. She ran a wildlife park in Florida with her very own tower of giraffes before falling in love and moving to Louisiana. (She'd argue that the move to Louisiana happened before the falling in love, but no one—not even the guy she fell for —really believes that.) The giraffes and her daughter, Princess Saoirse, moved with her, and she now helps run an even larger sanctuary there with the love of her life and his rambunctious, hearts-of-gold found family.

Cian, the youngest, enjoyed ten years of traveling the world, partying, and living life to its fullest. Then he met Her. The One. After a one-night-stand with a woman he believed was a stripper and his soul-mate (he was right about the second, but wrong about the first) he spent two years searching for her. When he found her, he swept her off her feet, and made her a real-life princess.

Which meant he was not interested in marrying either of the remaining Olsen grandchildren, granddaughter Astrid or grandson Alex.

Only one O'Grady prince was left to marry and unite the O'Grady and Olsen families. Oh, and produce the baby that will forever bind the two bloodlines. Which meant he had to convince Astrid somehow that a marriage of convenience was a good idea.

But Declan hasn't been back to Cara in more than fifteen years.

He also doesn't take well to being told what to do.

At all.

And Astrid doesn't think marriage to *anyone* is a good idea. Least of all the broody, bossy, billionaire who is eight years her senior.

So this marriage may not last. And even if it does, they have to be in the same room together at least once for their union to result in a baby, and so far that isn't looking promising...

The Drunken Poker Game That Changed Everything

Twenty-five years ago, Alfred, Diarmuid's best friend, and Diarmuid got very drunk while playing poker one night. As they often did. This night, however, Diarmuid was out of money. You might ask how a king runs out of money. And that is a fair question. That no one has been able to answer and that Diarmuid won't address even to this day.

Because he had nothing left to bid, Diarmuid lost a grandson to Alfred.

Yes, a grandson.

Not even a specific one. Any one of the three will do.

And what does Alfred intend to do with this grandson?

Marry him off to one of Alfred's granddaughters. He has two.

Linnea is the oldest. She's gorgeous, polished, classy, intelligent, and she loves Cara. She's everything a queen should be. Which makes sense since she's been raised to believe she will *be* queen since she was four years old.

Astrid is the younger sister. She's also gorgeous, but where Linnea is accommodating and patient and family-focused, Astrid is headstrong and independent and wants full control of her own life. She isn't interested in chaining herself to another person for life and the idea of being responsible for her family's entire legacy, not to mention the expectations of an entire country, is ridiculous to her.

The entire agreement between Diarmuid and Alfred was written out on the back of a playbill, and the words are smudged by spilled whiskey, but the family lawyer has informed everyone it's still legal and enforceable since the men both signed it in front of witnesses. Of course, that lawyer is also a very good friend of Diarmuid's and owes him money from another poker game. The same is true for the 'witnesses'.

The most important fact, however, is that in Cara, there's no need for lawyers and judges. King Diarmuid is the law. So the "contract" is enforceable in the stupid, archaic way that anything having to do with royal families is enforceable. With much manipulation, a lot of money, a pretty good dose of guilt, and a high tolerance for ridiculousness.

Pronunciation Guide (those Irish names can be tricky)
Cian—pronounced Kee-an
Diarmuid—pronounced Deer-mid

Linnea—pronounced Li Nay uh
Oisin—pronounced Osh-een
Roisin—pronounced Row-sheen
Saoirse—pronounced Sear-sha
Tadhg—pronounced Tige
Torin–pronounced Tore-in

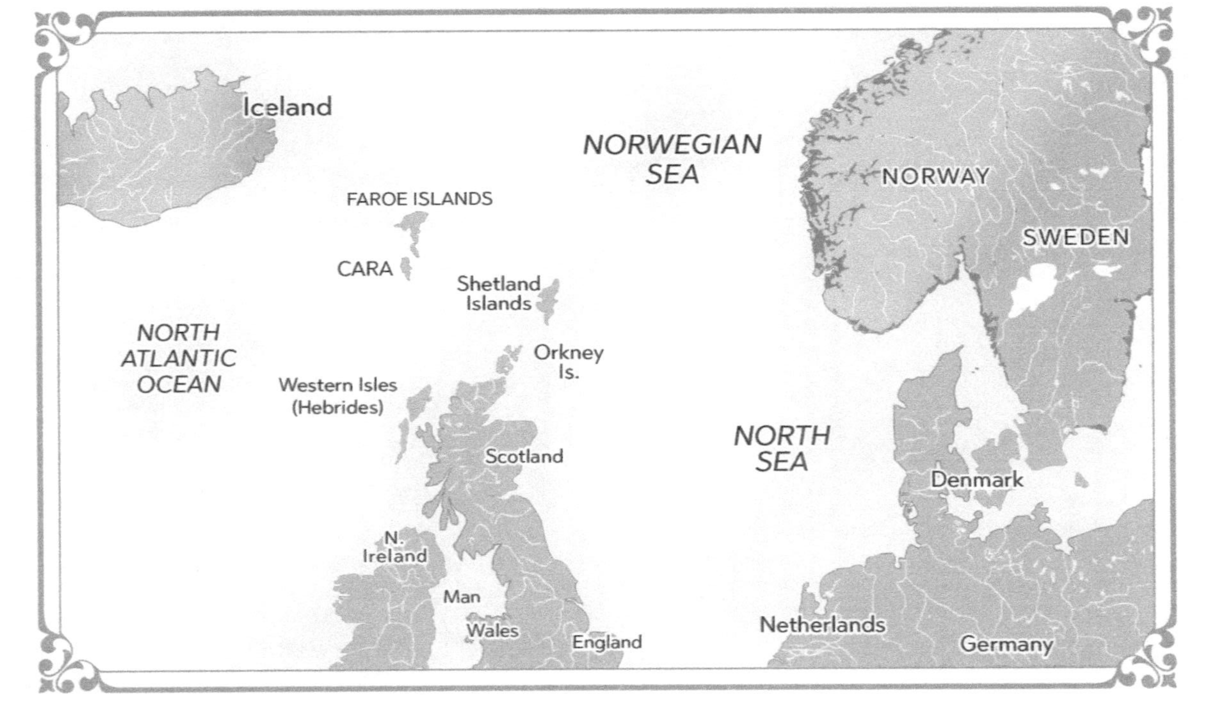

Iceland
NORWEGIAN SEA
NORWAY
SWEDEN
FAROE ISLANDS
CARA
Shetland Islands
NORTH ATLANTIC OCEAN
Orkney Is.
Western Isles (Hebrides)
NORTH SEA
Scotland
Denmark
N. Ireland
Man
Wales
England
Netherlands
Germany

CHAPTER 1
HENRY

"**D**o you take him as your husband?"

I'm standing in front of the king with the gorgeous, feisty, stubborn-as-hell brunette I am madly in love with.

And she is avoiding even looking at me, not to mention speaking to me.

"Ruby," I say softly for her ears only.

She presses her lips together, but she doesn't look at me.

I move closer to her, the sleeve of my suit jacket brushing her bare arm. "Dammit, Ruby."

"Not. Now." The words are soft but still firm. And she's still not looking at me.

"I do," Ruby's sister, Scarlett, replies to the king.

King Diarmuid looks at my best friend and smiles. "Cian, do you promise to love Scarlett with all your heart?"

The prince looks at Scarlett with a smile full of love. "I promise."

"Ruby, we need to talk," I say softly.

I knew she and her sister were on their way to the

palace. Ruby was the one who had called and told me Scarlett needed to get to Cian immediately. I arranged the private plane, for God's sake. Did Ruby really think she was going to avoid me once they got here? She's smarter than that.

Finally, the green eyes of the woman I cannot get over no matter how hard I try—and I have absolutely tried—meet mine. They are flashing with a mix of emotions.

"Stop it," she mouths.

"I'm not going to stop it," I whisper.

She frowns then turns her attention back to the wedding happening ten feet in front of us.

The king makes the rest of the ceremony short and sweet. He has full authority to join couples in marriage in this country and while some prior weddings have been longer and more sentimental, they don't need to be.

"Then I officially declare you husband and wife," the king proclaims. He raises his hand. "Go forth with my blessing."

And that's it. Scarlett and Cian are married.

And Ruby's and my lives are bound together for as long as we both shall live.

We are equally dedicated to these two people and will be running into each other for the rest of *their* lives. At least for the rest of their marriage. But theirs is a true love match. There is no reason to think that we don't have a good sixty years ahead of us to fight this frustrating, amazing chemistry between us.

Unless we stop fighting.

Cian finally releases Scarlett from their kiss, and they turn to beam at the room full of people. It's family and close friends only, but the room is still plenty full. Ruby steps forward and pulls her sister into a hug.

They are identical twins and closer than any two women I've ever met. I don't even have to ask to know that Ruby is feeling the same mix of emotions that I am.

Cian steps toward me and I also pull him into a hug, thunking him on the back three times. "Well done," I tell him, meaning it.

I might have been focused on Ruby through the ceremony, but I'm truly so damned happy for my friend. I've always wanted him fully cared for and Scarlett makes his heart full and whole in a way no one else ever could.

Scarlett Gale is the best decision my best friend has ever made.

And I'm forever grateful to her for choosing him as well.

She has my loyalty and friendship for the rest of her life for how happy she makes Cian.

He pulls back and gives me a huge grin. "Thank you for helping get her here."

I tip my head slightly. "You know I will always be there for her just like I am for you."

They're a package deal now. I'm more than Cian's best friend. I am his bodyguard. His right-hand man truly. And have been for the past twelve years. He was really only a job for about two months before I realized I'd found the best friend I was ever going to have.

We've grown up together in so many ways. He was seventeen and I was twenty when we met, but we were both lost, needing purpose, wanting to experience life, and the world differently than we had in the past. We did that together. We've traveled, studied, made mistakes, had adventures, and had a hell of a good time.

I'm so happy that Scarlett is in his life now. She's so good for him. I couldn't have chosen a better partner for him.

But him finding her, truly falling in love, deciding to spend his life with her, has left me feeling strangely restless. We are entering an entirely new chapter. For over a decade I've been the closest person to Cian O'Grady. I've been his first phone call, the one he asks for advice and for help. I've been the most important person to him.

That's changed.

His happiness has always been my second priority, only behind his safety and health. Yes, there have been occasions where I've had to choose safe and angry off over happy but in danger. But I am no longer the only person in charge of keeping him happy. Scarlett is his number one now.

That's going to take some adjusting to.

I glance over at Ruby. I know she's feeling the same.

She has been that person for Scarlett their entire lives. More than just keeping Scarlett company or being the one she asks for advice or shares secrets with, Ruby helped Scarlett navigate a very toxic relationship with their biological father, and raise Scarlett's daughter, Mariah.

They are incredibly tight. She has to be feeling happiness and love for Cian for making Scarlett so happy, along with a strange sense of loss and restlessness at this change in her life and role.

We're quickly surrounded by more friends and family, and I let Cian and Scarlett get swept into the crowd. But my eyes are on the beautiful brunette in jade green, not the one in white.

And ten minutes later, when Ruby tries to slip away, I follow her.

They've been here for three days. She's been *avoiding me* for three days. With the chaos of the entire O'Grady family here for the first time in years, the eldest brother Declan spontaneously marrying family friend Astrid Olsen, and wedding plans for Cian and Scarlett, along with her and Scarlett's mother flying in, it's been easy for Ruby to come up with excuse after excuse not to see me despite my many texts.

Until now.

I slip through the heavy door before it closes behind her and she's only taken three steps down the main hallway when I wrap my arm around her waist, my other hand covering her mouth. I lift her off her feet, taking us down the short hallway to our left.

I put my mouth to her ear. "We need to talk, Gem." I don't mean to use the nickname. It just slips out.

She doesn't fight me. She doesn't even squirm. She sighs heavily, not seeming surprised that it's me. Or that I'm man-handling her.

I have to uncover her mouth to open the door at the end of the short hallway but she doesn't say a word as I stride inside, kick the door shut, and turn the lock before setting her down.

"Is this the dungeon?" she finally asks once her feet touch the floor.

"Don't be ridiculous. The dungeon is two stories down." I flip the switch next to the door and sconces around the room come on, illuminating the cozy space with a soft, golden glow.

She looks around. The room is an inner, somewhat secret private space. There are no windows and while everyone in the palace is aware of the room, no one actually uses it.

"I would have expected the library to be bigger," she muses, taking in the floor to ceiling bookshelves along three of the walls, the overstuffed armchair and ottoman, the oak side table holding a lamp with a stained-glass lampshade, and the small writing desk just to our left.

"The palace library is much larger," I tell her. "This was the private sitting room of the king's friend and advisor, Oisin O'Connor. He's moved to the United States now, so this room doesn't get much use. But it still stores his private book collection."

She paces a few steps away, runs her fingers over a few book spines, then turns to face me. She crosses her arms. "Okay, so I am locked in a room that no one comes to. I guess you're finally going to get your way and we're going to talk."

"I always get my way." I tuck my hands into the pockets of my trousers. "And we were always going to talk. Things aren't over between us."

Emotions, including sadness, pass over her face. Then she says, "Things *are* over, Henry. They've been over."

"I love you," I say simply.

She sucks in a long breath. It's not surprise. It's frustration. I've told her this and she doesn't want to hear it. Not when we were both in Ohio, not over the phone, not in texts, and, apparently, not here.

"We can be together now," I say. "The things keeping us apart are not an issue now. Cian and Scarlett intend to go back to Emerald." Scarlett doesn't love her tiny hometown, but they've only been there for about a year and a half. Her daughter is a sophomore in high school, and Scarlett doesn't want to make Mariah move and leave her friends again. They'll stay at least until Mariah graduates. Wherever Scarlett is, Ruby will be. And wherever Scarlett is, Cian will be. And wherever Cian is, I will be. It's all working out.

But Ruby shakes her head. "It's not that easy."

I frown. "Of course it is. I had to leave you before. I had

to come and go. You said we couldn't make a relationship work when I had to be somewhere else and could only steal time with you. That's not the case now."

"But...Cian is still your first priority."

"He's my...job." I hesitate over that last word because my job is so much more than that. And Ruby knows that.

She gives me a small smile. "Henry, come on. We have to be honest about what's going on. You love me. I believe you. But you love the O'Grady family more."

My chest tightens. I shake my head. "Not more. Differently."

"But they come first. Cian comes first, and now..." She smiles and sighs softly. "My sister and niece, too, right?"

Yes, but...

"Right?" she presses. "Now that Scarlett and Mariah are princesses, they are a priority to you."

"Yes." I won't lie to her.

"And I love that." She shakes her head with a little laugh. "God, that's even more than I ever hoped for. All these years taking care of them, worrying about them, being there for them, I wished for people just like you guys. People who would *see* them, respect them, support them, lift them up, protect them." She has to stop and swallow. "You and Cian have given them safety and support but even more, you've given them a family, a community, a place to belong unlike either of them have *ever* had. I *love* that for them. But—" She holds up her hand when I open my mouth to respond. "That also bumps me even further down your list of people you can love and things you can take care of."

"Ruby, fuck, that's so unfair." I shove my hand through my hair. None of that is *wrong*, exactly, but it's not that simple, either. This is the first time I've fallen in love with a woman, and I *want* her in every way.

"Yeah, it is unfair," she agrees. "I don't want to take you away from Cian or my sister or niece. But it's unfair that it means *we* can't be together."

I take a step closer to her. "But we *can*."

"No. I mean... yes, I know it seems that way. Obviously, we can be in the same place at the same time now. We can spend time together. You won't be leaving like you have in the past. But..." She shakes her head. "Henry, I have big feelings for you, too, but I deserve more than this."

I scowl. "More than what? More than a man who can *not* get over you? More than a man who thinks about you constantly, a man who wants to make you happy and take care of you?"

She hugs her arms against her stomach, presses her lips together, and then, slowly, painfully, nods. "Yes. I deserve to be someone's number one."

I stare at her.

She watches me.

Several long moments tick by.

Then she says, "I can't be your number one, can I, Henry? If it comes down to me or Cian, it will have to be Cian."

I don't want to answer that question.

Because my answer will mean I lose her.

CHAPTER 2
RUBY

I already know the answer to the question. And I don't really want to hear him say it out loud. But I'm still going to make him say it.

Because *he* needs to say it.

I don't blame him. I'm not angry. I know what his job means to him. I admire it, actually. And I understand that it's one of the things we have in common.

I have been in a similar situation with my sister for the past thirty-six years. Scarlett has always been my number one focus. I've always dropped everything when she's called. I've lost sleep, friends, and money because of my sister. I've failed tests and relationships because of my sister. I've turned down or put off opportunities of my own for her.

And I'd do it all again. And again.

I understand Henry.

I *love* Henry.

But I'm thirty-six years old, and I've lived a life that has been anything but glamorous and privileged. I know this thing with us isn't going to work when his attention, energy, and heart are already spoken for.

He's amazing.

But I deserve more.

"Henry," I say, stepping toward him. "If it comes down to me or Cian, it will have to be Cian. Right?"

He's staring at me, his jaw clenched, his blue eyes dark. But, while Henry Dean is one of the most stubborn men I know, used to getting his way and bossing people—even a prince or two—around, he's honest.

"Right," he finally says. "It will have to be Cian."

"And now Scarlett and Mariah." This part is actually really important to me. It makes it all worth it. I can live without Henry—sadly and with a crack in my heart, sure, but alive—if I know he's there for my sister and niece.

"Yes. And now Scarlett and Mariah," he says, his voice sounding like sandpaper.

They deserve that. Him. All of *this*.

My god, my sister is now an honest-to-God *princess*. Cara is a tiny country that very few people have heard of or could find on a map. If they don't follow women's gymnastics or men's ice hockey, or celebrity royal gossip, they probably haven't heard of it at all. Cara's got a royal family that's been living in secret in the US for about a decade. They've also got an almost Olympic gold medalist and a rising hockey star who are now both living in the US. Brother and sister Alex and Astrid Olsen have helped raise their country's profile for sure. But Cara is still somewhat inconsequential in the overall global picture.

Still, my sister now has a family, security—physical, financial, emotional—and influence. She's going to get to have her dream job, running a foundation that will help single moms. And she's found true freaking love. Prince

Cian O'Grady loves my sister with everything he's got. It's big romantic movie love.

I tear up every time I think about all of this.

My sister deserves all of this. And my niece is set. She can go to college anywhere she wants, study anything she wants, travel the world, live anywhere, do all the amazing things she's dreamed of. Mariah will change the world with the O'Grady family behind her.

I'm so damned lucky to have a front-row seat for that.

So yes, I'm very happy that Henry will be there to take care of them, look after them, help them access everything they now have at their fingertips, and navigate this new world they are a part of.

It's going to make leaving them all so much easier.

"I'm glad," I finally say out loud to Henry. "I'm *glad* you're going to be there for them. I'm not angry. I'm not upset. I just..." I take a breath and meet his gaze. "You and I *have to* find a way to run into each other from time to time, to be friendly, but nothing more."

"No."

I roll my eyes. He's so fucking stubborn. He's four years younger than me, but he acts like he's my superior. It's annoying.

Unless we're in a bedroom.

We are not in a bedroom right now.

Yes, he's had a lot of life experience, but it's all been luxurious and extravagant. He's seen more of the world than I have. Eaten more exotic foods than I have. Experienced a wider variety of cultures than I have.

But I've been in the nitty-gritty of life. I've worked almost exclusively in bars and restaurants. I've put myself through college. I've lived paycheck to paycheck for most of my adult life. I've lived in shit-hole apartments, gone without...well, almost everything at one time or another... helped my sister navigate a pregnancy, the healthcare system, the childcare system, and the workplace all as a single mom.

And I've met people just like me and Scarlett all along the way.

Henry has dined and partied with royalty, politicians, and celebrities.

I know real people. Average people. Hardworking, just-trying-to-make-it people.

There are a lot more of the kind of people I know in the world than the kind of people Henry knows.

So his snooty, bossy, I-know-better attitude doesn't even make me blink. He's more sophisticated and can be demanding and a little intimidating, but he's also full of hot air.

There are definitely things he knows far less well than I do, and when I find one of those things, it delights me.

Right now, I think *I* happen to be one of those things.

Our chemistry is off the charts. I can't hide the fact that I react to him physically and, yes, as hard as I tried to hide it, that I'm in love with him. I wish he didn't know that. I wish *I* didn't know that. I wish it wasn't true. It would make all of this easier.

Because it's not *just* the in-love thing. It's that Henry and I are the same. We love big and hard. Once we love someone, we'll do anything for them.

So, it's incredibly hard to convince him that I can be in love with him and *not* want to be with him.

But he doesn't know that I have plans. Plans that don't involve Scarlett and Mariah. Or him.

He can't even imagine doing something that doesn't

involve Cian, so I know it hasn't occurred to him that I might be thinking of myself for a change.

"Then I'll have to just ignore you for the rest of my life," I tell him.

"No."

"Henry," I say firmly. "We are *not* going to date. Or sleep together. Or spend fun, family time together as if we're old friends."

"No, we're not going to do that last one. We *are* going to date and sleep together." He steps forward. "There's no reason we can't make this work. Yes, Cian is my responsibility. Yes, there are going to be times when I have to put him first. But that will be so much less now. It will mean going for a run with him or having lunch with him. It's Emerald, Ohio. He's going to be settled. Happy. He won't be jetting around the world. He won't be doing stupid things like deep-sea diving." He pauses. "Okay, he might still deep-sea dive. But he won't be...picking fights with men bigger than him in bars in Heppenheim."

I lift a brow.

"Germany," he fills in.

"But he *will* be traveling the country. He and Scarlett are going to be traveling for the Foundation."

"Sure. But those will be quick trips. A day or two. We'll be like any couple who has one partner who travels for work," he insists. He moves in until he's right in front of me. He lifts a hand to cup my cheek. "I'll be coming home. To you."

But see...that's the thing.

He won't.

I sigh and step back, away from his touch.

"The fact remains," I tell him. "I want to be the main character in my story."

He frowns.

"I want to be the number one thing in the life of my partner. Like Scarlett is in Cian's life."

That's kind of a low blow. Henry and Cian are more than friends. They're like brothers. And I know that this change in Cian's life—falling in love, getting married, giving Scarlett his time, attention, and energy—affects his bond with Henry. I know because it's affecting my bond with Scarlett.

But it's a *good* thing. Mostly. I think my jealousy is normal. I'm going to miss a lot of things about not being Scarlett's number one anymore. Yes, Mariah has been her main priority for the last fifteen years, but Mariah has been mine as well. She's really kind-of *our* daughter. There was nothing Scarlett did for her that I didn't do except actually carry her and give birth. Their natural mother-daughter bond is real, but Mariah and I are very, very close.

So yes, at times, I'm jealous that Scarlett is telling Cian her secrets, sharing her worries with him, spending most of her free time with him.

But mostly, I'm thrilled. Because I love her so damned much, and he is everything she deserves.

I know Henry feels all of this on the other side.

That doesn't mean I won't point it all out and make him face it to make my point, though.

"I want what Scarlett and Cian have. I want a guy who is willing to give everything up for me."

"Ruby," Henry says, his expression and tone of voice both pained.

"I don't want to hurt you," I tell him honestly. "I don't want us to hurt each other. That's why we need to agree to just avoid each other except when we absolutely can't. Obviously, there will be times when we have to see each other. But we need to be able to do that as adults. Adults who like and respect one another but who don't want to hurt each other."

He drags in a long breath but doesn't say anything.

"I'm going to be moving out of the house and getting an apartment so that—"

"No."

Here we go with the 'no's again. "Yes," I say simply. "I'm not going to live in the house with my sister and her new husband. And you." I tip my head. "I assume you'll live there with them?" Have they thought this out?

He hesitates. Then says, "Perhaps. Or we'll buy the house next door or across the street for me."

I laugh before I can swallow it. "People already live in those houses. They're not for sale."

"Everything is for sale if you find the right price."

See, this is what I mean. There are no actual barriers in Henry Dean's life. To anything.

Or so he thinks.

"Okay, whatever." This is not my problem. "I'm not going to be living there with them."

"They can buy a new house." He's frowning, but it's not really *at* me now. "You don't have to move out."

"I'm one person. There's three..." I lift a brow. "Maybe four of you. I don't need as much space. Plus, Mariah is settled there. It's not far from school or from Greta's house." Greta is Mariah's best friend and rock. "It's way easier for me to move."

Plus, my apartment won't be in Emerald...

"You're not moving. Brian gave *you* that house."

Brian was our stepdad but really the only father figure Scarlett and I had. We adored him. He died about two years ago and left Scarlett his auto shop and me his house. Both fully paid for with an additional trust to help keep things going for a while. Those two things were the main reason Scarlett had wanted to go back to Emerald after being gone for fifteen years, to see if anything had changed and if she could make some amends.

Nothing has really changed. Well, my sister has. She is more confident, knows who she is and what she wants, and she's happier.

I'm so proud of her. And I'm so excited about her next chapter.

And mine.

"Brian would not care if I gave the house to Scarlett," I tell Henry. "Trust me."

"I don't want you somewhere across town where I—" He abruptly bites off the rest of what he intended to say.

But I know what it is: *Where I can't keep an eye on you.*

He's protective. Overly protective.

Well, he doesn't need to worry about me being across town.

"This is the best solution. Scarlett and Cian can have the house. You and I are going to agree to be friends. And you're going to take excellent care of my sister and niece forever."

"I—"

"Promise that you're going to take excellent care of my sister and niece, Henry," I interrupt. "Promise me that they are as important to you and the O'Gradys as Cian is and that you'll do anything for them."

He frowns. Then nods. "Yes. I promise."

"Then everything is good."

"Except you and me."

"No. We're totally good. We're both doing exactly what we want to do."

"If I don't have you, I'm not doing what I want to do."

Both of my brows arch. "I know you're a spoiled, bossy rich boy, but even you know that sometimes you have to make choices. And you did."

His frown deepens. "And you're not upset at all?"

I shrug. "I'm human. Of course, I wish I could have it all. But this is how it has to be."

"No!" He steps forward again. "Dammit, Ruby, we *can* have it all. My job—okay, my brother—does come first sometimes, and I do promise to take care of your sister and niece, but we *can* be together."

I know I will never meet another man like Henry. I've met a lot of men. Even tried relationships with a few of them. None of them ever understood my relationship with Scarlett, not to mention it being one of the things they admired and loved about me. Not until Henry.

Some of them were jealous and quick to throw a punch at anyone who looked at me too long, but none of them were *protective* like Henry. He doesn't just want to keep me away from other men, he wants me safe in all ways. Physically but also emotionally. He wants me to feel good and strong and confident and fulfilled.

That's why I think, deep down, after he's thought about it for a while, he's going to understand and actually *like* what I'm about to tell him.

"We can't be together in Emerald," I say. "Because I'm moving back to New Orleans."

CHAPTER 3
RUBY

Henry's brows slam together, and he takes a quick breath. Then he puts his palm against the base of my throat and walks me backward until my shoulder blades meet the bookcase. Then he stares down at me, his hand heavy against my collarbones, possessive and commanding. This hold never fails to make me a puddle of lust. A *submissive* puddle of lust.

I know exactly what he's doing.

And it's working.

Be strong. Good lord. You have plans. Good plans. Plans that are more important than what this man can do to your pussy.

Probably.

See? When Henry's close to me, even my very determined inner voice gets a little mixed up. It's a problem, for sure.

"What did you say?" he asks quietly.

I swallow, my throat moving against his hand. "I'm going back to New Orleans. As soon as Cian and Scarlett get back to Emerald."

His blue gaze is sharp and angry. "No."

I nod, the movement restricted by his hold. "Yes. I start school in August. I want to get there, get settled, find a part-time job. Just...be there before I start the program."

That furrow between his brows deepens. "School?"

"Law school."

Just saying those words out loud to someone else gives me a thrill. I haven't told anyone. Not even Scarlett knows. I couldn't tell her. It was too much. There were too many things up in the air. Until about three weeks ago, I didn't think I was going to be able to go at all and yes, it was in large part because of her. I wasn't going to leave her in Emerald all alone. So I hadn't told her. There was no need.

Henry studies me, his gaze bouncing back and forth between my eyes. "You want to go to law school?"

"I'm *going* to law school," I tell him.

His hand is hot against my throat, and tingles race down my body. His body heat seeps into me. He's always so hot. Just hugging him warms me up almost instantly. Sure, some of it is the chemistry between us, but some of it is just that he's a human furnace. He's also hard. And big. And I *love* being pressed between him and firm surfaces. This is certainly not a first.

But it might be the last.

It would be better for my mental health if it were the last. I can't stay on this emotional rollercoaster with him. I need to move on.

Being a thousand miles away from him will help.

Drowning myself in my dream *finally* coming true will also help.

I hope.

"Law school," he repeats. "I didn't know you wanted that."

"I haven't told anyone," I say.

"You got in? It's for sure?"

I nod. "I actually got in two years ago. Right before Brian died."

He moves his hand from the front of my throat to the back of my neck. The slide of his slightly rough palm against my skin makes shivers dance through my body, and my nipples tighten. He continues just to hold me, close enough I can smell his cologne and feel the warmth of his breath against my cheek.

"But you didn't go," he says.

"I couldn't. I had to go to Ohio with Scarlett. I called the program to tell them I was declining the spot, and they told me about deferment. They let me postpone starting for a year. Then, when we were still in Ohio, and it didn't look like anything was going to change, I called them again and tried to withdraw. They said I was such a great candidate, they really wanted me, and would I like just to defer another year. I said yes. And then you and Cian showed up and..." I let out a breath. "Now Scarlett is okay. She's safe and secure. She doesn't need me like she did before. So I can go." I can't help the smile that curves my lips. "Finally."

He's looking at me with what almost looks like wonder. "How did you...how did you get through college? I didn't even know you did that. Does Scarlett know that?"

Henry and I talked about our relationships with Scarlett and Cian, talked about what it was like to help raise Mariah, talked about him helping raise Cian's niece when his sister was a single mom, talked about the places we've both lived and the places he's traveled to. I've filled him in on my childhood, my mom, my biological father, and my stepdad.

But there's plenty we haven't covered yet. His visits to Emerald were always stolen time from his job and weren't long. And, if I'm honest, we spent a lot of our time together naked.

So, he doesn't know about this part of my life. He thinks I've been a stripper and bartender all my adult life. Which is true. It's just that I haven't been *only* that.

"I took my college classes one by one, as I could afford them, over the past fifteen years," I tell him. "I took most of them while we lived in New Orleans. I made the most money there." Bartending and stripping in the French Quarter paid better than any of the bartending or waitressing jobs I'd had prior. "I took them from Loyola because they gave me scholarship help. And that's where I got into law school."

He nods slowly. "Wow."

I smile.

"You're so...amazing." His thumb strokes up and down the side of my neck.

My panties get a little wetter, and I struggle to concentrate on our conversation. I wet my lips. "Thanks."

"Why do you want to be a lawyer?"

That one's easy. "So I can help people. I don't like when people are taken advantage of by people more powerful than they are—big corporations, landlords, bosses, predatory lenders. I want to be more than a cheerleader or someone who can loan someone my car to go talk to legal aid."

"You don't have to go to New Orleans," he says.

"I do." I frown. "I'm in the Loyola program. They've been holding my spot."

"Isn't there a law school at Ohio State?"

Columbus is only twenty minutes from Emerald. I sigh. "Yes. But I haven't applied or been accepted there."

"So you should apply. If you can get in at Loyola, I'll bet you can get in at Ohio State."

That is not necessarily true, of course. But I know what that means coming from Henry. He'll pull strings and get me in at Ohio State if that's what I want.

I shake my head. "I'm going to Loyola."

"That's very far away from Scarlett and Mariah."

"Yes. It is. Which is why I had to wait until you and Cian came along. I'm very grateful to be able to leave them in such good hands."

"You should stay closer."

I put my hands on his chest and push. He takes a step back. "I don't want to stay closer."

"It's still law school. It's still what you want."

"I want Loyola."

"Why?"

"Because I want to see what *I* can do on my own." I blurt it out, but it's the truth. I've *thought* it several times, I've just never said it. I take a breath. "Scarlett's never been on her own without me, but I've never been without her either. I want to see how I do. It's three years. It's not like it has to be forever if I hate it."

"You will hate it," he says.

I frown. "Hey."

"You will. You are one of the most big-hearted, community-oriented people I know."

I like that. But I try not to let it sway me. Or give me doubts. I do like having a community of people I know and like and trust around me. And while I've built that in each place Scarlett and I have lived, my sister and her little girl are the common denominators in my community, the center of it for me.

"I can find that in New Orleans. I'll have classmates,

and I'll have people at work. I still have friends there." But it will be two years since I've been back or even talked to a few of them.

"Stay closer," he says. "Let me take care of you, too." His voice is still rough, but now it sounds more pleading than commanding.

"I want to take care of myself," I tell him.

"You'll be lonely."

I nod. "Maybe. Probably. Sometimes at least. But being lonely isn't bad."

Now, he looks upset and confused. Probably upset to think that I might feel something negative. Henry isn't good when "his" people, the people he's decided he should take care of, whether or not he's been hired to do that, aren't happy and secure.

But I think he's also confused because he truly doesn't understand the statement "being lonely isn't bad". I sincerely doubt he's been lonely for one minute since becoming a part of the O'Grady inner circle. Just from what I've found reading about them online, and listening to the gossip podcast out of Cara, and watching him with Cian, and now with the family over the last few days, the O'Gradys are only alone if they want to be. No one gets *lonely*.

"I don't want you to go."

"Noted."

"But you're still going to."

"Yes."

"So just when I am coming to Emerald to stay, you're going to leave."

I shake my head. This guy...

"I'm not leaving *you*, Henry. This isn't about you. Like I said, all of this was in motion long before I even knew who you were. This has been my plan and dream for a long time and, though ironic, I can actually go pursue it now *because* you're in Emerald."

"I can...come to New Orleans to visit. You'll come back to Emerald too, sometimes. We can—"

I cut him off. "No."

"You won't even try long distance?"

My heart squeezes. I want to be in love. I'm pretty conventional that way. I want a solid, strong, happy relationship.

But Henry Dean isn't a conventional guy. In a lot of very wonderful and interesting ways, sure, but still, definitely not conventional.

"Come with me," I say, knowing it's a huge risk. "Permanently. We can be together in New Orleans. But you have to be all in."

Emotions flicker through his eyes.

"It's not fair of you to ask me that," he says, his voice tight.

"It's a real solution," I say.

"It's not. And you know it. And you're going to make me be the bad guy."

"You could at least think about—"

"Stop it."

He looks legitimately upset.

I let that sink in. He won't leave Cian. I can't stay in Ohio. So...

"Then we need to just be friends," I tell him firmly.

He stares at me for a long, long moment. I feel like I'm holding my breath.

Finally, he shakes his head. "I can't do that."

I deflate. He's going to make this difficult. He's going to

keep trying to persuade me. And I don't know if I have the strength to resist.

I need to get my ass to New Orleans ASAP.

"Henry, I—"

"I'll just ignore you, like you said. Pretend you don't exist. Live my life as if we never met."

My heart drops into my stomach. So he's *not* going to try to persuade me. That's...good. Very good. We'll ignore each other. Treat each other like strangers.

That sounds awful.

But probably for the best.

"Okay."

"And you'll do the same," he says.

It's not a question.

I nod. "Yes. I'll do the same. We'll only spend time together when it's required by our relationships with Scarlett and Cian and Mariah, and then we will talk only as much as is needed, and we won't ask about one another, or contact each other, or..."

"Think about one another," he says as I trail off.

Suddenly, I want to cry. I swallow hard against the lump in my throat and make myself nod. "Right."

He looks at me for another long second. Then he says, "Right." He goes to the door, opens it, then pauses. He doesn't look back when he says, "If you need help finding a place to live in New Orleans, assistance moving, anything like that, let me know."

"That's very nice of you."

"The sooner you're away from Emerald, the better."

Ouch.

I swallow hard. He's right, though. And I'm sure he'll hire people to help get me out of Emerald. He won't do it himself.

"I agree," I tell him.

"Take a right out of this room. You'll find the main hall-way. Take a left to get to the staircase to the upper levels."

I was on my way to my bedroom when he carried me in here.

I definitely don't feel like going back to the party now.

"Thanks," I say softly.

Then he leaves me, shutting the door behind him.

CHAPTER 4

HENRY

I've been a growly asshole for the past two days, since my 'talk' with Ruby—okay my break-up with Ruby—so I'm not surprised that it takes me nearly thirty minutes to find Jonah. I'm also not surprised to find he's not answering my text because he's at a little party that I wasn't invited to. So no one's answering my texts or wanting to hang out. I'm not in a good mood and they're sick of me. I get it.

But I'm still annoyed when I walk past Cian and Scarlett's room and find the doors open and not only Mariah and Saoirse inside the front sitting room but Linnea and Jonah looking very comfortable, as if they've been here for a while.

"Didn't think we'd be welcome across this threshold for a few more days," I say dryly,

"Welcome is a strong word," Cian replies.

My friend has sequestered his new bride in this room for the past forty-eight hours. We've left them alone, of course. Her daughter, Mariah, has been warmly welcomed into the family, and her new cousin, Saoirse, who is only a couple of years younger, has kept her constant company, showing her around the palace and grounds.

Cian and Scarlett haven't been needed for anything, so they've been left alone.

Until now, I guess.

I look around as I cross the room to take the chair near where Cian and Scarlett are sitting. I'm acutely aware of the fact that Ruby is not here.

"I was just filling them in on the trip to Portland to open up the new moms' community there," Linnea says. "And telling them how excited Christian is to have us come to New York and open one. He'd like to sit down and meet. He has some great input on locations."

Linnea, Jonah's new wife and long-time royal advisor, is helping Cian and Scarlett with their new foundation. The foundation funds communities that bring single moms together to live and help each other with childcare, cooking, housework, laundry, and all the other activities of daily living that are made easier when they have people they can trust and depend on.

She discussed a number of plans with me, including a trip to Portland and one to New York. She's already reached out to Cian's brother Declan to help with the new site in Portland and Christian Waite, one of the senators from New York, to get him involved with the one there.

"Of course Waite is interested," Jonah says, his hand moving from the back of the loveseat where he and Linnea are sitting to the back of her neck in a very possessive, almost second-nature gesture.

"*Anyway,*" Linnea says to Cian and Scarlett. "The trips are all planned. I think a couple of interviews would be interesting for you as well, but we can check on those as we go. And I love the idea of talking to the podcast. In fact, I'm going to pitch having Mariah come back after we've gone around the country and opened some of these homes. I'm sure they would love to have a young woman's perspective on this kind of work."

Mariah sits up straighter. "That would be really neat."

Why isn't Ruby here? She'd love to know all the ways they're involving Mariah in the project.

Linnea smiles at her. "You're going to be so great at all of this. As an ambassador for the royal family, but also for all of the wonderful things your mom and Cian are doing."

Mariah looks over at her mom and Cian, almost as if she's stunned.

"As much as you want to do," Cian assures her. "Your call."

Saoirse leans over and nudges Mariah with an elbow. "It gets easier as you go along."

And is Ruby going to be traveling with us? Has she told Scarlett about law school and New Orleans yet? If not, when is she going to? Are they making plans to involve her in the foundation? If so, she needs to tell them that she's not going to be around for that instead of springing it on them after they've planned a whole future with her in it.

I realize I'm scowling when I lean over and ask Cian, "Where is Ruby?"

He looks surprised at the question. "She left. Last night, actually. She texted Scarlett when she landed in Ohio this morning."

She *what*? My frown deepens. "She left?"

"You didn't think she was going to stay with us indefinitely, did you?" Cian asks, smiling.

But his smile dies almost immediately as I continue to scowl. I *know* that she didn't plan to stay indefinitely but I bloody well expected her to keep her ass on this island until we *all* left. Together. So that she isn't back in Emerald alone.

"She wanted to get back," Cian says. "She has a life in Ohio. She had to get back to work. She's got a house. Friends. She can't travel around the US with us."

I shake my head. "Why not? You could support her."

I know that's not her plan, but Cian doesn't know about law school. I know Ruby didn't tell her sister that she plans to leave them for New Orleans while Scarlett is still essentially on her honeymoon.

Hell, Ruby might not have even *seen* Scarlett with the way Cian has kept her to himself for the last two days.

"That's not the issue," Cian says.

"Then what? A bartending job she does only out of necessity in a town where she lives only because Scarlett wanted to move back there? Emerald was never Ruby's plan."

Okay, that was a dickhead thing to say. I mean, it's true. But it's not as if Ruby is upset with Scarlett. In fact, Ruby is sweet and accommodating and patient with her sister almost to a fault. Scarlett has been calling the shots in their relationship for...ever.

Am I annoyed because if Scarlett had just stayed in New Orleans instead of going back to Emerald two years ago to try to make amends with a town that doesn't deserve her we could *all* be living in New Orleans, together, happy and in love?

Yes.

But it's not Scarlett's fault.

Cian glances at Scarlett but she's listening to Linnea and Mariah talk.

He lowers his voice and leans closer to me. "Well, I don't know what to tell you, Henry. She came in and said her goodbyes. I arranged the plane. She texted Scarlett when she got home." He studies me. "I take it she didn't say goodbye to you?"

I blow out a breath. Okay, *that's* why I'm annoyed. "No."

"Maybe that's for the best?" Cian asks.

I grind my back teeth together. But then I nod. "Yeah, maybe."

Just then, Scarlett's phone rings.

"Sorry," she apologizes, pulling the phone from her pocket. She glances at the screen and frowns, then looks at Cian. "It's Ruby."

My heart thuds against my ribs just hearing her name.

"Take it," Cian tells her. "It's fine."

Scarlett stands and takes a few steps away from the group, lifting her phone to her ear.

I can't help but watch her.

It's clear immediately that this isn't just a friendly phone call.

My heart starts beating faster.

"Something's wrong," I tell Cian.

Scarlett comes back over to the couch. "We might have to rearrange our trips a little bit."

"What is it?" I ask, my voice clipped.

"We just need to go back to Ohio. Or I do. Maybe you can go on without me," Scarlett says to Cian.

He frowns. "No way. Why do you have to go back?" He stands. "Is Ruby all right?"

I do too. I need the answer to that question *now*.

"Yes. Kind of. She's...taking someone in."

"What the fuck does that mean?" I demand before Cian can speak.

She looks at both of us, then glances around the room. Everyone is listening.

"You can tell everyone," Cian assures her. "They're all here for you and for Ruby."

What is going on? I nearly shout, but I manage to keep my cool.

I can't yell at one of Cara's princesses.

Who is technically my boss.

Scarlett's shoulders relax a bit at that. "A woman who knows Ruby from the bar has decided to leave her abusive husband and reached out to Ruby for help. Ruby invited her and her young son to come stay at our house until the woman can get her legal stuff in order and figure out a plan."

"No," I say firmly.

Scarlett frowns at me. "She's not asking for permission, Henry. From me or you. She was just informing me."

Too bad. "Why do you need to go home then?" I ask.

Obviously, I'm not going to let Scarlett go to Emerald. She's on her honeymoon. This isn't something Scarlett is going to deal with.

This is something her bodyguard will take care of.

Scarlett shrugs. "I know the guy. We went to high school with him. He's definitely not a good person. I am afraid he's not going to let his wife and son leave peacefully. And I'm afraid he's going to blame Ruby directly."

"So she's not safe," I say.

Goddamn it, Ruby. But, of course, she wouldn't say no to someone asking her for help. Not even this kind of help.

Maybe especially this kind of help.

Scarlett grimaces. "That's what I'm worried about."

"Then I'll go," I say easily.

I'm definitely going. I made that decision the minute I found out Ruby was back in Emerald and Scarlett and Cian were making at least two stops before they went back to Ohio.

"You're going to go to Emerald? And you'll do what? Protect Ruby?" Scarlett asks.

"Yes." Obviously. "I'm trained for this, for fuck's sake. She couldn't have better protection. It makes perfect sense."

"Except that she doesn't want to see you anymore," Scarlett points out.

I see the sisters found time to talk before Cian locked his bride in his suite.

Yeah, well, too fucking bad that she doesn't want to see me. "This isn't about that. She needs to be safe. We both know we're not going to talk her out of doing this. So I need to be there to make sure she's all right."

"But—" Scarlett starts.

"Even if you did go, you will not be as good at protecting her as I will," I say. "And if you and Mariah go home, there are two more people for this asshole to threaten. You, Mariah, and Cian will stay away until we get this woman and her kid settled. I'll be there to be sure they're okay. And Ruby, of course."

There is no other way this is going to go, but I have to make Scarlett feel as if she's a part of this decision.

"It makes sense, Scarlett," Cian says.

She frowns. "What about Cian?" she asks me. "I thought you always had to be with him."

We *are* going to figure this out.

"He's got you now," I say.

Scarlett looks puzzled. "What?"

"You can keep him from doing anything stupid." Thank God. That's part of the job I'm happy to have some help with.

"I..." She looks from me to him, then back to me. "I was thinking more of the keeping him from being assassinated thing."

Thankfully, that's very rarely been a true threat.

"He can't be anywhere safer than here in Cara," I say. "And when you go to the US, Jonah will be with you." I turn to Linnea and Jonah. "Right?" Jonah will be with them because of Linnea. He's been protecting a much more head-strong prince for ten years. Cian is far more easy-going than Torin.

Linnea nods. "Right."

Jonah looks at his wife and then at me, "Yeah. Right." Clearly this hadn't occurred to him before now, but he's rolling with it.

I turn back to Scarlett and Cian. "So he'll have a babysitter and a bodyguard with him."

"Hey," Cian protests.

We all look at him.

After a moment, he shakes his head. "No, never mind. That sounds good."

Exactly.

"I'll call you from Emerald." I don't wait to see if anyone has anything further to say.

It doesn't matter.

There's a sassy, stubborn brunette I need to...talk to.

Yes, we're going to *talk*. I can keep from yelling. I'm pretty sure.

But she left without telling anyone. To go home alone. Then let a woman move in with her who has an abusive husband who is "not a good person" and who will blame Ruby for his wife leaving him.

Okay, I'm going to yell.

But Ruby knows me. She'll be expecting it the second she sees me.

And the fact that my yelling won't faze her a bit will make me want to kiss her. And fuck her against the wall.

I blow out a breath.

This trip to Emerald is such a bad idea.

But am I still going? Of course, I am. I've been Cian O'Grady's bodyguard and best friend for twelve years. Something being a bad idea has never been a deterrent before, so why start now?

CHAPTER 5
HENRY

I am *very* aware that right now, I should be sitting in a bloody *palace*, drinking eighteen-year-old scotch out of crystal tumblers and telling a *prince* that no, he really shouldn't buy his new stepdaughter a teacup pig just because she sent him that adorable video that happened to have a teacup pig in it.

Instead, I had to *text* that to him. Which is not as effective as telling him. And then sitting there and making sure he doesn't start looking up 'how to buy a teacup pig' and 'what do teacup pigs eat' and 'good names for teacup pigs'. Especially that last one. Obviously, Mariah should get to name her own pig.

The odds are that Cian is going to own a teacup pig—okay, more than one, because he never does anything small—by this time tomorrow. And that he won't have noticed the fact about the pigs that says the 'teacup' size can still get to be two hundred pounds.

Which means that I'll be living with a small herd of teacup pigs. All more-than-a-thousand-pounds of them.

And no, I don't look up if a group of pigs is called a herd. But I'm eighty-percent sure it's not.

I *do* send him an article titled "Ten Things About Teacup Pigs That Aren't So Cute" but I know Cian well and figure he'll only read to about item four, so I also send the article to Scarlett.

But that's all I can do. Because instead of preventing my future backyard from turning into a small barnyard *in person*, I'm stalking across this dingy room in small-town Ohio where the beer options are pitiful, and I wouldn't even consider ordering a scotch to tell the guy leaning on the bar that he'd better back the fuck up, or we're going to have a *huge* problem. A much, much bigger problem than figuring out how to house half a dozen not-so-little pigs.

"Come on, Jeff, this isn't something you need to worry about," the beautiful, friendly, small-town bartender—the woman who has made my life *very* complicated—is saying to the guy. "We've all known each other a long time. Just let it go."

"I can't let it go," Jeff says, very stupidly leaning in even closer to her. "He's my *friend*. I have to try to help him."

Ruby plants a hand on her hip and frowns. "No. You don't. This isn't about you at all. And you *know* they have problems. Don't tell me you don't."

"Chris has always been hot-headed," Jeff says. "You know he's a good guy deep down."

She barks out a laugh. "No, I don't know that. April left. It's over. The best thing you can do to help is help *him* get used to that truth."

"Goddammit, Ruby!" Jeff slams his hand down on the bar. "Don't be a bitch about this! You don't want in the middle of this."

Ruby steps closer to the bar and points a finger at him.

"Do *not* raise your voice to me, Jeff Messer! You need to leave." She thrusts her finger at the door.

"I don't have to go anywhere."

"Actually, you do." She points at the sign behind the bar that says the employees have the right to refuse service to anyone. "Don't make me call Danny."

I don't know who Danny is. Maybe he's the local cop. Maybe he's just another friend. It doesn't matter.

I'm here now.

Because of her. This woman whose heart is bigger than her common sense.

This woman who has reminded me daily for the past eight months why I have intentionally resisted falling in love. Until now.

"No need to bother Danny," I say from right behind Jeff. "Jeff's on his way out."

The man swivels on his bar stool quickly. He scowls at me. "Excuse me?"

I'm aware of him. I'm cataloging his body language in case he takes a swing. But my eyes are on the gorgeous brunette behind the bar. She's wearing blue jeans, a sunshine yellow tank top, and several necklaces and bracelets. Her long, dark hair is down, hanging nearly to the middle of her back, and her blue eyes are locked on mine.

Lots of labels go through my mind as I look at her. The two primary ones are *love of my life* and *pain in my ass*.

Then she sighs. "What are you doing here?"

Also, the last person on the planet who wants to see me. Right now. Maybe ever.

"Helping Jeff find the door." I look at Jeff. "Right?"

"I'm not goin' anywhere," he tells me belligerently. "I don't know you. I was talkin' to Ruby."

"You were being an asshole to Ruby, and that's not okay

with me. You can walk to the door, or I'll carry you there. Choose," I tell him.

"You work for Danny?" he asks.

"I don't know who Danny is," I tell him.

"He owns this place."

I just continue to look at him.

"Are you a cop?"

"No."

"You're not from here," he states unnecessarily.

"No."

"Then why should I listen to you?"

"Because I can make you very sorry you didn't."

To his credit, he seems to take that seriously. "This is bullshit." He turns to Ruby. "We'll talk about this later."

I step forward quickly, grab his arm, yank him off the stool, and start for the door. "You will *not* talk to her about this, or anything else, later." I march him to the door, open it, and shove him out into the October night. "You will not come into the bar during *any* of her shifts. You will not stop by her house. You will not approach her at any other business or on the street. You will not call her, text her, send an email, send a letter, postcard, or carrier pigeon. Do I make myself clear?"

He blinks at me. "Carrier pigeon?"

I growl. "Stay the fuck away from her. And tell your friends too. Ruby Gale is off limits. In all ways. Or you'll be talking to *me*. And trust me, you don't want that."

He straightens but starts backing away toward the parking lot. "I suppose you'll beat the shit out of me?"

"Maybe," I agree. "Or I might make you miserable in some other way. Or maybe I'll do both. There are lots of options."

He frowns but then just turns and heads for his truck. I

watch until he's pulled out of the parking lot, and his tail-lights have disappeared.

Then I go back inside.

To confront my biggest problem of all.

The woman I can *not* get over.

The one I'm going to be living with for the foreseeable future.

CHAPTER 6
RUBY

"I thought we agreed to ignore each other for the rest of our lives."

"We did." Henry Dean plants his fine ass on the stool in the middle of the bar, directly across from where I'm standing.

I try very hard not to catalog the way the dark gray button-down shirt pulls across his broad shoulders and thick biceps or how the sleeves rolled up to the elbows reveal the tattoos on his right forearm. Even though he's wearing his usual dress pants and shoes—both in black—he looks hot. Like rich-asshole-CEO hot. He stands out so obviously in the rundown small-town bar that it should be laughable, but if anything, he looks bored. Maybe mildly irritated. Not at all uncomfortable.

I've never seen Henry look uncomfortable, and I can't imagine the situation that would make him feel that way.

And don't even get me started on the accent. He's British, and he sounds even better than Henry Cavill.

It's not fair.

I just saw him yesterday...or maybe it was the day

before—the time difference between here and Cara throws me off—but I still notice that his beard has grown in a little more, and there are dark smudges under his gorgeous blue eyes.

"Then what are you doing here?"

"Emerald is my hometown now, too."

That statement makes my breath lodge in my chest.

Hearing it out loud from him like that makes it *really* real.

I've been trying very hard not to think about Henry at all, because it hurts so much when I do. And it makes me all itchy and jumpy because I don't know when I'm going to see him again. Or how to act when I do.

But I did expect to have notice before he just showed up. I figured Scarlett would let me know when she was coming home. Which would be when Henry would be coming to Emerald, since he's practically a conjoined twin with her new husband.

I clear my throat. "You came back early? Without them?"

"Your sister tells me you have a houseguest."

I sigh. And study the man who, even when he is thousands of miles away with an ocean between us, can make my panties wet. But with only a beat-up slab of wood separating us, I'm tempted to both launch myself into his arms and punch him in the jaw.

Henry Dean is a huge pain in my ass.

Things were pretty good in my life before he showed up.

And really, if I hadn't fallen in love with him, things would be going *great.*

Ignoring him for as long as Scarlett and Cian stay married—yes, fine, forever—was never going to be *easy,* but I figured it would only be select holidays and things like

Mariah's birthday and graduation. Once I leave Emerald, he and I won't run into each other much.

Stomping into my place of employment, inserting himself into a conversation, and throwing a customer out, was definitely not how I pictured things going.

Even if that was pretty hot.

"My houseguest is not in need of butler services," I say. "I have no idea why you would think your presence is required."

He gives me a look that clearly says he doesn't like my attitude or my sass. Too fucking bad.

"Scarlett informed me that your houseguest has a husband who is not very pleased with the fact she's staying with you." He arches a brow and glances toward the door where he just escorted Jeff out into the night. "Jeff confirmed a few things as well."

"No, Chris isn't very happy." I cross my arms. "But I didn't order a bodyguard."

"Perk of being an in-law to the royal family," he says with a shrug.

"Cian sent you?"

"I volunteered."

"You didn't have to do that. I was calling to inform Scarlett, not ask for help. I've known Chris Duncan since high school. He's definitely a jerk and has a terrible temper, but I'm not afraid of him."

"Scarlett was about to get on a plane to come herself. She's on her honeymoon with my best friend. I'm here so that she stays *there*."

I shake my head. Of course, Scarlett was going to come home. She knows Chris, too. Plus, she's probably feeling as weird as I am about this time and distance between us.

My sister and I haven't spent a lot of time apart, literally, since we were conceived. As identical twins, we've always been in each other's personal space. The only time we really had any physical or emotional distance was when she went to live with our biological father in high school. It was a very emotional time for both of us. Time neither of us wants to repeat. Obviously, her being happily married and on her honeymoon is a whole different situation. That doesn't mean that her first instinct to come home and be with me was any different, though.

"If you think I'm going to let you face down some abusive asshole ex of your friend by yourself, you don't know me very well," Henry says.

The problem is, I know Henry very well. We are very much alike.

"I am actually shocked that you can be this far away from Cian without breaking out in hives."

"Who says I don't have hives?" he asks.

Good point. I blow out a breath and focus on his muscular, corded forearm. "They haven't spread to your wrists yet," I comment.

"It's only been a few hours," he says.

Dammit. His self-deprecating humor and self-awareness about how codependent he and Cian are is one of my favorite things about him.

I know that Henry was hired as Cian's bodyguard when Cian abdicated the throne and came to the United States at seventeen. Henry posed as his college roommate and almost literally hasn't left his side in over a decade. They've traveled the world, had numerous adventures—and a few misadventures—and become more like brothers than boss-employee or even friends.

It's not another woman or a romantic relationship I

have to be jealous of. His heart is already spoken for by the Royal family, and specifically Cian O'Grady.

And ironically, it's one of the things I love best about him. I am not interested in breaking him and Cian up.

"So what's the plan here?" I ask him. "You're going to tell Chris to leave us alone? His friends?" I glance toward the door where he escorted Jeff out as well.

"I'm staying until your friend's situation stabilizes."

I frown. "Can you be more specific?"

"Why don't *you* be specific," he tells me, his tone firm yet frustrated. "What's going on? She's staying with you. For how long? What is her plan? What is *your* plan? Let me guess, just whatever this woman needs for as long as she thinks she needs it."

I glance around the bar to be sure that no one needs anything, almost wishing that some of these guys were a little more difficult. But everyone here tonight is a regular, and they've been here long enough to be settled into either the game they're watching on television or their conversation.

"It *just* happened today," I tell him, keeping my voice low. "So no we don't have a whole big elaborate plan. *Yet.* But we will."

"But you're not in a hurry," he says.

I frown. "What does that mean?"

He shakes his head. "You act like I don't know that the reason this woman and her kid are *living* with you, less than seventy-two hours after your sister got married, is because Scarlett now has someone else taking care of her, and you're feeling a little unneeded."

I widen my eyes. I know him very well. And he knows *me* very well. "You act like I don't know that you're only here because the guy *you* take care of now has a new babysitter and *you're* feeling a little unneeded."

He just looks at me for a long moment. But he doesn't argue.

Yeah, not only are we a lot alike, but we both acknowledge it.

"Scarlett told me you went to high school with the asshole husband, but not April. And she's got a little boy who's four."

I nod. "Yes."

"Tell me more."

Fine. He's here. He's not going to leave, I know that. And I *wish* I was madder about seeing him. But I'm not. We're just going to need some rules.

I take a breath. "April moved here a few years ago. She covers the day shift here at the bar. That's how I met her. Chris is ten years older than she is. They were dating, things got a little serious, then she wanted to break it off, but found out she was pregnant. So she agreed to marry him. Their little guy, Elliot, is four. Chris has never been a great husband or father. At first, it was verbal and emotional abuse. Then financial. He's always been very controlling. But more recently, it's become physical. I've only known her for about a year since we moved back, but I've been encouraging her to leave since we met. Chris knows that, and he's been pissed at me. He's come in here and yelled at me a couple of times. But anyway, when I got home today, I got a phone call from her. She was crying and said she was finally ready. So I said come over right now." I shrug. "They're staying at our house. I don't know what else you need to know."

Henry's jaw clenches. "How long is she staying?"

I narrow my eyes and give him the answer I know he's expecting. "As long as she needs to."

"Dammit, Ruby. There needs to be a plan. Is she filing for divorce? Is she wanting to leave town? Does she have any money? Does she have anywhere to go?"

He's almost yelling. I mean, not really. Not by normal standards. But by always-in-control-of-every-damned-thing Henry standards, definitely.

How interesting.

I give him a slow blink I know will drive him nuts. "I've barely seen her. I gave her my keys when I came in tonight, and she was going to pick Elliot up and go straight to my house."

He blows out a breath. "*We* need to go to your house."

I roll my eyes. "I plan to. After I'm done *working*."

It's not like Henry doesn't have a job. I mean, his gig is twenty-four-seven-three-sixty-five. But how he makes a living is *very, very* different from what I—and most of the world—means by "work".

He doesn't say anything to that. Instead, he pulls his phone out, taps in a number and lifts it to his ear.

I lean onto the bar, propping my chin on my hand to watch. I can't help it. He's interesting. And amusing. In an I-want-to-strangle-you-and-fuck-you-so-bad-I-almost-can't-stand-it way.

"Is this Dan?" he asks a moment later.

I frown. Dan? That's the name of the bar owner. My boss.

"This is Henry Dean. I'm a friend of Ruby's. She needs to leave early tonight and I was wondering how much you think you'd typically bring in the rest of the night?"

He pauses, obviously listening to whatever Dan is saying.

I roll my eyes. Seriously, I don't think Henry Dean or Cian O'Grady—or any of the other royals, as far as I can tell —have ever learned the meaning of the word audacity.

But they live it. Out loud.

"Okay, I'm going to double that amount," Henry says a moment later. "If you give me your account information, I'll wire it right now. Then we're going to close the bar down, and I'm going to take Ruby home."

He pauses again, then holds his hand out to me. I lift a brow.

Instead of using his words, he leans in, plucks out the pen I have tucked behind my ear, and writes a number on a napkin.

Oh my God, Dan just gave a total stranger his bank account number over the phone. I'm going to have to have a talk with my boss, the sixty-eight-year-old man who has lived in the same town all his life and lets people run tabs for months at a time. He named the bar Big Dick's when he and his best friend, Kevin, started it. Not because of their names or because of any body parts, but because they both were well-known, well, jerks.

Dan has mellowed, though, in the three years since Kevin died. Not completely, but definitely some.

Still, just handing his banking info out? *Come on, Dan.*

"Thanks, Dan. Sending that in the next five minutes. I'll text you when it's gone through," Henry says.

Is it the accent? I wonder, watching this transpire right before my eyes. The British accent does make him sound... I don't know. Sexy as fuck, to me, but that's probably not what's working on Dan. Maybe posh? Serious? Sophisticated?

The accent is sometimes more obvious than at other times. He can turn it up or down depending on the situation and his mood. I noted that when we first got to know each other. He explained that he often adopts an American accent, as does Cian, and as a bodyguard trying to blend into the background, over the past decade-plus, he's dropped a lot of British words and slang from his vocabulary. Both he and Cian have Americanized their speech.

Once in a while a word or term will sneak in. *Bloody* is common when he's worked up. French fries are chips. And he can *not* call pants pants. They're trousers. He also sometimes calls panties 'knickers' but it always makes me giggle for some reason. It's a funny-sounding word, what can I say?

Henry disconnects the call but then starts swiping over his phone screen. Presumably, transferring some stupid amount of money—though it's a Tuesday night in Emerald, Ohio, and it's already near eleven p.m. It's not like Dan brings in half a million dollars a night and certainly not in the three hours left before we close up—to Dan's account.

"You just always do whatever you want, don't you?" I ask, already knowing the answer.

"I do," Henry confirms without looking up.

He hits a final button, then pivots on his stool. "Last call, guys!" he tells the mostly empty room. "And this final round is on the house since we're closing up early."

Everyone perks up at that, but I frown. "We?"

"I'm going to buy the bar tomorrow," he says, turning back to face me.

I straighten. "*What?*"

"That's just easier than calling Dan and paying him every time I need you to be available. If I'm your boss, I can decide when, and if, you work."

I stare at him. He doesn't say that in a sexy, flirty way. If he'd made that into a hot *when I'm your boss* kind of way, I might have smiled and gone along with it.

As it is, I plant a hand on my hip. "You're insane."

"Actually no. I have a full physical and mental exam every year. Perfectly fit in every way."

That calm tone of voice and the way he watches me with an impossible-to-read expression makes me feel very much like slapping him. Which would not be the most composed, in-control thing to do.

Which infuriates me.

"Let's put aside for a moment that you wanting to control when and if I work is a bright cherry red fucking flag," I say, pretty sure I sound calm-ish. "I need this job. If I don't work, I don't get paid. If I don't get paid, I don't have things like food and electricity."

He rolls his eyes. "Of course, you'll have food and elec-tricity. I'm not going to not pay you."

"Even when I don't work?"

"Yes. How much do you want? I'll just transfer money to your account now, too."

And he would. Cian is the prince with...I have no idea how much money, but *lots* probably covers it. But Henry also has plenty. He's paid well, I'm sure, and he has no expenses. He lives where Cian lives, eats what Cian eats, travels with Cian. I suppose he maybe buys his own clothes —though I don't know that for sure, and he has very expen-sive taste—and, I don't know, toothpaste? But he doesn't really have to worry about things like rent and heating bills.

"Don't be ridiculous," I tell him, moving down the bar to give the ten bar patrons their free final drinks.

I'm grateful for the space and distraction. Henry Dean is too hard to dislike even when he's being a pompous, controlling, bossy ass.

You really like his controlling, bossy ass sometimes.

That inner voice that insists on reminding me about Past Henry is *not* helpful.

Past Henry is the Henry who I met eight months ago, happily flirted with, enthusiastically kissed, greedily fucked, and stupidly fell in love with.

Present Henry is, well, the bane of my existence.

After all the drinks are passed out, I start cleaning up. I guess I'm closing early. It's not like I mind that. I work at the bar because the hours work well for my home-life balance with Scarlett and Mariah, and I'm a good bartender—I've been doing it long enough—and it's pretty low-key. Dan's a rough-around-the-edges guy, but he's easy to work for. And most of the regulars are okay. I grew up here, so I know everyone, or at least know *of* them, and that helps.

Small towns are like that, I guess. Bartending and dancing in New Orleans was different. There were good things about dealing with strangers and new faces every night. People who hadn't known me since the cradle. But there are definite benefits to having a history in town too.

People here know who I am. They know I'm not a bitch unless I need to be, but I'm also not a pushover. They know my friends, and don't really want me to tell the loan officer at the bank they might need to talk to one day, the high school football coach who coaches their kids, or the local contractor they might need to hire, what assholes they are. None of my friends would let that affect how they do their jobs, but it can make relationships tense and people do care about reputations and how people look at them and talk about them in small towns.

Within forty minutes, everyone has finished their drinks and left—which is about thirty minutes longer than Henry seems to think it should have taken them. Henry is picking up their bottles and glasses the second they set them down and wishing them a goodnight while their asses are still in their seats.

No one seems to want to argue with him.

None of them know who he is. Not really. They don't know he's a trained bodyguard or that he's probably got a gun tucked somewhere. He doesn't need them to know that. He's just got this don't-fuck-with-me air about him.

He moves behind the bar with the final empty bottles, dumping them in the bin, then grabbing a rag without a word and heading out into the main room to wipe down tables.

At least he's helping me clean up.

He actually seems at ease tipping chairs upside down on tables and even grabbing a broom, and I wonder about his life. He's so obviously comfortable in suits and drinking expensive liquor and looked completely at ease in the *palace* in Cara. But here tonight, he's as comfortable sitting in this bar as any of the small-town guys I know.

I finish balancing the register and pull off my apron, tucking it in the laundry basket with the dirty towels.

When I turn, he's right there. In my space, close enough I can feel his body heat and smell his cologne. Something that reminds me of a library full of old books and leather chairs. I'm sure it's expensive. I used to think that I liked the smell of just regular guys. Outdoorsy smells like pine or sandalwood or some shit like that.

But no.

Expensive scents like freaking jasmine or musk or bourbon or whatever the hell Henry Dean smells like makes my pussy clench, and my nipples tighten, and dammit…he hasn't even touched me.

But I remember every time he *has*.

Because Henry Dean's touch is never accidental or casual. At least not with me.

And it's very freaking memorable.

"Here's another," he says, holding up a towel.

His voice is husky and I feel like my gaze is actually caught on his. I can't look away.

"Ruby."

The word rolls over me.

"Huh?"

"Gem…"

Oh, fuck. That nickname does me in. Short for 'gemstone', taken of course, from Ruby, he started calling me that after he kissed me that first time. He only uses it when we're alone, close, intimate. When he also says things like I'm precious, priceless, his treasure.

"Dammit, Henry," I mutter, as I grip the front of his shirt and pull him down, pressing my lips to his.

His hand cups the back of my head, his fingers gripping my hair, holding me in place as he immediately deepens the kiss.

His tongue boldly strokes mine as he tips my head, allowing a fuller fit of our mouths.

I moan, and he walks me back until my ass hits the counter behind me.

Then he presses into me.

And so much for ignoring each other.

CHAPTER 7
HENRY

Well...so much for ignoring each other.

I kiss Ruby like I haven't kissed a woman in years.

No, I kiss Ruby, as if I'll never get enough of *her*. Which I'm beginning to fear is the truth.

How this woman, a small-town girl from Ohio that has mostly worked as a bartender and stripper, is the one who got under my skin and made me rethink everything I've been so sure of in my life is beyond me. I haven't wanted to fall in love. And I certainly didn't fall in love with Ruby Gale on purpose. But now that it's happened, I have absolutely no idea how to get out of it.

I lift my head, my fingers still tangled in her hair so that I can hold her still as I stare into her gorgeous face.

I know every detail of this face. Every swirl of blue in her eyes, the two freckles at the corner of her left eye, the sweet bow to her lips, the exact shade of pink the tip of her nose turns after I kiss her the way I just did.

I toss the bar towel I came back here to discard, then rest my hand on her hip.

"I'm going to be staying at your house," I tell her. She needs to know that simply because it's a fact. But also because, obviously, we have a hard time keeping our hands off one another.

Her eyes widen as what I said sinks in.

Then, as expected, she flattens her hands on my chest and pushes me away.

"What? No. You can stay at the bed and breakfast."

That's where Cian and I stayed when we came back for Cian to win Scarlett over.

But in my previous visits to Emerald, I stayed at Ruby's. In her room. In her bed.

"I'm staying at your house," I repeat. "I'm here to protect you and your friend from her husband. I can't do that if I'm not right there."

"You're overreacting," she tells me, taking a step to the side and sliding out from the small space between me and the counter.

"I don't care. This isn't up for negotiation."

"It's my private property," she tells me. "You can't just move yourself in there if I say no."

"And how do you think you're going to prevent it?" I ask.

She takes a breath, preparing to respond, but then thinks about the question. And frowns when she realizes she doesn't have an answer.

Exactly. She can't physically throw me out. She can't change the locks. I'll pick them. She won't call the cops on me. I'd find a way around that anyway. And she cannot emotionally manipulate me. I'm too stubborn, and being there to protect her is more important than her feelings about it.

I give her a slow smile. "I will stalk you. I'll break into

your house in the middle of the night. I'll follow you everywhere you go. Just try to get rid of me, Gem."

I see the quick breath she takes at my use of the nickname. It comes out so easily when we're alone.

Then she crosses her arms and presses her lips together as she studies me.

Her phone starts ringing before she decides on what to say. Which is probably for the best. For both of us.

She pulls it from her back pocket. Neither of us ever lets calls go without at least checking who's calling.

She frowns. "It's April." She lifts the phone to her ear. "Hey," she greets. Then her eyes widen and she starts toward the back room. "We'll be right there. Don't open the door and do *not* go outside."

I don't know what's going on exactly, but I hear the change in Ruby's voice, and I immediately prepare to leave the bar. I shut the lights off, make sure everything important is shut off behind the bar, and meet Ruby at the front door, my keys in my hand.

"Chris is at my house. He's banging on the front door and yelling." She's got her bag and her keys in hand as well.

I push the door open and she steps outside. "Should I call the cops?" she asks.

"No need. They won't get there before I do," I tell her. I start toward the car I rented.

I turn back when I realize she stopped walking.

"Is that a *Porsche*?" she asks.

I grin. "They didn't have any Jaguars for rent." I'm going to be buying something soon since we're going to be here long-term now, but I needed a car tonight.

"You rented a regular car last time," she says, staring at the silver beauty.

"We were hiding out last time. Trying to stay under the

radar." We've been doing that for years. I'm anticipating not needing to do that anymore.

Her eyes finally come to my face. "And that's over now?"

I shrug. "Everyone knows who we are now. I might as well like the car I'm driving."

She opens her mouth to reply, then shuts it and shakes her head. "Right. Of course." She starts for her blue Honda Accord, muttering something I can't hear.

"Hey," I call after her.

"What?"

"Wait a few minutes before following me. I want to get there well ahead of you."

"But...why?"

"I need to deal with Chris."

"And you don't want a witness?"

I roll my eyes. "I don't want you getting in the middle of it."

"You think I'll try to defend Chris?" she asks.

"I don't want to risk him trying to grab you or something," I tell her. "Just hang back."

She sighs. "I'm not afraid of Chris."

"Well, you probably should be."

I know Ruby and Scarlett have been on their own for a very long time. I can only assume that Ruby has had to deal with men at the strip club and bar who were aggressive or just assholes—drunk or not. I actually don't want to know if they ever had to defend themselves at any of their homes. I'm not sure I want to know.

She frowns. "Henry—"

"Don't make me handcuff you to a chair in the bar until this is over," I say.

Her frown deepens, then her mouth drops open. Probably when she realizes I'm not fucking around.

"*Henry*."

I cross my arms.

"You can't just *handle* all of this *for* me."

"Of course I can." She's ridiculous, and not thinking clearly, if she thinks I'm not going to do exactly that.

"But...what about..."

"What about what, Ruby?" I ask, a bit exasperated. "I need to get to your house where your *friend* and her little boy are being harassed."

She presses her lips together and nods. "Fine. Go. But I'll be behind you."

"*Several minutes*," I tell her firmly.

She sighs, but says, "Yes, *several minutes* behind you."

"And don't make any stops on your way home."

"Where would I stop?"

"Ruby," I say. "Can you, please, just say 'yes, sir'?"

I can see her eye roll even from several feet away in the shadowy parking lot.

"No, actually I can't."

I don't smile. I just say, "I'll settle for a 'fine'."

She blows out a breath and gives me a soft, almost inaudible, "Fine."

Good enough. For now.

I have a feeling we're going to be having this conversation, or something much like it, again, so I get in my car and pull onto the highway to make the short drive into the tiny town of Emerald. I pull into Ruby's driveway a few minutes later.

Sure enough, a man is pacing back and forth across the porch. He's in blue jeans and a flannel jacket with work boots and has a cap on.

The porch light is on, but it's not enough light for me to

tell anything about a weapon other than he's not holding anything in his hands.

I get out and slam the door hard.

He comes to the top of the steps, where he stands with his feet braced apart, his hands on his hips.

"Who the fuck are you?" he asks as I approach across the grass.

"I'm the guy who's going to tell you *one* time nicely to leave. Then I'm the guy who's going to *make you* leave if you don't."

He gives a short laugh. "Sure, I'll leave. As soon as my *wife and kid* come out here and go with me."

I stop at the bottom of the steps. I take a quick inventory. Chris is shorter and wider than Jeff, but it looks like his width is muscular and not from too many burgers and pints.

He looks angry, but he also looks tired. I don't think he's been drinking.

"That's not going to happen," I inform him.

"That is not for *you* to say."

"Oh, but it is," I tell him in a tone that I know is very condescending and will likely infuriate him.

"Are you fucking her?"

I lift a brow. "April? No. I haven't even met her. But she's here because of Ruby. And that makes it my business."

"You're fucking Ruby," he says bluntly.

I haven't in a while, and that's starting to wear on me, I'm not going to lie. "That's none of your business," I tell him. "But you're trespassing and harassing our guests. You need to leave."

"They're my *wife and kid*!" he shouts. "You don't get to tell me what I can or can't do."

"I do while you're standing on this private property," I

tell him firmly. "And *April* does when it has to do with her. She can leave you whenever she wants to."

"The fuck she can!"

"You need to lower your voice," I tell him, keeping my voice calm.

"You can call the cops. We're friends."

Of course, they are. "I don't need to call the cops."

"I'm not leaving without my wife."

"Yes, you are. By yourself or with my help. Your choice. You have to the count of ten."

He scoffs. "You think you can physically remove me?"

"I absolutely do." I step up on the first step. "But I won't need to. I can make you absolutely miserable without ever laying a finger on you." I take another step up. "I know how much you owe on all of your credit cards. I know which porn sites you visit and how often. I know everything in your personnel file. I know about the DUI that your friend, the cop, covered up for you." I take another step up. "Trust me when I say that I can make any of those into a problem if I choose to. There are a lot more miserable things than a broken nose or jaw. Things that don't heal as quickly. Not that broken bones don't really suck too."

Now I'm only three steps down from where he's standing.

He's staring at me with worry now rather than anger. "How do you know all of that?"

"I have resources that you can't imagine," I tell him. "Which is why you're going to leave right now. And you are *not* going to come back. April is going to stay here as long as it takes for her to figure out what she wants to do." I take one more step up. "You are not going to harass her here, or at work, or in public. You're going to leave her alone."

"She's my *wife*," he says one more time.

I nod. "And if you'd treated her as such instead of being an abusive asshole, she might want to stay with you, but you fucked up, Chris. Now be a man and face the fact that this is all your own fault."

"Oh, I see," he says, taking a step back. "She said I hurt her?"

"Yes."

"And you believe her?"

"I do."

"It never occurred to you that she might be lying?"

"No."

He shakes his head. "The guy never gets the benefit of the doubt, right?"

"No." I narrow my eyes. "If she wants to get away from you enough to lie, then she still really wants to get away from you."

"Fuck this," he spits. He steps around me. "I'm leaving."

"And staying away," I say, watching him stomp down the steps.

He doesn't answer.

Ruby pulls into the driveway just then. She gets out quickly, standing in the open door of her car. Which is the opposite of what I told her to do. I roll my eyes. Of course it is.

She's watching him go. "Ruby," I say. "Come on."

She slams the door of her car and hurries up to the porch, pulling the strap of her purse up on her shoulder. "What happened?" she asks, breathlessly.

"I told him to leave and not come back," I say, grabbing her purse and digging inside for her keys.

"And?"

"And he won't come back," I say. I mostly believe that. I

think he believed me when I said I have a lot of ways of making his life very miserable.

That doesn't mean he's going to go away entirely or sit quietly by while April works through what she wants to do.

Which means, I'm going to have to push this. Make it happen as quickly as possible.

I won't have Ruby in any kind of danger. Even if it's just the danger of some guy bad-mouthing her, being a creep while she walks down Main Street, or sending his asshole friends to harass her at the bar.

None of that is going to happen.

Her keys are not in her purse, so I slide my hand into the front pocket of her jeans.

"Hey," she protests, but her voice is breathless.

I pull the keys out, and she says, "oh," softly.

I wish I could linger over that reaction. This situation is extremely frustrating.

I shove the key into the lock and push the door open. "Where does Chris work?"

"He's an insurance agent."

"I know that. Where is his office?"

"How do you know that?"

"It's a long flight from Cara to Ohio," I remind her, nudging her across the threshold and stepping into the house behind her. I shut the door and lock it, engaging the deadbolt as well.

"You read about Chris on the flight?"

"Among other things," I say. I also faced the fact that I was going to be living in small-town Ohio for the foreseeable future. "I got a bunch of information from your sister and then did my research on him and April."

Ruby kicks her shoes off and shrugs out of her jacket.

"His office is downtown. The tall building across from the coffee shop."

I know the building. I spent a lot of time in this town and patronized all of the businesses at one time or another during the time Cian was here winning Scarlett over. I got to know the layout of the town, got to know the names and faces behind the businesses. Which means Chris is an associate, not an owner of the insurance company.

So he works mostly out of an office. He'll be easy to keep track of. I'm going to need to get a couple of extra guys here. That or someone Chris works with on my side. I need to know what the guy is doing and saying until April and her little boy are safe and stable somewhere he can't easily get to them.

I'll also have to put in a call to Iris. So far, I've not told my boss that I'm in Ohio. She might understand why. Maybe. Cian will always be Iris's first priority. She'll also expect him to be mine. But now that he is more settled, and his future is at least partially mapped out with Scarlett and their foundation, surely Iris will ease up on how much of my constant attention Cian needs.

Still, she won't like that I just took off to come to Ruby's aid. That was reckless and very unlike me.

The only times I'm truly impulsive are when I'm following Cian on one of his adventures, and hell, that's my job.

Ruby is just my...obsession.

Okay, Iris probably won't understand, or like, this.

I follow Ruby into the living room. I take in the scattered toys, and a half-filled popcorn bowl. But April and Elliot are nowhere to be seen.

"What is all of this?" Ruby asks.

The plastic and cardboard that had encased the toys are

lying on the floor in a neat pile in front of the stone fireplace.

"I had some things sent over."

She turns to face me. "Things? You sent toys over?"

"Toys. A few books. Some bedding. I also had dinner delivered. And a few things for April."

Ruby stares at me as if she's never seen me before. "What kind of things for April?"

She almost looks jealous. Interesting. "Just some self-care things. Bath salts, lotion. A bottle of wine. Though I'm not sure what she drinks. I went with a sweet white. Some new pajamas."

Ruby's mouth falls open now. "*Pajamas*? You're a stranger to her. Why would you do all of that?"

"I'm assuming she assumes it's all from you," I say.

"But..." Ruby frowns. "Why? You don't think she has pajamas?"

"I have no idea what her frame of mind was when she left home. In any case, I wanted her and Elliot to feel comforted and welcome here on a scary night that is probably full of second-guessing and stress. At least, as if it was a fun stay away from home. But it's a subliminal message that this is a fresh start that is going to be easy and full of good things." I lift a brow at her continued look of puzzlement. "I've been around women and kids, Ruby. And I knew you were busy. So I just had some things sent over. It's not a big deal."

She crosses her arms. "Have you dated a single mom?" She looks like she's just now considering the women in my past. And as if she doesn't like it at all.

"I *lived with* a single mom and her daughter," I remind her.

Her frown pulls tighter. "You *did*?"

I can't fight the small smile that tugs my lips up. I like her jealous. I won't deny it. "Fiona and Saoirse," I say.

She knows that I lived with Cian and his sister and her daughter. And Fiona's bodyguard. And their brother Torin and his bodyguard, long before Torin was crown prince of Cara.

Understanding dawns on Ruby's face and she nods. "Oh, right. Of course."

She breathes out, and I wonder if she's relieved.

Then she frowns again. "Only them?"

We haven't discussed our past relationships. We haven't actually spent a lot of time together one-on-one. And when we have been alone, a lot of our conversations have been focused on present day situations. Her sister and niece. Cian and Cara. My job. Her living in Emerald and being estranged from her father who is the pastor at the megachurch just outside of town. That's a whole can of worms that took up plenty of time.

And then there was the time we spent together *not* talking.

"Fiona is the only single mom I've ever lived with," I confirm.

Ruby props a hand on her hip.

"I haven't dated a single mom either," I add. That would have been far too complicated. I've had enough extra family to consider with the O'Gradys. "But I have dated women who liked to be pampered," I say with a shrug. "And I know kids like new toys and pizza."

That wasn't a huge stretch, though I haven't been around many little boys. I *was* a little boy, though, and lived with two princes and three bodyguards. While our "bachelor pad" had expensive espresso machines, high thread count sheets, and a housekeeper when we lived in Florida, boys still like their toys, gross jokes, and junk food even when they're in their late twenties.

Ruby takes a step towards me, and it almost seems subconscious. "It *is* kind of a big deal. You're a man. A stranger to them. But you did all of that to make their first night more comfortable?"

"I want April to feel that leaving was a good decision. She's got to be scared. I'm sure she's second-guessing everything. Maybe a bubble bath and some flannel pajamas will at least make her feel like she can relax tonight and that there are good things ahead."

Ruby studies me with a tiny furrow between her brows. "So you understanding women and kids isn't a shock. But how do you know what a woman leaving her husband or a kid leaving his dad is feeling?" She has a thoughtful look now as if it's occurring to her that something deeper might be going on here.

I shake my head. "I don't. I haven't been in that exact situation myself. But I have been alone in a new place, by myself, wondering about my choices."

I haven't told Ruby about my childhood, my mom, what happened with my brother, or my relationship with my father. I'm not keeping it from her. We just haven't gotten to that yet. Not that I'm eager to tell her, exactly. It's not a happy story.

"And did new flannel pajamas make that situation better?" she finally asks.

I just lift one shoulder. "I don't know. I didn't have new flannel pajamas there." I pause. Most of what I remember of being sent off to boarding school, dropped off by no one but our driver, was the gray cloudy sky, the gray stone walls of my private room, and how bloody cold everything was, literally and metaphorically. "But I'd had them one

Christmas when I was younger. And I know when I finally got to a place where I was with people who wanted me and wanted to help me, it kind of felt like new flannel pajamas."

The O'Gradys are definitely like soft, very colorful flannel pajamas. They are comforting and warm, and they never fail to make me smile.

I wonder how the king would feel about that metaphor.

He'd probably love it.

Ruby just stands there not responding for a long moment. Then she says, "I didn't think about having anything here for them. April's been taking care of herself and Elliot for a long time. She's had Chris around, but he hasn't been a lot of help, so I just told her to make herself at home and that she was welcome to anything in any cabinet or closet."

I nod. "Because you're used to women being able to take even the shittiest situation and make it better. It never occurred to you that she might need some bath salts because you and Scarlett never did." I blow out a breath. "I wasn't assuming that she couldn't handle it."

Ruby steps toward me again. "I didn't think that's what you meant. And the thing is, maybe Scarlett and I didn't *need* bath salts or flannel pajamas. But there were lots of nights that they still would've been really nice. We didn't know what we were missing."

My chest feels tight. I hate the idea that this woman spent so many years having to be tough. I recognize that all of that has made her into the woman that I respect and love, but I still resent the fact that her life hasn't been easy. And it's fucking hard as hell to squelch the nearly constant urge I feel to make her life easy now.

Did I possibly project that in part onto April? Maybe. It is just a fact that I have the resources to make things better for the people around me, and when I know that someone needs something, it's ridiculous for me not to provide it.

Before either of us can say anything more, there are footsteps on the staircase.

"Ruby," a soft voice says.

We both turn.

April is slender and pale, with long blond hair that hangs in a thin braid over her shoulder and looks like she could easily pass for seventeen or eighteen, but the little boy hugging her leg has dark hair, big, brown eyes, and has a round face with chubby cheeks.

He looks like his father.

Ruby's expression lightens. "Hi, guys."

"We were upstairs. It was a little quieter up there," April says carefully.

"We were playing games on my mom's tablet," Elliot tells me.

I assume April took her son upstairs to get away from the commotion Chris was causing at the front door. Or at least as far away as they could get.

"Definitely quieter up there," Ruby agrees. "That's where I take my tablet to play on and read too."

Elliot nods. "Did you hear that man? He was so mad."

I glance at April. She's giving Ruby a look.

Okay, so Elliot doesn't know the man banging on the front door was his dad. That's probably good.

"I did," Ruby said. "He was at the wrong house and Henry helped explain that and told him where he was supposed to be instead."

That's one way to describe what I did, I suppose. I nod when Elliot looks at me.

"You did?" he asks.

I tuck my hands into my pockets and rock back on my

heels, working on looking at ease. "Yep. He's gone now, and he won't be back." I need the kid to understand he's safe here from all the loud, angry men, father or not.

"That's good," Elliot says. Then he descends the steps and comes to stand in front of me. "Want to see the new toys Ruby sent me?"

"I really do," I tell him.

He takes my hand, startling me, and I look up at his mom. But April is just watching us with a mix of relief and obvious fatigue.

She says to Ruby, "You really didn't have to do *all* of this for us. The toys and pajamas and pizza. It was too much."

Ruby shoots me a look. I just wink at her as Elliot leads me into the living room. Taking care of people is never too much. Someday, Ruby will understand that.

I settle at the coffee table with Elliot and he starts explaining how he and his mom got to Ruby's house and found all the packages on the front porch with their names on them.

I grin. I love that I was able to surprise them. I had to pay the shopper from Columbus a ridiculous amount to make out gift tags, go to so many stores, and then come all the way over to Emerald, but it had to be done.

I look around the living room, feeling a familiar sense of comfort being here. Ruby inherited the house from her stepfather, and the classic two-story farmhouse style boasts walnut woodwork throughout, including real wood floors on the first floor. But I'm guessing Ruby and her sister and niece are responsible for the buttery yellow color of the walls.

I take in the multicolored throw pillows, blankets on the blue sofa, and matching armchairs that are so different from the carefully coordinated color schemes in the palace and that the professional decorator gave to the house we remodeled in Autre, Louisiana, when we moved there. Ruby's bedroom is similar. The duvet on the bed is pink, her pillows are green, and her sheets are blue. Not because she's chaotic or just loves bursts of colors, but because she simply buys whatever she needs at the moment, likely on sale, without thought to things like color coordinating or aesthetics.

I'd be willing to bet very good money that all of the furniture in this room was Brian's and left over, or is hand-me-down, or was bought from friends or people in town at garage sales.

Ruby and Scarlett don't do excess. They don't do extravagant. They don't do over-the-top.

Marrying a prince is by far the most over-the-top thing Scarlett Gale has ever done or will ever do and I know it's going to take her a long time to fully adjust to her new lifestyle.

Leaving her sister and niece to pursue a law degree in another state is as extravagant as Ruby Gale will ever get.

And that shouldn't be something that's extreme in someone's life.

The urge to kidnap her and force her to let me take care of her gets stronger every time I'm with her, I swear.

I listen to Elliot happily babble about the toys, pleased that he's so excited.

"I got *planes*." Elliot moves around the coffee table and pushes the LEGO airplanes he put together earlier toward me.

"I *love* planes," I tell him honestly.

I'm very happy to see the toys. I ordered them, but I haven't *seen* them. I love LEGOs, especially airplane sets. Cian doesn't like all the instructions and steps that go into sets like this and prefers to just dive in and start sticking things together, which never works, of course. There's a reason step one comes before step two. Jonah, Saoirse, and Fiona don't like to sit that long. Torin will do them with me sometimes but I'm usually on my own with building sets, puzzles, and things like that.

When Scarlett told me Elliot was into planes and rockets and not into sports or many "outdoorsy" activities, I took a chance on quieter things like coloring books and age-appropriate LEGOs.

"Wow, these look great," I tell him of the three planes he's put together on the coffee table.

Elliot giggles. I like hearing that. He doesn't seem withdrawn or scared, at least at this moment. I assume he knows Ruby at least well enough to be comfortable staying in her house, and I'm apparently acceptable because I'm with her.

Elliot goes to another box and starts to open it but April protests from the living room doorway. "Oh, not another one tonight, buddy. It's bedtime."

She looks exhausted.

I jump in before Elliot can protest. I yawn and stretch. "I'm *so* tired," I tell him. "Ruby is, too."

We both look at her, and she also fakes a big yawn. "*Really* tired," she says.

He looks so disappointed.

"But," I tell him. "I'm going to need help in the morning. Like early. I'm making..." I glance at April and Ruby, then lean in to share a "secret" with Elliot. "Pancakes," I whisper. "But I can't do it alone."

He looks at me with a puzzled frown. "My mom makes pancakes alone."

I nod. "Because she's a mom. Moms are amazing. But I

need help when I do it. Do you think you could be my helper?"

He nods. "Yeah. For sure."

"Okay, so we have to get a lot of sleep so we do a good job."

He jumps to his feet. "Okay!" He runs to his mom. "Come on!" He takes her hand and starts up the stairs.

April looks at me with surprise.

"April, this is Henry," Ruby says quickly. "He's a friend. He's also a—" Ruby pauses, then spells, "B-o-d-y-g-u-a-r-d."

April's eyes widen. "Really?"

"Really," I tell her. "And I'm going to be staying here with you all until everything is settled."

It's clear she's not sure what to say to that.

"He's good at what he does," Ruby says. "This is probably the best solution for now. We'll talk about a plan tomorrow."

"By the way, you don't have work tomorrow," I tell April. I'll get a hold of Dan before the bar is set to open and buy it outright. Then I'll hang up a CLOSED sign on the front door, and that will take care of both of my main issues —keeping April and Elliot away from Chris until we can get them set up out of town and keeping Ruby by my side.

"Wait." April pauses. "What do you mean?"

Ruby jumps in, hands on April's shoulders, turning her and nudging her up the stairs again. "That's all going to be fine. I'll talk to him. You don't need to worry about it."

"But Charles..."

"I know."

"And Mandy and Ada."

"I know." Ruby nudges her again.

"And the—"

"April, I *promise* it will be okay. I've got it. But you need to relax and you don't need to get up early. Just sleep late, have a day off with Elliot, and let me and Henry take care of things."

I like the sound of us taking care of things as a team. But I'm taking care of Ruby right now too.

I can't see them now from where I'm sitting on the floor by the coffee table, but it sounds like April has stopped at the top of the staircase, and Ruby is still at the base.

"But the money..." April says, either trailing off or finishing quietly enough that I can't hear.

"Henry will make sure you don't miss any money."

Damn right.

"How?" April asks.

"He's got even more money than he does, good looks, and audacity."

I roll my eyes. But I can easily cover April and Ruby's salaries for a couple of weeks until we can get her divorced and relocated.

April laughs softly. "This is a little crazy."

"Yes," Ruby agrees. "But good crazy. I promise."

I'm glad to hear her say that. Being stuck under the same roof for even a day will make it very hard to keep our feelings in check, and this will take longer than one day, even with my people pulling strings. But the less Ruby fights me on, the easier this will all be.

Finally, April gives a soft laugh and says, "Thank you. Seriously. Dinner tonight, the new pajamas. You thought of everything, Ruby. You didn't have to do any of that, but I started crying when I saw the way you worked to make us feel welcome here. You're a very good friend."

Ruby clears her throat. "I know that you are completely capable, and you don't actually need help. You are an amazing mom and a kick-ass woman, and you can handle whatever comes your way. But—" She glances at me, then back up the steps. "We're here for you. Whatever you need. If it's just dinner, that's fine. If it's something bigger, that's fine too. We'll do whatever we can."

I love this gorgeous, stubborn pain in my ass. She's not doing this to take credit, she's doing it to make everyone comfortable. And we feel like a team. I know that she means what she says when she tells April that we'll do whatever we can to help. And I know she would've done that even if I hadn't shown up. But I love that she's going to let me help. At least that she's going to let me help *April*. I have a feeling getting her to let me take care of her won't be quite as easy.

Maybe I should buy her some new pajamas and LEGOs.

CHAPTER 8
RUBY

I follow April and Elliot up the stairs to be sure they have everything they need.

And to give myself a few minutes outside of Henry Dean's gravitational pull.

Lord. Of course, Henry has thought of everything. More than everything.

The guy is even harder to resist now. How the fuck did that happen? He barged in here—well into my *job*, first—taking over everything and being bossy and grumpy and I *should* be annoyed. But no. He also had to buy my friend who just left her husband *flannel pajamas* and her son toy airplanes. Not to mention handling Chris. I could have if I had to, but of course, it's nicer that I don't. I'm not an idiot.

So yeah, this is all going to be a huge problem for me. Henry and I are under the same roof now for the foreseeable future. And it's not a huge roof.

We have a three-bedroom house with one bathroom upstairs. There's a half-bath on the first floor, and we've got a shower in the basement, but we all use the one upstairs. That's the main bathroom. And it's not like our bedrooms are in separate wings, like at the palace. Our doors are a few feet apart.

It's just the right size for me, Scarlett, and Mariah.

Even when Henry stayed here in the past. Because he was in my room with me.

That can't happen now. I'm not over him. I won't even pretend that I am. But I have to *try* to keep from getting closer. And making it harder to leave.

"You guys need anything?" I ask from the doorway of Scarlett's room.

Elliot crawls up on the bed and April gives me a tired smile. "I don't think so. I can worry about everything else tomorrow."

The sheets on the bed in Scarlett's room where I've put April and Elliot have little colorful airplanes all over them. This is clearly part of what Henry had sent over for them. How did he know that Elliot likes airplanes? Was it just a lucky guess? Or do all little boys at age four like airplanes? In any case, Elliot is excited to show them to me and it does help to get him into bed and under the covers to read a book—also obviously sent tonight with everything else— with his mom. He snuggles up next to April, and I slip out of the room.

I hesitate in the hallway.

The unoccupied room is Mariah's, but it feels weird to me to put Henry in there. Mariah is a teenage girl. Who knows what she's got lying around or stuffed in drawers? Not that Henry would snoop, but I should at least get Mariah's permission. She loves Henry. She'll probably say yes. But...

Fine. I want him in my room.

I don't know why. Maybe so it will smell like him after he leaves? Maybe because it might drive him a little nuts while he's here? That room is full of memories—very hot, dirty memories—of us.

It's probably a little of both.

I'm so screwed here.

I'm an adult—we both are—so I should probably go downstairs and talk about the sleeping arrangements with him.

Instead, I pull out my phone and text him.

You're sleeping in my room. I'll be in Mariah's room. Goodnight.

He answers almost immediately. I should just ignore that. I told him how it's going to be. This is my house. I didn't even invite him to stay. So, he should just do this the way I say.

I read the message.

Don't be ridiculous.

I don't really know what that's supposed to mean. *You want the couch? Go for it. Pillows and blankets are in the hall closet. GOODNIGHT.*

There. Capital letters. That should do it.

I wait.

I shift my weight. I scratch an itch on my shoulder. I bite my lip. I start to text him more but then delete it. I check that my message went through. It did.

So he's just not going to respond?

Okay, good.

That means he got the message. And is going to do things my way.

Right?

I almost laugh. Henry Dean doesn't do things anyone's way but his.

Well, that may not be true. The king probably gives him directions.

But Henry pretty much always gets his way. He can probably charm and sweet-talk King Diarmuid too. Wouldn't surprise me a bit.

I frown. Wait. Does this mean he wants to sleep on the couch?

And why do I feel a twinge of disappointment that he's not fighting me harder on this?

I should be grateful. Resisting him is nearly impossible —fine, so far it's been impossible because I have not successfully done it yet—so if he just lets it go, I'm in much better shape.

Still, this is very unlike him.

The guy flew seven hours across most of an ocean because he thought I needed protection. The guy kissed me in the bar like he was starving for me.

Because of the creaky floorboards, I tiptoe to the top of the staircase and listen carefully.

He's moving around down there. I'm sure he's checking the locks on all the doors and windows.

It's funny how when Henry is in the house, I'm less diligent about those things myself. That's always a part of my before-bed routine.

I hear paper rustling, and I creep partway down the stairs so I can lean over and look through the banister. He's cleaning up the living room, gathering the plastic, boxes, and paper that wrapped Elliot's new toys.

I sigh. He's cleaning up my house. Why can't he be a slob? Or inconsiderate? Or terrible with kids?

He's a bossy asshole sometimes, but, unfortunately for me, that makes me hot.

I listen as he makes his way across the room and into the kitchen. The back door opens, then closes and I know he's going out to the trash receptacle. I wait but he doesn't come right back in.

He's probably checking the perimeter of my yard for threats.

My nipples tingle and my traitorous pussy clenches.

I'm not used to being protected.

I think my mom and Brian worried about me. I know Scarlett does. A few friends here and there did too. But no one's actively, physically, *protected* me.

That's usually my job. I give people what resources they need—at least what I can—and I'll get in someone's face if needed. But I'm obviously not as confident, nor as effective, as Henry.

He's over the top. He has been since the first time I met him, even when he thought I was Scarlett and the woman who had a hot weekend fling with his best friend and broke his heart. But, if I'm being honest, I like his extremes.

It's nice to have someone care that much.

He's probably going to set up cameras, or hell, some booby traps or something around my property.

And I should find that ridiculous.

Instead, I'm hot and tingly.

When I hear him come back in, I scoot up the stairs quickly.

He can sleep on the couch. Fine. Whatever.

He can also sleep in my room. His choice. He knows his way around the house. And even if he didn't, he's the type to just make himself comfortable wherever he is.

But I am sleeping in Mariah's room. And I'm going to push a dresser in front of the door. Not to keep him out, but to keep myself *in*.

I head for my room first though. I need to get some of my things out of there and need to do it before he's in there.

Pajamas, a book because there's no way I'm going to be able to fall asleep right away, one of my pillows, my hairbrush, and body lotion. I pause beside my bedside table. Where my vibrators reside.

Yeah. I am probably going to need one of those. Damn him anyway.

Of course, even when he's thousands of miles away in another country and I think I'm not going to see him again for months, I'm still using these things and thinking of him.

Of course, I'm going to be using one when he's *in* my house. And just kissed the hell out of me.

And was amazing to my scared friend.

And was amazing to her little boy.

And has been amazing to every person I've ever seen him interact with.

Except for Chris. Which was amazing in its own way.

With a sigh, I yank the drawer open and grab my favorite little pink friend.

I step out into the hallway, turn left to go to Mariah's room, and run directly into a hard, very good-smelling chest.

My book slides out of my arms and my vibrator drops right on top of it.

We both look down. Then up, our gazes colliding.

"I'm not sleeping on the couch," Henry tells me.

"Fine. Your call." I bend, grab my vibrator and book, and try to step past him.

He steps in my way.

"What do you think you're doing?"

"Going to bed."

"Not with that."

I hug everything closer to my chest. "I like my pillows

way better than Mariah's. Hers are too flat." I know he's not talking about my pillow

He reaches out and plucks the vibrator out of my fingers. He holds it up.

My body immediately flushes hot. We've used that exact vibrator together, in the room just behind me, and my body reacts like he's turned it on and touched it to my clit.

"You're not taking this."

"If you need one, there are more in the drawer." My attempt to sound bored and unaffected fails spectacularly as my voice comes out breathless.

"I do like that purple one," he says, his voice low and husky.

Fuck, we had fun with that one.

"Just be sure you clean it up after." I try to grab the pink one back, but it holds it up, out of reach.

He leans in, our noses only a couple of inches apart, his breath hot on my lips. "You are not going to be in the next room with just a wall between us, getting yourself off with a vibrator, thinking about me, Gem."

My pussy clenches hard. "Fine," I manage somehow. "I'll think about Taylor Zakhar Perez. No problem at all." The actor has dark hair, dark eyes, and medium brown skin, smiles a lot, and has no British accent. In other words, he's not like Henry at all.

Henry's eyes narrow, but one corner of his mouth tips up. "I'm not worried." He reaches up and strokes the tip of the vibrator down my cheek to my lips, then over my bottom lip. "I know very well that you think of me whenever anything is between these gorgeous thighs." He presses the vibrator more firmly against my lip and I catch my breath. "Up against your sweet clit." My lips part and he slides the tip of the vibrator just inside my mouth. "Inside your tight, hot pussy."

Then he withdraws it and tucks it into his pocket. I give a little gasp of indignation.

"No orgasms that I'm not giving you while I'm under the same roof. You want to come, you come to me."

Now I narrow my eyes. "Absolutely not. That is *not* ignoring each other."

"You blew the idea of me ignoring you when you got involved with April and Chris."

We're keeping our voices low so that we don't disturb April and Elliot but the husky whispering makes me think of all the nights we were in bed together. The dirty talk. The sweet talk.

I frown at him. "Now that you know the situation, you know I had to get involved."

He gives a single nod. "And you know that once *I* understood the situation, I had to come and make sure *you* were okay."

"You're not going to be able to keep doing that," I say softly.

His gaze is intent as his eyes lock on mine. "Yes. I will."

A ribbon of heat and need snakes through me and it's not simply the usual I-want-you craving. It's also the desire to be taken care of that way. To have someone drop everything and just show up. Someone who will take away some of the stress and worry.

But I can't get used to that.

He's not coming with me to New Orleans and even if he thinks he can just show up whenever he thinks I might need him, he's not Batman. He won't know every time I could use a hand, every night I'm just a little lonely, every single situation where a hundred dollars could make all the difference. There will be *lots* of all of those. But I'll be over a thousand miles away. He won't be able to get to me within minutes. Regardless of what he thinks, he can't just snap his fingers and make everything better.

He's making the choice to stay here with Cian and there's no doubt in my mind—or probably his—that I'll find more people to take care of and more situations to get mixed up in. Fighting "the bad guys" is what's drawing me to law school. Trying to even the playing field a bit, making things fairer between the 'haves' and the 'have nots' is my mission.

And there are a lot of 'have-nots'.

I lift my chin. "You can take all of my toys and make all the declarations you want to. I still have fingers, you know."

Heat flares in his eyes and he leans even closer. "Yes. You do. And I have a hand. I guess turnabout is fair play, then. And I'll be in your bed, won't I, Gem? Surrounded by your scent. In the sheets where I fucked you over and over. With a drawer full of your pretty little knickers *right there*."

My eyes widen. Clearly, he's promising to jerk off *with my panties in my bed*. I don't smile at his use of 'knickers' this time. I'm concentrating too hard on not begging him to take me right here against the wall.

"Henry—" I start, but he takes my hand and lifts it to his mouth.

He slides the index and middle finger of my right hand into his mouth. He runs his tongue along my middle digit, making me moan. Then he sucks. Then lets me go.

Yes. The fingers he just wet are the ones I would have to use. As he knows. I'm right-handed. And those are the ones I used when he made me give myself an orgasm while he propped up between my thighs and watched.

God, that was so hot.

And yes, I've replayed it in my mind many times since then. While having my fingers between my legs in the bed where he'll be sleeping.

Damn him.

"Don't cry my name too loud," he says, his smirk saying he knows everything I'm thinking. "Wouldn't want to wake up our guests."

Then he steps around me, goes into my bedroom, and shuts the door.

With my vibrator still in his pocket.

But as the air cools my wet fingers and I pad the few feet to Mariah's room, I'm not focusing on my tingling nerve endings or my racing heart rate. I just keep hearing Henry's words in my head—*our guests*.

As if this is his house. As if this is all his responsibility too.

And dammit, it feels that way.

And I really like it.

He's already made all this easier. Oh, not on my hormones. Or my heart. But now that I've seen April and Elliot in person, and witnessed Chris reacting to their situation, I realize that I'm glad Henry is here.

I close Mariah's bedroom door and try to push the dresser in front of it.

It's too heavy, of course, but I do push her futon in front of it at least. It won't stop me, but it will at least slow me down if I decide to go climb in bed with Henry in the middle of the night.

CHAPTER 9
HENRY

The house is still quiet when I step into the kitchen through the back door after my run the next morning.

Good. I'm glad they're not awake yet. Last night was a lot and April and Elliot need the sleep.

I didn't expect to see Ruby. She's a night owl and a late sleeper.

She'd told me once that she and Scarlett made perfect co-parents because Scarlett was a morning person while Ruby didn't mind doing midnight or even two a.m. feedings when Mariah was a baby. Her bar and strip club jobs had always worked great for them raising Scarlett's daughter together.

I scrub a hand over my face as I head to the fridge for water. I should still be sleeping. But I'd had a fitful night in Ruby's bed, surrounded by all of her stuff and her scent. Then I got up to go for a run despite sleeping like shit and jet lag. I will never get used to the time change between the States and Cara, but I know the sooner I resume a normal schedule, the better off I'll be.

I take three long gulps of water.

I've had sleepless nights because of Ruby before. Some because we'd been up all night, naked in each other's arms. Some because we were apart and I was missing her with an ache I couldn't relieve no matter what I'd done. The ache hadn't just been in my dick, but deep in my chest. Hell, in my bones.

But none of those nights had been as bad as last night.

She was right next door. I was in her bed. My heart—and yes, my dick—were wondering what the fuck we were doing apart.

Not falling further in love. Getting over each other. Moving on.

Right. We are *not* sleeping together and falling further in love, on purpose.

It's a good plan, everything considered.

I peruse the contents of Ruby's fridge, grabbing milk, eggs, and bacon before nudging the door shut.

It's just after seven and I need a shower, but I want to get the pancakes started before Elliot comes down. I don't want him to think I forgot.

As I open packages, measure ingredients, and crack eggs I think about what I'm really doing here.

Twenty-four hours ago I was in Cara, preparing for a trip to the US with a prince and his new princess. I was looking at the layouts of the penthouse suites in expensive hotels, thinking about how many cars we'd need for each trip, exchanging messages with the security teams for the VIP guests who would be at each site to bring out the media and raise awareness.

Now I'm making pancakes for a little boy in small-town Ohio.

And I have no regrets.

Well, except for missing the lobster at DaVinci's in Portland. The chef there is amazing.

But there's no way Ruby really believed that I wouldn't show up when I found out about April and Elliot.

Maybe she thought she could just walk away and ignore me, but she forgot that neither of us can ever *really* walk away and ignore problems around us.

We have a lot in common. And right now we have Elliot to take care of. Together.

I'm going to figure out a plan for the kid and his mom today. We're going to put things in motion. I'm not going to tolerate Elliot being scared and hiding out from his own father. That's bullshit.

I gather flour, baking powder, sugar, and salt and start combining everything in a bowl. If Ruby has a problem with me rummaging in her kitchen and helping myself to bowls, spoons, griddles, and food, we're both in for a long next few weeks. Because this is nothing compared to how involved I'm going to be in everything she's got going on.

She's going to argue with me. Protest. Push back. But it won't matter.

She's feisty, but she's not stupid. She'll understand that I'm right. About everything.

And my focus will be on Elliot to start. She'll see that, and there will be no way for her to fight me on the things we need to do for that little boy. She won't want to.

I'm going to fix things for Elliot. And April. But April is an adult whose choices have to be respected, even if they suck. Elliot is a kid and he's at the mercy of the adults around him.

But I'm one of those adults and I'm going to make *extremely* good choices.

I whip the ingredients in the bowl hard with the whisk I

pulled from Ruby's very messy middle drawer full of utensils.

I know how it feels to dread seeing your own father and I'm going to do everything I can to change that for Elliot. I was powerless to change my own situation but I'm not powerless anymore. I know what it's like to have someone come in and fix your shitty reality. The relief, the weight that lifts, the happiness when you learn that your father doesn't get to write all the rules, and that other people can care even more than your own flesh and blood.

I'm going to be sure Elliot knows those feelings too. He's a lot younger than I was, but that only means he has more years of happiness and security to look forward to.

I'm going to get Elliot and April somewhere safe where Chris can't bother them. Ever again. Then I'm going to make sure they are secure and set up for ongoing success.

Then I'm going to do the same for Ruby. With or without her knowledge. Or permission.

But, until everyone's awake, I'll make pancakes.

Twenty minutes later I have bacon, scrambled eggs, and airplane-shaped pancakes in casserole pans, keeping warm in the oven. I saved some batter so that Elliot can help make a few pancakes too. I told him he could be my helper and I meant it.

If I tell him something is going to happen, it will. If I tell him I'm going to do something, I'll do it. Airplane pancakes are just the start.

Since the house is still quiet, I head upstairs for a quick shower.

I pass the closed bedroom doors, grabbing a towel out of the hall closet. I'm in and out of the bathroom in less than ten minutes, deciding there's no need to shave today.

But the bedroom doors are still shut when I pass them again and there's no noise behind them at all.

Okay, maybe I'll have to have a pancake or two by myself.

I return to the kitchen and make coffee. I've only taken one sip and dug the syrup out of the pantry when my phone rings.

I check the screen.

It's Ruby.

I frown. What the hell?

"Hey, Gem."

"Hey, can you bring those rolls down soon? They're getting restless."

I pull the phone away from my ear and look at the screen. Yes, it's Ruby. "Did you mean to call me?" I ask her. Then another thought occurs to me. "Are you upstairs?" Did she dial me in her sleep or something?

"Henry," she says with a sigh. "Of course I meant to call you. No, I'm not upstairs. I need those cinnamon rolls. Like right now."

"Cinnamon rolls? What cinnamon rolls?" I look around the kitchen. Then I frown again. "What do you mean you're not upstairs?"

"Wow, you are a *great* bodyguard," she says dryly. "We left forty-five minutes ago."

While I was running. I'm off the stool and stomping to the front window. Sure enough, her car is gone.

So is the car I assumed was April's.

Ruby said *we* left forty-five minutes ago. What the *fuck*?

"Is April with you?" I ask.

"Yes. Actually, *I'm* here with *her*. I heard her get up and I couldn't come down here instead of her because I don't know how to operate the stupid espresso machine either, but I assumed that you wouldn't want them to come down here alone."

"You have Elliot with you too?"

"Of course. We weren't going to leave him at the house alone. And *you* weren't there."

"I was just out for a run. You could have waited."

"We couldn't. They were all calling both of our phones!"

"Who was?"

"*All* of them."

"Who is—"

"Just a minute, Ben! I'm coming!" she calls to someone.

I frown. Who the hell is Ben? "Where the hell are you?" I head for the stairs, taking them two at a time.

"The bar."

I stop outside her bedroom where my boots are. "The bar? Big Dick's?"

"Of course Big Dick's!" she snaps. "Just a *second*, Will. If you want your milk frothed, you'll have to wait for April. I only do cold flat milk!"

I scowl. "The bar I own and told you not to go to today?"

She sighs heavily. "Yes."

"That bar is not open today." I grab my boots and shove one foot into the first one.

"Well, the thing is, you can't buy a business at midnight and then not *tell* anyone that is used to showing up at said business at seven a.m. that there's been a change in management and hours," she says.

I hear a bang behind her, then a hissing sound.

"There are people there?" I ask. "Bloody hell! It's seven-thirty in the morning!"

"It's seven forty-eight in the morning and yes, there are

people here!" she snaps. "And they're annoyed they had to wait forty-five minutes past their usual time for coffee and breakfast. *Please* bring the rolls down here."

I stomp back down the stairs. "I don't know what fucking rolls you're talking about. I—"

The doorbell rings.

"I'll see you soon," Ruby says in my ear. "Hurry up."

Then she hangs up.

I stare at my phone.

She hung up on me. *What* is going on?

The doorbell rings again. Then there's a knock.

I'll admit, I open the door with trepidation. I don't like not knowing what's going on. I'm always the one in charge. I call the shots. I make the plans. This all feels very out of my control, and that makes me wary. And grumpy.

I brace myself, then swing the door open anyway.

Three women are standing on Ruby's front porch.

"Good morning, Henry," the white woman in the middle says. She has blond hair with gray streaks, a friendly smile, and a plate of cinnamon rolls.

"Um. Good morning, ladies."

"I'm Mandy. I have the cinnamon rolls." She's in blue jeans, a pink T-shirt, and a long light blue cardigan.

"Well, I guess that's good. Ruby mentioned I was supposed to have rolls. Maybe you can tell me what they're for."

"For Dick's." Mandy hands me the plate. "April and Ruby need them."

I take the plate. "Yes, so I gathered. Is there a reason you're bringing them here instead of taking them to the bar?" I'm happy to take them. I'm definitely heading to the bar. But I'm very curious about what's going on.

"Oh, I can't take them to the bar," Mandy says. "Will's there. He might see me."

"Who's Will?"

"My husband."

Okay. "Your husband is at the *bar*? This early in the day?" I look down at the plate. These look amazing. The plate is slightly warm, the icing is thick and is melting just a bit, sliding down the sides of huge, fluffy, golden-brown rolls, and I can smell the buttery cinnamon scent even through the plastic wrap covering the plate.

"He goes to Dick's every morning at seven for coffee and breakfast."

"To the *bar*?" I clarify. "That seems...odd, doesn't it?"

"It's where their friends are. They can sit around and watch TV, bitch about politics and the weather, play their games, and stay out of our way," the Black woman to Mandy's left adds. "I'm Ada. My husband Ben is there too. And if those rolls don't show up soon, he might come home, so you need to move it." She's wearing a purple pant suit, a multi-colored silk scarf, and her long dark hair falls in braids nearly to her waist. Multiple gold bangles jingle at her wrists.

"But it's a bar," I say again. Though why do I care?

Because if these guys are there, Ruby has to be there. And April. That's really the only reason. If these men need a place to go and everyone has decided that should be a run-down bar on the edge of town, that's none of my business. As long as it doesn't get in the way of *my* plans.

"It's a building that has everything they need," the taller white woman behind Mandy and Ada says. Her silvery hair is cut in a bob and she's wearing gray linen trousers, and a baggy gray sweatshirt that says A Woman Without A Man Is Like A Fish Without A Bicycle.

"You need to get moving," Mandy says, pointing at the plate. "Don't want those to get too cold. They need to think April baked them in the kitchen at the bar."

"It's that big of a deal they don't find out they're from you?"

"It's good for them to know someone other than their wives can do things for them," Mandy says.

"If they're not going to learn to do things for themselves," the woman at the back says with an eye roll.

"We've tried, Cecelia," Ada says. "You know that. Ben can do everything *but* bake." She looks up at me. "How a man who taught college physics for forty years can't figure out how to make a fucking chocolate chip cookie is beyond me."

"But April doesn't actually make cinnamon rolls?" I ask.

"Oh, for God's sake," Mandy says. "That girl has way too much going on to worry about baking rolls every damned morning."

"We're happy to do it," Ada adds. "Having her keep track of them for us while we get work done is worth it, believe me."

"You make cinnamon rolls too?" I ask Ada.

"Oh, no, Mandy does the cinnamon rolls and all the muffins. I do the caramel pecan rolls and the apple crumble bars."

I look at Cecelia. She holds up her hands. "I'm widowed. None of them are mine, so I don't have anyone in husband daycare."

I snort before I can swallow it. "Husband daycare?"

"Basically." She shrugs. "April makes sure they stay busy at Dick's, that they eat, take their meds, and she watches for signs of low blood sugar and high blood pressure. And she keeps Charles from wandering. She's defi-nitely babysitting. But they love it."

"And it lets Mandy get her painting and reading done," Ada says. Her smile is fond as she looks at her friend. "She retired two years ago and finally has a chance to paint. She's amazing. But when Will is there, he's loud and in the way. He plays the piano and the violin."

Mandy nods. "And Ada is still working. She's busy from eight until three and Ben's a huge distraction."

"I can do whatever I want," Cecelia says with a shrug. "But I still support the husband daycare with monetary donations toward coffee supplies and puzzles and shit because I like having my friends free for lunch and book club."

I feel myself smiling. "I understand."

Mandy narrows her eyes and points a finger at me. "You better. Because you can *not* shut the bar down like you tried to today. It has to stay open. April needs the job and those guys need a place to go."

"So do Holly and the girls," Ada says.

"And the kids," Cecelia adds.

I sigh. Shit. "I didn't know about all of this," I tell them. "I'll...work something out. But, April needs...something else."

Ada frowns. "Why?"

"Some things are going on." I don't know how much to tell these women. They seem to know April fairly well, but her personal life isn't mine to discuss. Besides, the fewer people who know about my plans for April, the more secure she'll be.

"That job is extremely good for her," Cecelia says. "You need to leave her there."

"You could raise her wage though," Ada says.

"And she'll need a health plan now that she's getting rid of Chris."

"You know about that?" I ask.

"Of course," Mandy says. "And we know that you paid Dan a million bucks for the bar."

"Which is outrageous," Cecelia adds.

"So you obviously can afford to pay both April and Ruby more *with benefits*," Ada says.

"And add a couple more streaming channels," Mandy says. "Will would love the channel with all the murder documentaries."

I could definitely pay both women more and add benefits but neither of them will be working at Dick's much longer. I'm smart enough not to get into that with these women right now, though. I simply nod. "Which channel is that?"

"You'll have to ask him. But you should get them a bigger TV too," she says.

"Maybe I'll add surround sound and some heated recliners," I say dryly.

Ada and Mandy's faces both light up. "That would be *amazing*," Mandy says.

I narrow my eyes. I think both of these women are bright enough to catch my sarcasm and are choosing to miss it on purpose.

"Maybe I should just get April a better job than waitressing at a bar," I say, one eyebrow arching. Jonah calls this my British Asshole look, but I can't stop it. "Surely you agree she can do more."

All three women plant a hand on their hips in a seemingly synchronized motion and my instinctive reaction is "oh crap". My British Asshole look drops.

"She is more than a waitress," Mandy tells me. "I'm sure

on the surface, that's how it seems, but she is a very sweet, loving girl who finds a lot of happiness in taking care of others. I've told her that when her life settles down a little, she should consider being a teacher or a social worker or something. She is so good with everyone who comes in there."

Ada nods. "She is so patient with Charles and his dementia. She's taught Michael Spanish. His son married a wonderful Hispanic woman whose mother doesn't speak much English. Michael wanted to be able to talk with her and asked April to teach him some basic phrases. I guess she did very well in Spanish in high school and then after he asked her to teach him, she went online and studied even more."

Mandy smiles. "And though she doesn't have time to bake first thing every morning, she does love to make lunch down there for everyone. She absolutely glows when people compliment her. I think being needed there is very important to her." Mandy's smile turns to a frown. At me. "She doesn't just pour beer."

"In fact, she rarely pours beer. Dan doesn't serve alcohol until after six. That's when Ruby's shift starts," Ada informs me.

Cecelia leans forward, pinning me with a direct look. "I assume you're concerned about Christopher and the trouble he caused last night."

Mandy and Ada both look at her. She nods at them. "April left him and came to stay here with Ruby last night."

I frown. "How do you know that?"

She points across the street. "My dead husband's sister lives right there. She saw April arrive and witnessed what happened with Christopher on this porch. It's a small town, Henry."

I blow out a breath. "Then you understand why I need to keep her away from Christopher. That means she needs to be somewhere more secure than the bar."

"We can help with Christopher," Ada says.

I give her a questioning look. "Do I want to know what that means?"

Mandy laughs. "If poisoning some cinnamon rolls and burying a body was all it took, we would have gotten rid of Cecelia's husband twenty years ago."

I look at Cecelia. "Was your husband abusive?"

"No. Just a boring misogynist."

"Why did you stay?"

"Because I didn't become friends with these two until he had stage three brain cancer. If I'd known them when I was younger, they would have talked me into leaving sooner."

Mandy gives her a smile and Ada bumps her with her hip.

Cecelia just shrugs. "Anyway, I'm not above threatening Christopher with a meat cleaver to the balls," she tells me. "But I don't need to do that. I can do something much worse." She looks at her friends. "*We* can do something much worse."

"What's that?"

"Make his life miserable if he's an asshole to her," she says.

I study her. That's very similar to what I said to Christopher myself last night. "He's already been an asshole to her."

"But we didn't know that," Ada says. "Now that we do, we can make sure it stops."

I think about that. "Do you know Christopher well?" I ask. "What kind of work are you in?"

Ada laughs. So do Mandy and Cecelia.

"I know him well enough. And it doesn't matter what kind of work I do," Ada says. "My work doesn't have to affect him. I live in the same town that he does. I interact with the same *people* he does. I also interact with the same people April does."

"Meaning?" I ask.

"It's hard to blend in in a small town. It's hard to have anonymity. It's hard to disappear into a crowd. If you're a terrible person, people find out. And people generally don't want to associate with terrible people. Especially when the rest of the town will then assume you're a terrible person too."

"Peer pressure," Mandy says. "It doesn't just work in grade school."

"You think you can bully Christopher into being a good guy?" I ask.

"I think we can make it easier for Christopher to *behave* like a good guy, than it is to behave like an asshole," Mandy says. "We might not be able to change his heart, but we can make it damned uncomfortable to *act* like a dickhead. And that's what we need, right? For him to treat April well, no matter how he actually feels. She's not going to stay married to him. She doesn't need him to love her. She just needs him to not be abusive toward her or Elliot."

I nod. "Christopher cares enough about what you think of him?"

Ada laughs lightly. "Christopher probably barely knows who the three of us are. But we know people who know people Christopher does care about. If the right people tell someone who matters to him the right information, it can influence him."

"And you would do that?" I ask.

"Of course. Even if we didn't know and like April, men abusing women and children is not something that's going to stand in Emerald," Ada says.

Mandy and Cecelia both nod.

"There are a lot of people in this town I don't like," Cecelia says. "But there are none who are going to publicly defend an abuser. I can confidently say that."

"None who will *publicly* defend one," I say. "Are there some who will privately support him?"

"Well, that's the thing about a small town," Cecelia says with a smile. "It's damned near impossible to keep things private here."

I think about that and realize that these three women know this town far better than I do and I should defer to their expertise. "Okay, if you say we can keep April safe while she's working at Dick's, I'll keep it open."

"How about you keep it open because it's the right thing to do for everyone who needs it to be open?" Mandy asks. "And you trust us that April will be safe there because we say she'll be safe there?"

I study them again for a long moment. I always get to call the shots and people always assume I know what I'm doing and that I'm right. Until now. Here in Emerald, I'm meeting resistance every time I try to make a decision.

"Your husband really drives you so crazy that you'll help me keep Dick's open so he has a place to go in the mornings?" I ask Mandy.

Mandy shakes her head. "My husband has been diagnosed with clinical depression. His medication and therapy help, but he needs to get out of the house, have hobbies, see his friends, feel like he's a part of a group. Going to Dick's is good for him."

Well, damn. Fine. Dick's stays open.

Closing it down was probably extreme anyway. But it was supposed to just be a bar. Now it's…something else. I'm not entirely sure I understand all of it, but I'll deal with it. Like I always do. Emerald, Ohio, can't be more of a handful than the Cara royal family.

Probably.

"But Ben *does* drive me crazy enough that I'll help you," Ada says, unapologetically. "I find him charming and interesting even after forty-two years together which means he's very distracting when he's around. So he needs to be out of the house when I'm trying to get work done."

I arch both brows. Did she just tell me that she can't keep her hands off her husband when he's in the house with her?

She gives me a wink. "Yes, I mean that just how it sounds."

I laugh. "Fine. I'll keep it open."

"Good boy," Cecelia says.

"As if I really had a choice."

The three women smile. We all know the truth.

"I guess I better get these cinnamon rolls down to the bar. We wouldn't want Ben and Will to decide they miss their lovely wives."

"Definitely not," Ada agrees, starting for the porch steps.

"Be sure you go in the back door," Mandy says as she turns to leave. "Don't want the guys to see you coming in with them."

"And do *not* send any of them home before two p.m.!" Ada calls from the passenger side of the car they all rode over in.

I simply lift my hand and wave as they pull out of the driveway.

So, this is what it feels like to be ordered around.

It's annoying. I'm not sure how Cian's put up with me doing it to him all this time.

CHAPTER 10
RUBY

I feel my phone vibrate in my pocket and pull it out praying it's Henry.

I'm at the back door.

Thank goodness. I push through the swinging door to the kitchen and hurry to the back door to let him in. Surprisingly the cinnamon roll scented candle burning in the kitchen has convinced the men upfront that the cinnamon rolls are baking in the oven back here. But since we were an hour late opening, they're getting grumpy despite having their coffee and their bacon and eggs already.

"He's here," I tell April, who's dishing up more bacon at the stove.

Personally, I think bacon can totally take the place of cinnamon rolls, but the guys in the next room don't seem to agree.

"Finally," she says with a smile. "I probably should learn how to actually make those."

I give the younger girl a smile. "Sure, in all your free time."

She shrugs. "I'd enjoy it. And Elliot is getting old enough now to be a helper."

I know it's not so much that April wants to bake as it's that she wants all of the "these are amazing" and "you always start my day out right, sweetheart" exclamations to be about things she's actually doing.

We've shared quite a bit about our backgrounds in the time we've been working together. Her parents weren't big on encouragement and building her up and she now looks for external validation wherever she can get it.

That's unfortunately why Christopher was able to charm her with easy accolades like "you're so pretty" and "you're so sweet" and "you make my life so easy".

All of those things are true and I am sure Christopher meant them, but his appreciation of her is superficial and selfish. I am so glad April is finally seeing that. And while she eats up all of the praise from our customers, I want her to find something she truly wants to do for *herself*, not just for the admiration of others.

"I'm going to take this out to the guys and see who needs more coffee," April tells me, picking up the plate of bacon.

"Sounds good. I'll bring the cinnamon rolls."

I watch her back through the swinging doors.

She's another person I worry about leaving.

She's not my responsibility. I know that. But I'm so proud of her for finally deciding to get away from Christopher and I feel like this is a precarious time to leave town when she could use a friend or an older sister type in her life.

I shove all of that away as I push the back door open for Henry.

It *is* okay for me to think about what I want. It really is. It's not selfish.

"Here you go." He immediately hands over a huge platter of cinnamon rolls. I note that he is also carrying a casserole dish.

"Did they send something else?" I ask as he steps past me.

He shakes his head. "These are Elliott's pancakes."

"You made Elliot pancakes?" I ask, surprised.

"I told him I would last night."

"But...then you brought them down here?"

"I told him he would have pancakes this morning," Henry says firmly as if that should be obvious.

Right. Henry Dean does what he says he's going to do. "I'm sure he'll love them." And that's true. Elliot will definitely love the pancakes Henry made. He thinks Henry is very cool. And...they're pancakes.

"They're shaped like airplanes." Henry more or less mutters that.

I can't help my smile. Or the way that makes me melt a little. "Oh," I say softly. "That's adorable."

He frowns. "It would have been nice to have them in the kitchen at your house. I put the syrup in a separate container so it didn't make them mushy, but we'll have to reheat them and they're not going to be as good. And he was supposed to make them *with* me."

I know he's irritated but that's all adorable too. I want to hug him. And kiss him. And spread pancake syrup all over him. But I don't say any of that.

Instead, I sigh. Because I kind of wish I was eating pancakes, of any shape, in my kitchen instead too. I mean, I could be watching this hot, grumpy guy cook. I could be drinking coffee instead of serving it to people.

I am *not* a morning person. I'm here because, well, I'm a fucking angel, I guess. I could not let April come down here by herself. Just in case Christopher got some stupid idea about showing up. And no, neither April nor I could ignore the people in the next room.

"Look, Henry, I don't know what to tell you. The guys came to the bar like they always do. Dan let them in, of course. But he doesn't know how to use the espresso machine, so he called April when it was a quarter after and she still wasn't here. And as I told you, I figured you wouldn't want her coming down here alone...without you or me anyway...so here I am."

"Wait... *Dan* let them in?"

"Of course. No one else has a key. Other than me and April."

"But..." Henry seems very confused. "I paid Dan a million dollars last night. He's literally a *millionaire* now. Why would he come down and open up the bar he just sold?"

I shrug. "His friends and his favorite cappuccinos are down here."

"These retired guys come down here every morning to drink *cappuccinos?*" he asks, distracted for a moment.

"A couple of them. Dan especially. Will likes lattes. With hazelnut syrup, and no, don't try to sneak in the sugar-free kind, he *will* know and he won't drink it. Charles drinks straight-up espresso."

Henry runs a hand over his face. "What the hell is going on around here?" he mutters. He drops his hand. "I'm glad you at least didn't take Elliot to daycare."

I unwrap the casserole dish. Those are definitely airplane-shaped pancakes. A lot of them. God, that's *adorable.* I put a few on a plate and put them in the microwave to heat up. "Oh, we did take him to daycare." I wait for Henry's reaction. I know I shouldn't mess with him, but it's so fun.

He's so buttoned up and so used to being in charge and there's just something about seeing him out of his element that I enjoy *so* much.

I've been picturing the scene with him on my porch with Mandy, Ada, and Cecelia for the past thirty minutes. And grinning.

"*What*?" he exclaims. "Dammit, Ruby. I didn't want you all down here where Christopher could easily get to you. But dropping Elliot off at daycare without proper security in place was..."

I think it's good he trails off before he finishes that sentence.

"We have security in place," I tell him. "There's even a trained bodyguard."

"There's a bodyguard at Elliot's daycare?"

I turn to face him. "One of the best. Or so he tells me."

"*I* will be vetting any security around you, April, or Elliot."

I cross my arms. "Of course, the three people he's supposedly looking after right now, left the house this morning and were gone for forty-five minutes before he even realized. Actually, he never did realize. I'm not sure how long it would've taken if I hadn't called him."

His brows slam together as realization dawns. "Where is Elliot?"

I take the warm pancakes from the microwave and hand them to him, along with the covered container of syrup.

I point toward the door that leads to the main room of the bar. "In the daycare."

Henry looks like he has a lot more to say—and I'm sure he does—but instead of saying any of it, he turns on his heel and stomps out into the bar.

I'm smiling imagining Elliot's reaction to Henry and the pancakes as I unwrap the cinnamon rolls, warm them up slightly in the microwave as well—not enough to melt the frosting, but enough for them to be nice and gooey—and carry them out into the main room. I hum as I move amongst the tables, distributing them to our not-so-patient patrons.

"Man, smelling these baking has been killing me," Charles tells me.

I grin at him. That is a *really* good candle. "I know. Thanks for waiting without complaining *at all*."

He laughs. "I'm sorry."

I pat him on the shoulder. He seems to be having a good day but his memory decline makes me so sad. Some days he doesn't remember a funny occurrence from the week before or one of the kids' names which bothers him and hurts the little one's feelings. The kids are all patient and kind and we've explained that Charles can't help it and it doesn't mean he doesn't care. It's still hard sometimes.

Yes, I worry about leaving him too.

"I know I say it all the time," Will tells me as I set a cinnamon roll on the plate that held bacon just a few minutes ago. "But these are better than Mandy's. I'll deny it if you ever tell her though."

He does say that all the time. And I've already told Mandy and she laughed and rolled her eyes. "They are the best cinnamon rolls in town," I tell him with a nod.

"These look amazing, sweetheart," Will calls to April.

She gives him a big grin.

Henry comes back into the room through the wide

doorway that leads from the backroom Dan converted into a playroom eighteen months ago. He had plenty of volunteer help. Will was in construction before he retired, Ben had sold insurance but had done plenty of home improvement projects over the years. Even Charles was very good with a paintbrush.

The women who come in every morning after their three-mile walk contributed ideas for color schemes, more hands for painting, and had gathered so many books, gently used toys, and colorful cushions that we'd needed to build additional shelves and storage units.

The room has big windows that look out onto an open field that has never been built up. Dan owns that land as well. I'll have to ask him if Henry got that acre or so of grass and weeds with his million dollars.

Dan and his buddy, Paul, who had originally built the bar, had used the room for an office and extra storage. But it's been a long time since Dan sat at a desk for any length of time and he's not the type of guy to hole up in a back room alone. So I suggested he stick a tiny desk in the storeroom behind the bar and that he turn that big back room into a room for a few kids. When I mentioned that April would be able to work more shifts and longer hours if Elliot could come to work with her, Dan had easily agreed.

Now the adults take turns spending an hour or so in the room with the kids, reading, playing, doing crafts or music —depending on the adult and their particular interests and skill level—or supervising snacks or naps. Yes, Charles and Will thumb wrestle over nap time. And take a nap on the sofa back there while the kids sleep.

Mandy donated that sofa as soon as she found out about the kids' room and nap time.

Henry locates me immediately across the bar and strides toward me.

"Come with me," Henry says as soon as he's close enough for me to hear his low, gruff command.

"I'm—" I look around, trying to come up with an excuse not to obey, only to find that with the cinnamon rolls finally here, everyone has finally settled into their morning routine.

It's not only the kids in the back room who have regular activities here. The adults spend their time in various ways. There's a three-hour block of crazy game shows on television, there's chatting, gossiping, and arguing that must be done, and crossword puzzles and a gigantic jigsaw puzzle that must be worked.

I sigh, then look up at Henry. He has a strange expression on his face. He doesn't exactly look happy, but he's not angry. He looks a little...befuddled.

I love that word. I also love that look on Henry Dean.

That is definitely a new look, and a new feeling I'm sure, for this man. He is always in complete control, in charge. People listen to him without question.

But Big Dick's bar in tiny little Emerald, Ohio, full of retirees and preschool kids, bacon and cinnamon rolls, cappuccinos and jigsaw puzzles, has him a little flummoxed.

Yeah, I definitely like that word for him too.

I try to follow him, but he falls in next to me, his big hot hand settling on my lower back.

Dammit. How can even that simple touch make me feel warmer?

I slept like crap last night. I'd known I would, but it was even worse than expected. Knowing he was right on the other side of the wall, in my bed, I could not get the images of him out of my mind. I wanted so badly to tiptoe into the room, slide between the sheets next to him and say fuck it. Yes, it would make it harder to get over him. But I'm not so sure that getting over him is in the cards anyway.

He guides me toward the swinging door into the kitchen.

April is behind the bar, now making fruit smoothies. The four ladies who walk together every morning, always stop in for smoothies and to "catch their breaths"—ie, catch up on the gossip and give their friend Maggie a chance to flirt with Dan.

"You okay for a minute?" I ask April.

She smiles and waves me away. "Of course." She handles this crowd by herself every day.

"'Morning, Ruby," Wendy says. "I haven't seen you down here this time of day in a long time."

"I know." I look up at Henry again. "Unusual morning."

Henry holds the kitchen door open, waiting for me to pass.

"I'll say," Wendy agrees, checking Henry out with obvious interest.

I wonder what everyone is saying about Henry. I wonder how April is going to explain him. I wonder how *Dan* is going to explain the guy who now owns the place.

"Oh, um, Henry?" April asks.

He looks over at her.

"I need to place our weekly supply order today. Food, napkins, toilet paper, stuff like that. Dan said that since you—"

Henry has already dug his wallet out and he tosses her a credit card. "Get whatever you need."

April catches the card and looks from it to him. "Do you want to look the order over before I place it?"

"No."

"Oh." She seems confused.

"I have no idea what you need here. You're the expert," Henry tells her. "Get whatever you think you should get."

"Oh." She looks surprised. Then pleased. She grins. "What if I buy a new car?"

"Do you need a new car?" Henry asks.

Her smile drops at his not-kidding-around tone. "No. I mean...no. I would never do that."

"If you need a new car, we can talk about that," Henry says.

I pinch his side. "Lighten up," I whisper.

He clears his throat. "But for now, just get whatever the bar needs. And the kids. Whatever they need."

"I want to try caramel syrup!" Will calls. "Sneak some of that on the list. Dan wouldn't let me try it."

"You don't need two kinds of syrup," Dan grouses. "This isn't a damned coffee shop."

"Isn't it?" Henry mutters. "Definitely get caramel syrup," he says. "Vanilla too."

"Oh yes, vanilla sounds good!" Will calls.

Henry rolls his eyes but the corner of his mouth tips just slightly. No one else sees either thing, but no one else is studying him as if he's the most incredible thing they've ever seen. The way I am.

April smiles at him. "I've got it covered. I promise we won't go *too* crazy."

"I trust you, April," Henry says.

Her eyes widen and her smile says she's touched. "Thanks, Henry."

Damn him. He's so...good. And I don't think he even knows how much that meant to her. Dan had her do all the ordering too, but he always checked the order over, even after her working here for three years.

Henry nudges me into the kitchen and lets the door swing shut behind us.

"There are three other kids in that room with Elliot," are his first words to me.

I nod. "I'm aware."

"Are they April's friends' kids?"

"Yes. Two belong to Taylor and one belongs to Amber. The kids are friends of Elliot's obviously."

"How much do they pay for daycare here?"

I think he already knows the answer. "Nothing."

"Because April is just watching them while she works and her boss is okay with it?"

I lift a shoulder. "Basically. I mean, we all help watch them. The kids are never back there without an adult."

"Is this place licensed as a daycare?"

"Is the room in the back of the *bar,* filled with hand-me-down toys and supervised by retirees and two bartenders *licensed* as a daycare?" I laugh. "No. We're pretty much just babysitting for friends."

He steps closer and lifts a hand to cup my cheek. "It was your idea, wasn't it?" His voice is low and rumbly now.

The sound causes a warm tingle to start in my chest, then move through my belly to my pussy.

I nod. "Yes, initially. Generally. I told Dan I thought it was a good idea. He agreed. We all pitched in to make it happen. We still do."

"Everyone does it because they like you."

I shake my head. "Dan might have agreed because he knows I have good ideas. But everyone does it because they like *April.* And Elliot. And the other kids. The older people really like spending time with the kids. The kids like spending time with the older people. All day long they get a variety of people reading to them and playing with them and telling them stories. Sarah is teaching them how to tie their shoes. Ben teaches them about animals. It's like having eight additional grandparents."

Henry just stares at me for three heartbeats. Then he mutters, "Dammit, Gem," before he leans in and seals his mouth over mine.

I don't think there's ever going to be a time when Henry Dean is going to kiss me and I am not going to respond.

I am stubborn. I have a temper. I know who I am and what I want.

But I am not stupid. And I am not strong enough to resist the wave of lust and longing that goes through me whenever this man touches me.

I kiss him back. I open my mouth when his tongue demands it. I moan when he cups my head, and tips it back. I sigh when his fingers tangle in my hair. I arch closer when his tongue strokes over mine and heat licks through my body.

He kisses me for long, delicious, devastating-to-my-panties minutes.

Finally, he lifts his head. He takes a deep breath, staring down at me. "How am I supposed to get over you?" he asks. "Your big heart, the way you dive in to help, the way you just meet people where they are... there's no way I could ever ignore you, Gem. That's never going to work."

My heart thumps against my chest.

"Henry." But I don't say anything else. I'm not sure what to say.

I love that he knows that I had the idea for the daycare, and I love that he finds that attractive. It's just like the things he does that I find attractive.

The way we care about other people and try to impact the world around us is what draws us together, even more than the intense chemistry between us. The way we go about fixing things is different, of course, but I love his heart too.

"We need to make a plan for April and Elliot," he tells me. His voice is firm, almost as if he expects me to argue with him.

"I know," I tell him. We do need a plan. The sooner April and Elliot are safe and secure, the sooner Henry will focus back on Cian, Scarlett, and Mariah. And the sooner I can focus my attention on my move to New Orleans.

He stares at me for another long moment, then lets go of me and steps back.

"Is she able to sit down and talk soon?" he asks. "Or tonight?"

"We can do it here. She should have all the smoothies made."

Henry runs a hand over his face. "I guess you should introduce me to everyone," he says, not sounding all that enthusiastic about it. "Then you and April and I need to talk. She can't leave, I assume?"

"Not unless her new boss is going to take over the shift," I say giving him a little grin.

"He doesn't know how to run the espresso machine either," Henry says dryly.

"Well, they shouldn't have any more coffee, anyway. We need to switch them over to water. Will doesn't drink enough water as it is. And Ben will start on soda if you let him but just because it's diet, it still has caffeine. He doesn't need all of that."

Henry gives me a look. "I'm not going to memorize

what they all need and don't need to be eating and drinking. No matter how intimidating their wives are."

I laugh. I love those ladies. "I suppose you could go out and announce to everyone that the bar is closing down. If you really want to keep April from working."

He grimaces. "I was informed I'm not allowed to shut the bar down."

I am not surprised to hear that. "It's not just a bar, Henry."

He glances toward the swinging doors. "I know. It's a damned community center that just happens to serve alcohol at night."

"Pretty much," I agree. "How did you not notice the huge table with the five-thousand-piece jigsaw puzzle on it before today?"

His gaze roams over my face. "Because when I've been in here before, I've been very focused on something else."

Me.

He's been so focused on me before that he didn't take in details of the room we were in.

Yeah, the idea of ignoring him really was a stupid one.

"Why don't they just hang out at an actual community center? Or go have breakfast at the diner or the coffee shop in town?" he asks.

That's an interesting question. But it's got a pretty simple answer. I tuck my hands into the back pocket of my jeans. "My father."

Henry seems surprised for only about two seconds. Henry knows all about my father. I told him about my family and our history when we were first getting to know each other. Then he learned even more when Scarlett refused to let Henry tell Cian where she was. Then he really saw up close how Mariah was affected by our family issues when Henry brought Cian to Emerald.

"These men don't get along with your father?" Henry asks.

"These men and their families don't go to my father's church. They didn't want to become a part of his congregation and give him money. They don't agree with the amount of power my father has in town and they don't like the way members of the church try to manipulate and intimidate everyone in Emerald. So they've found the one place in town they can come and spend time and not be confronted."

"Confronted?" Henry asks. "What do you mean?"

My father is the pastor at the church where just a little over half of the town worships. If you aren't a part of that church, you are considered less than by the members of that church and are reminded of that any chance they get.

My father and I have never been close. He turned his back on my mom—a fling he'd had with a girl passing through town just as he was building his church—when he found out she was pregnant. He and I have only spoken a handful of times, and I don't regret that. My mom and my stepfather made up for any gaps my father left. But I resent the way he came between Scarlett and me in high school, and I will never forgive him for the way he made Scarlett feel and the way he publicly shamed her when she got pregnant with Mariah. Many of those issues stayed with her until very recently. Some might stay with her forever.

"Members of the church work all over town," I tell Henry. "And they hold Bible studies and mini-services they call "Live Rights"—reminders of how to live right every day no matter where you are—in places like the diner and the coffee shop. It's supposedly for the people participating, but they make a point of sitting right in the middle of wherever they are and being loud enough that everyone can hear."

"Every single day?"

"Yep. There's a group each day in each place, sometimes just two or three people, sometimes more, but it's every day, all over town," I say. "And they do it during their breaks at work too. So even if you don't go to the church and you don't have time to stop at the diner or the coffee shop, there's a good chance you'll walk into your breakroom at work, and there will be three or four of them talking about a Bible verse or praying, or whatever."

"They're essentially going out and preaching to everyone all the time."

I nod. "Sounds innocuous, I know. It probably even sounds good and godly to some. But it's just so in your face and the louder they get when you're there, the more you know they judge you."

One corner of his mouth curls up. "Are they loud when you're around?"

I smile. "*Very.*" Henry knows I don't give a rat's ass what my father, or his followers, think of me. Everyone knows that, actually.

His smile almost looks proud. He glances at the door leading back out to the bar. "So these men and women come here to avoid that?"

"Yeah. Dan doesn't let them do that here. One group tried. He cranked up Highway to Hell on the jukebox and played it until they stopped talking. He offered them coffee and rolls then, but they just wanted to pray for everyone. He told them fine, but if he could hear one word of it over at the bar, he'd *sing* Highway to Hell, acapella, and nobody wanted that. They left soon after."

Henry is outright grinning now. I *love* his grin.

"Dan isn't religious?" Henry asks.

"It's not that. It's just the whole having it shoved down your throat. And that they take over *everywhere*. You can't avoid it. It really should be something people *choose*, you know. They know how to find the church if they want that."

"That church is very hard to miss," Henry says.

I laugh. My father's church is big and gaudy and right on the edge of town as you come in on the main highway.

Henry takes a breath. "Let's go talk to April. We need to get a plan in place."

"Okay."

I don't warn him that this isn't going to go his way either. He'll find out soon enough.

CHAPTER 11
HENRY

E veryone in the bar turns to look when I walk out of
the kitchen.

My steps actually falter. Why do I get the feeling I'm
about to be interrogated? And why does that idea, here of
all places, make my palms sweat a little?

My gaze finds April. "Can we talk for a few minutes?"

She nods. "Okay, everyone, it's time."

"Time for—" I start but everyone in the room gets up
from their seats and starts rearranging the tables.

When there are four tables pulled together into one and
everyone has their chairs pulled up to it, they sit and look at
me expectantly.

"This isn't a town hall," I say. But I accept my fate
before anyone even speaks. This is obviously a group
project.

"Of course not," Ben says. "We don't want the whole
town involved. Just us."

"Right." I look at April. "I want to talk about what's next
for you and Elliot."

She nods and takes a seat between Wendy and Charles. "I know. I'm ready."

"You want everyone involved in this?"

She looks around the table. "Well...they all know the situation and they have some good ideas."

"You've already discussed this?"

"Of course."

Why does that surprise me? Because April only left her husband last night, she seemed overwhelmed and unsure when I met her, and it's now only nine a.m. the next morning.

But she seems different today. She's smiling. She's laughing. She's moving around here with confidence, and she seems relaxed and at ease.

Maybe she just needed some sleep. Maybe she just needed to be in her usual routine. Maybe I'm making her feel secure.

I'd really like that last one to be the case, but something niggles in my mind telling me that's not it.

I know what it is.

She's here with people who care about her, who she can care for, and she feels needed and appreciated here.

That's what's doing it.

I know that feeling well.

I pull out the only empty chair and sit. I'm next to Ruby with Dan on my other side.

"Okay, so the most important thing is keeping you and Elliot safe," I tell her. "We need you somewhere Christopher can't get to either of you. To intimidate you, to coerce you, or to hurt you."

She nods.

"How long until Scarlett and Mariah and..." Ben glances at Will.

But a woman in a bright yellow tracksuit answers, "Cian."

"Right. Cian. How long until they're back?" Ben asks.

"I..." I wasn't expecting to be the one answering questions. "I'm not sure exactly. They'll be gone for at least another week."

"Oh, that's plenty of time," Will says.

The woman who had been at the bar getting a smoothie from April leans in and nods. "We can definitely have the room remodeled in a week. So they'll stay with you until then?"

She's asking Ruby, not me.

Ruby nods. "Of course, that's fine."

"Great," the woman says. "We'll get started tomorrow, but a week is fine."

"What's fine?" I ask. I find myself looking at Ruby. She's reasonable. She understands the goal here.

She looks from me to the woman. "What room, Wendy?"

"The room at Will and Mandy's."

"The bathroom needs some work too," the woman in the tracksuit says.

"Uh, Henry, this is Maggie," Ruby says. "Her dad owned the hardware store in town for years and she took it over and has been running it for about eight years now."

"Hi," I say as Maggie smiles and extends her hand for me to shake.

I am being steamrolled. And they're all so smiley about it.

"Everyone, this is Henry. He's a good friend and—"

"A bodyguard," Charles says. "We know."

Ruby laughs. "Yes. He's here to help keep April and

Elliot safe. Until we can figure out something more permanent."

"That'll be about a week," Will says. "Though she hardly needs a bodyguard."

"I'm simply—" I start.

"Christopher is an asshole," Ben says. "But what are you going to do? Shoot him?"

"Of course not, I just—"

"I'll bet he can do some major damage without a weapon." This comes from another woman who came in with Wendy and Maggie. She's giving me an appreciative once-over.

"How many ways do you know to kill a man?" Charles asks me.

Seventeen, but I'm not going to tell them that. "That's not really—"

"It only takes one," Dan says, chuckling. He's sitting back in his chair, with one ankle propped on the opposite knee. He looks like *none* of the other millionaires I've met in my life.

"It's handy to have options though," Wendy says.

"And some are more painful and slower than others," Ben says, nodding. "With guys like Christopher, that would be tempting."

"I'd really like to focus on—" I try again.

"Oh, honey, I can get one of those amazing rainfall shower heads for you at a steal," Maggie says to April. "We can easily convert that tub and shower into a walk-in shower."

"But she'll want a tub for Elliot," the other woman whose name I still don't know, says. "Does Elliot like baths?"

"He does," April says. "I do, too."

"You can keep the tub. I'll take the rainfall shower head in our bathroom," Will tells Maggie.

"We're not remodeling two bathrooms," Wendy says. "We don't have time for that."

"Still, get me the deal and I'll do our bathroom down the road," Will says.

"Can we knock that wall out between the bedroom and that hallway closet?" Maggie asks. "That would expand the room really nicely. If you say yes to that, I'll get you the showerhead *and* a great deal on tile."

"Yes," Will says without hesitation.

"Do you need to ask Mandy?" Ben asks.

"Nah, she'll be so excited."

I finally slap my hand down on the table. "*What* the *hell* are you talking about?"

Ruby's hand moves to my thigh and squeezes. I take a breath as I look around the table at the wide-eyed stares.

"I think Henry is just feeling a little lost," Ruby says.

"I just—"

She squeezes harder and I clamp my jaw together.

"Somebody catch us up," Ruby says.

"Oh, right," Ben says. "You weren't out here."

"Nope," Ruby says. "Sounds like you've all done some big talking."

"Yeah, we've decided that April and Elliot will come live with me and Mandy," Will says.

My mouth drops open. "Wha—"

Ruby squeezes my leg *hard*.

I shut up.

"Oh, wow," Ruby says. "Really? Why's that?"

"Initially we thought our house made the most sense," Ben says. "We have three extra bedrooms, the big fenced-in yard, the playset outside, all of that."

"And you're closer to here," Maggie adds.

"Right. But then we remembered the whole situation and keeping them safe and Will and Mandy live across the street from Rich Looper," Ben says.

"I mean, they have two extra bedrooms and a nice yard too," Wendy says.

"We can easily fence it in," Dan comments.

"For sure," Wendy agrees. "And we'll have to do a little remodeling on the bedroom, but that will be fun."

Everyone around the table nods.

I just look from one of them to the next.

They're serious.

Not only about moving April and Elliot in with a couple who are not their family—that I know of—but everyone is going to pitch in to fix things up.

"Who is Rich Looper?" I finally ask.

"Bill Looper's brother," Ben says.

I wait. He doesn't add anything more. I lift a brow. "And?"

Will jumps in. "If I say that Christopher is being problematic, bothering us, trespassing, harassing any of us, Bill will believe me because Rich and I get along great. We've been great neighbors for like twenty years."

I sigh. "Give me a break, please? Who the fuck is Bill Looper?"

"Oh, right. Bill was the town cop until about three years ago," Will explains.

"But he's not now?" I clarify. "How does that help?"

"Everyone knows and respects Bill," Maggie says.

They all nod.

"If Bill says Christopher is being problematic, people will believe us. And the current cops will act on it," Ben says.

"The current cops won't act on a harassment complaint until *you* all say it's real?" I ask, frustration tightening my neck. I need to just get April and Elliot the hell out of here.

"Sure, they'll talk to everyone, but if it becomes a he said-she said with Christopher, April will have influential people on her side," Wendy further clarifies.

"Just because you all say so?" I ask.

They all look at one another, then back at me.

"Well... yeah," Ben says.

Dan leans forward in his chair. "We all grew up here. We've worked here, raised our kids here, and been a part of the community. We've got some pull."

I think about that. Do they have the power to protect April? Just by being a part of the town for a long time? Just by reputation?

I sit back. Ruby starts to slide her hand from my thigh, but I cover it with mine, keeping it right there.

"Will your opinions, your word, still matter?" I ask Dan.

He frowns. "Still? What do you mean?"

"I have to ask," I tell him. "This is April and Elliot's safety. So humor me. You've all lived here a long time, but most of you are retired now. You hang out here together, away from town, in your little bubble. And I don't blame you. But other people in town might feel they know Chris and his allies better."

"Just because they go to that cult church?" Charles asks with a scowl.

I lift a shoulder, squeezing Ruby's hand. "Maybe for some people. But for some it might not be the church specifically, so much as it is that they're just out in the community, patronizing the businesses, being around. They can't really know there's another side if that side is invisible."

"They know we're here," Ben says, grumpily.

"And I'll bet they're intimidated as hell coming in here," I say with a laugh.

"Intimidated?" Maggie asks. "Of us? A bunch of people drinking smoothies and watching game shows and coloring with little kids?"

"They don't know that's what's going on," I tell them. "All they know is it's a bar and you don't really want them here. You've basically built yourselves a clubhouse and put up a sign that says membership is closed."

No one says anything immediately. But they all look grumpy or surprised, or both.

"I'm just telling you how it looks from the outside," I finally say. "And that might not help April."

"Well, if they're intimidated, then maybe that will keep Christopher away from her," Wendy says.

Yeah, maybe.

"You could also consider going to stay with your sister," I tell April, finally finding a chance to tell them *my* idea.

She frowns. "My sister lives in Cincinnati."

"I know." I've done my research. Of course.

"That's..." April looks around. "So far."

"That's the point," I tell her. "It would be much harder for Christopher to just show up there. He'd risk issues with work, at least, if he did that." It's a little over a hundred miles between here and Cincinnati. It would be drivable, but more difficult than her just being a couple of blocks away.

"But I don't want to leave Emerald," April says. "My friends are here. My job."

"I'll help you with money," I say. "We'll get you another job." She works in a bar. It can't be that difficult to find her another job.

But even as that thought goes through my mind, I realize that's not entirely accurate.

It would be difficult to find her another situation like she has here. Or maybe impossible.

Not that she couldn't build a new community and find more people to care for. God knows the world is full of people who need cared for.

I glance at Ruby as my chest tightens.

That's exactly what Ruby will do in New Orleans. She'll find people who need her. People who need a community. She'll build that up for them the way she has here.

Sure, these people have known each other, have been friends, have had this connection, but I guarantee she's nurtured all of this, and encouraged Dan to keep this going. She might have even pushed him to add rolls and coffee and game shows in the first place. Though it's more likely Mandy and Ada volunteered the rolls to keep their guys here and happy.

I have to fight a smile.

Maybe Ruby learned some of her nurturing from those women. Either way, I'm sure Ruby has continued working the night shift so April could have these early hours because Ruby knew that April needed all of this as much as these older people did.

April is shaking her head. "I don't want to leave, Emerald, Henry."

"You want to live with Mandy and Will?"

She looks at Will. "I do. I can be a lot of help to them and they'll be so good to Elliot."

"Better than your sister? His aunt?" I press.

She laughs. "So much better." She shakes her head. "My sister loves us, but she's got her own kids, her own career, her own life. Mandy and Will's kids live in Omaha and Chicago.

I'm not saying we would ever take their places but I know Mandy misses them so much and she's so great with kids. And Will..." She trails off, looking at Will with clear affection.

"I'm depressed," Will says with a shrug. "I'm doing pretty good right now, but it's up and down, you know? And having other people around, people to focus on, to help, to care about, helps me a lot."

I let out a breath and feel Ruby squeeze my hand.

"Okay. Well..." I run a hand through my hair. "I can at least speed up the divorce process. Let's get you untethered legally as quickly as possible."

I'm losing options here to help her. And Elliot.

"What do you mean?" Ruby asks.

I look down at her. "That process can take six weeks minimum and that's if Christopher doesn't give us any trouble. I think we all know that's not going to happen."

"But how can you speed it up?" she asks with a frown.

"I can..." Pull strings, use my connections, call in favors. I'm certain I know someone who knows someone who knows a judge in Ohio that can make a divorce happen quickly. "Grease the wheels."

Ruby's eyebrows arch. "You're not talking about paying off a judge! Henry, please tell me..."

"Of course not." I'm sure it won't come to *that*. We know important people who can just make things move faster.

"Then what?"

"I can just bump her up in the queue."

Ruby shifts on her chair to face me more fully. "But if you move April up, that means someone else gets moved back."

"Well...yes."

"No." Ruby looks at April. "Sorry, babe. But we can't do that. Other women have been waiting. They need this too. Maybe more than you do. You've got us. Some of them might not have anyone. We'll keep you safe. We'll help you navigate things."

April nods. "I know. We should do it the right way. I can wait."

Ruby nods. She meets my eyes again. "No power plays, Henry."

I lean closer. I don't know why. Everyone here is hanging on every word everyone is saying. "The advantage of knowing people with power is being able to get things done. Easier. Faster. Better. This is what I can do."

It's starting to look like this is *all* I can fucking do. And I'm not happy about it.

"I have to believe the system can work for everyone," Ruby says. "That's really important to me. I know some people get favors and have privileges, but I *have* to know that the people I know can still have good things happen doing it the regular way. The system has to also work for people who don't have power and money, Henry."

"Isn't that why you want to go to law school? To have more power?" I ask.

She swallows. The room is completely silent.

I'm guessing she hasn't told them she wants to go to school.

Finally, she nods. "Yes. But I'll have to use the system. I'll have to follow the rules. No skipping steps. No favors. I want to be a lawyer so I can help people navigate that system. Not to find work-arounds."

"The system sucks sometimes."

She nods. "I know. But maybe I can make it suck less for

some people by being there, helping them, being on their side."

"Ruby," I say, my voice tight with frustration. She's going to be everyone's favorite lawyer. And it will break her heart multiple times.

"Just help us file the papers the *usual* way."

"I need to do more," I say quietly.

"You can help us knock down walls at Will and Mandy's house," Ben says.

I look at the other man.

Then I look at the other people at the table, my eyes meeting April's last.

They're going to remodel Will and Mandy's house so that April and Elliot can move in there. Across the street from the brother of the last town cop. Because April doesn't want to leave this town. This crazy bar. Or this quirky group.

Bloody hell.

I've been knocking down metaphorical walls for a long time. Now, those walls in Will's house might be the only ones I get to knock down.

I sigh.

Fine.

Honestly, slamming a sledgehammer into something doesn't sound too bad right now.

CHAPTER 12
RUBY

"Is there a group like this that comes in at night too?"

Henry has been over in the corner working on the jigsaw puzzle with Charles. I don't know what they've been talking about, but they've both smiled and laughed and gotten a good chunk of the puzzle done.

The meeting with everyone didn't go according to Henry's plan, I know, but he did seem a little excited about sitting down with the puzzle. Not quite as excited as he was about the LEGOs with Elliot last night, but he wasn't over there just to entertain Charles.

He also volunteered to help at lunchtime with the kids and I couldn't help but peek in on that as well.

Ugh. It was so cute. I wanted to climb in his lap and eat banana pudding with him too.

It's not like I'm under any delusion that I'm not crazy about the guy.

His swooping in and saving the day—or even just wanting to so much that he's annoyed when he can't—is so sexy.

He's leaning on the bar now watching me wash glasses.

"No, the night shift is not like this," I tell him with a little laugh. "It's a pretty typical bar at night. I guess that's also a reason that you might've missed some of this ambiance when you've been here before."

Henry's only been here during the hours I've worked. The earliest he's ever showed up at Dick's was when he and Cian came to town after he told Cian that he'd found Scarlett. That had been early afternoon and I had been filling in for April. Luckily we'd been past the breakfast and lunch craziness and Dan had been here to cover me when I needed to leave.

But Henry had definitely been singularly focused when he'd been here. I doubt he'd done more than scan the room to take in the number of people. I'm sure he hadn't cataloged details like their ages or the fact that they were drinking water and soda instead of liquor.

"That's the fourth time you've yawned in the past fifteen minutes," he comments as I cover my mouth, dragging in air with a big yawn.

"You've been counting my yawns?"

"I've been paying attention to…a lot of things."

I'm not surprised he's noticed. Whenever we're in the same vicinity, at least a portion of his attention is on me.

I love that.

It makes me feel like a silly high school girl with a crush—something I never felt when I was a high school girl—but I can't help it.

"I didn't sleep very well last night," I tell him.

He meets my gaze directly, a little heat in his. "Me either."

"And this isn't my usual shift," I remind him.

"I know. So I'm closing the place down for the rest of the day. And night," he says.

I open my mouth to argue. But yawn again.

He gives me a look that says he knows I was going to argue. "I'm closing the bar for the rest of the day and night. We're going home."

I really do want to go home.

There isn't a regular crowd in the evenings. At least not like this group. And none of these people will stay past four.

"Okay," I agree. "I drove April over. I can just give her my keys."

He frowns. "Well, obviously, she and Elliot will be coming with us."

"She's going over to Will and Mandy's tonight for dinner. They're going to tell Elliot that they're moving in there next week. They're also going to let him pick out what color he wants to paint his bedroom."

Henry takes in that information, then shakes his head. "Someone's driving her over there and picking her up."

"Okay," I agree. I'm easy. Not only am I too tired to argue with him, he's right. We are protecting April until we can get everything settled. She's come up with a plan that she likes, regardless of Henry's feelings, but we can still do our best to make sure that she is constantly surrounded by allies. "But April wants to stop at the grocery store so she can make a salad. She wants to contribute to dinner."

"Fine. I can take her to the grocery store. Or she can give me a list and I can just get the stuff."

I smile. "How about I take her to the grocery store and then over to Mandy's? I'll grab something for us for dinner too." I lean onto the bar. "It'll just be the two of us. What do you want?"

I don't miss the way his gaze drops to my mouth. "I am pretty hungry now that you mention it."

"I'll pick something quick and easy."

I don't really care what we do for dinner, but I want it to be simple. Because Henry and I need to talk. April is basically taken care of. I think the plan with Mandy and Will is just fine. They'll all be happy with it and April will be safe.

I understand Henry's side of it. April going to stay with her sister in Cincinnati would put distance between her and Christopher, but April shouldn't have to leave her home. If she wants to stay in Emerald, then we need to find a way to help her do that and still be safe.

She has a huge community of people around her. I also understand that she doesn't want to start over somewhere else. I've done it a lot of times. I'm good at it. But I've always moved out of necessity. I've found new people because I need people around me. That doesn't mean that I wouldn't rather just stay in one place where I'm comfortable and happy, with people I know, trust, and love.

I feel my throat tighten.

I've lived in New Orleans before. It will be fine. I'll be fine.

I focus on April again. This is about April and Elliot, not me.

There will no doubt be some kind of arrangement that has to be made for visitation and custody of Elliot. Being here in Emerald will make that easier, too.

I blow out a breath. Yes, this plan for April is good, and so Henry and I don't need to do much more. Or anything more, really. We helped. Now our part in this situation is done.

Henry can go meet up with Cian and Scarlett in Portland.

They just got there this afternoon. He hasn't even really missed anything yet.

We finish cleaning up the bar, Henry pitching in, and

everyone is out the door by four-thirty. Will takes Elliot home with him so April and I can stop by the grocery store.

"To the store, then to Will and Mandy's, then home," Henry says as he walks us to my car.

"Yes. Promise," I tell him.

"Call me if there are any problems."

"There won't be any problems."

He sighs. "Just say, 'Of course, Henry'. Is that really that difficult?"

I smile up at him. "Of course, Henry."

"That's better." Again, his gaze drops to my lips. "Don't be long."

A hot ripple goes through me.

Dammit.

It would be so great if I was going home to have dinner with my boyfriend.

Or even if I was just going home to have dinner with a really great, rich, hot British guy that I wanted to have hot sex with.

Which, I guess, technically, I am...

"Ruby?"

"Yeah?"

"Get in the car."

I realize I've been staring at him.

Okay, at his mouth.

Dammit.

Sleeping with him again is a really bad idea.

I'm pretty sure. I'm having a hard time remembering why, though.

April talks non-stop about the day. How Dan said he was going to donate some of his new money to a town project. How popular Elliot was with the other kids because he and Henry were friends. How living with Mandy and Will means that Elliot will have a pet.

I just let her talk. I'm happy for her. I really am. I'm happy for Mandy and Will too.

I guess I was just expecting to be helpful to her for longer than a couple of days.

I thought I'd be… I don't even know. I feel like I haven't really done anything at all.

April and I pass the meat counter, where I grab some chicken thighs and then head for the produce section. I figure I can throw together a salad as well. Something simple. And something light. Something that won't sit like a lead ball in my gut while I tell Henry he can now leave Emerald.

I'm squeezing avocados when I hear, "Christopher is a good man. You're making a mistake."

Dammit. We were so close to the end.

I look over to see Crystal Dumont standing behind her cart, glaring at April. Behind her is her mother, Kelly. Crystal has a very high opinion of herself, but Kelly thinks Crystal is even more perfect than Crystal does.

"If you like him so much, you can have him," April says.

"I have a husband," Crystal says. "I know what it's like to have a good man and to be *grateful* for that."

I move up next to April and start to open my mouth to defend her, but April says, "Grateful? Is *that* what keeps you with Luke? I've always wondered. Because it can't be the way he treats you with respect and love, or the way he supports you, or the way he defends you or believes in you."

I snap my mouth shut and settle back on my heels. April seems fine. I'm here for the show now.

"You are such a bitch," Crystal says. "I told Luke when

Chris first started dating you that you'd be trouble. Luke never wanted him to get serious about you."

"I know," April says. "Because he was afraid that *you* might figure out that your whole world didn't have to revolve around him and you might grow a spine. He was afraid you'd take after me."

"And *leave him* when I got bored?"

"Or leave him when you realized he's an asshole," April says, her voice still calm. "Or after he cheated on you. *Again.*"

Crystal's face is pink now.

"Are you saying Christopher cheated on you?" Kelly demands. "I don't believe it."

"No," April says. "He hit me. And I was *not* going to let him hit my son."

Kelly scowls. "I'm sure it was a mistake or an accident. Christopher is a good man."

"I suppose we may have different definitions of good," April says. "But mine doesn't include physical or verbal abuse. So *I* am going to leave *my* marriage when those things start happening. You do you."

She starts to push our cart forward, obviously done with the conversation, but Crystal steps in front of it. "No one will believe you. Everyone here has known Christopher his whole life. You're not from here."

"I don't care," April says.

I can see the tension in her shoulders, but I'm impressed with how steady her voice is.

"I don't need anyone to believe me other than the people I care about. And you don't make that list."

"But when you try to get custody, or another job, or make new friends, everyone will just know you as the lying bitch who tried to ruin a good man who is a steady part of our community," Crystal informs her.

I feel like she just slapped me.

This isn't about me, I know that. And that sentiment shouldn't surprise me. That's the way this town, and so many like it, are. If you're from here, you belong more than 'outsiders'. And even some of us born and raised here are still outcasts if we don't conform.

I'm fine with that. I've always been fine. Being my father's daughter has always put me in a precarious position in the community, but my mom didn't let him define us. We found our people, we lived our lives, we did good things for the right reasons, and let our actions speak for themselves.

But how can I leave April when this is what she'll be facing?

She's got everyone out at Dick's, but they're not exactly her peer group. I'm not as worried about her job, because I know Henry will look out for her, but he's not going to be her girlfriend. Her call-me-up-if-you-ever-just-need-to-talk-or-vent person. Her I-don't-even-know-why-I'm-sad-but-can-you-come-over-and-make-me-feel-better person. Her it's-a-random-Tuesday-but-let's-get-nachos-and-watch-trash-tv-and-do-mani-pedis-like-it's-Friday-night person.

Everyone needs that person.

My person just married a prince and we'll be getting nachos less often when I live in another city in another state.

But I don't want to think about that.

Right now, I'm worried about April. Can I leave *her* when she's likely to be ostracized by this damned town she's so intent on staying in?

"Ooh, honey, that color of green does *not* go with what you're wearing."

I catch the narrowing of Crystal's eyes just before April and I turn.

Amber Connors has just strolled up behind us, a plastic shopping basket swinging from her arm. She looks amazing, as always. She owns the salon downtown and her hair, makeup, nails, and clothes are always perfect. But she also comes off as genuine, kind, and accepting of everyone.

I adore her. She's gone out with me and Scarlett a few times. Scarlett often helps her out with little things like making treats for her daughter's class or grabbing last-minute items for a class project because Amber and her husband Tony both work long hours and Scarlett knows how much an extra hand can help.

But Amber and Tony are new-ish to Emerald and Amber has tried not to take any "sides" in town rivalries. Especially between those who attend my father's church and those who don't. It's important for her business, which is vital for her family, that she has clients from all over town.

Scarlett and I understand, and we've worked hard not to put her in the middle of anything.

But now, she walks right up to us, her eyes on Crystal.

"She's not wearing green," Kelly says.

Amber doesn't take her gaze from Crystal. "Her jealousy is obvious and *bright* green. And it's quite ugly."

Kelly gasps, but Crystal just crosses her arms. "Jealous? Of *April*? Seriously?"

"Oh, for sure," Amber says.

Amber is a little younger than me and a little older than April. Probably right about Crystal's age.

"I do not want Christopher if that's what you're implying," Crystal says.

"Well, at least you're smart enough for that," Amber says. "But no. I'm talking about how you're jealous of April being brave enough to do what you can't. Or won't."

"Leave my husband?" Crystal scoffs. "Believe it or not, I don't *want* to make my husband the subject of scandal and gossip."

I note that Crystal is pressing her arms against her stomach and won't meet Amber's gaze directly.

"I'm not talking about leaving Luke," Amber says. "Though no one would blame you."

Kelly gasps again. Crystal doesn't say anything.

"I'm talking about April being able to stand up for herself and make herself happy. I'm not saying you have to leave Luke for that. That's up to you. But everyone knows you're not happy, Crystal. It's why you're so mean and judgey. Happy people don't worry about other people's lives so much. They want to spend their time and energy in their *own* lives." Amber finally looks at April. "I'm sorry that you had to leave your husband to be happy. Obviously, at one point you thought you could be happy with him and I'm sorry that's not how it turned out. That's hard. But I'm glad you realize that you deserve to be happy and don't have to stay in a situation where that's not the case."

April gives her a wobbly smile. "Thank you, Amber."

"Also, your highlights look amazing."

April's smile grows. "Thanks."

Amber looks at Crystal again. "I really hope you find something that makes you happy, Crystal. Because I really don't believe that walking up to people in the grocery store and berating them for their life choices is it. But, if it is...just know that there are lots of people who aren't going to just stand by and let it happen."

Crystal sucks in a deep breath, but she doesn't say anything.

Amber looks over at me and gives me a smile. "Hey, Ruby."

"Hey, rockstar."

She laughs. "Good to see you. Come down for a mani soon, 'k?"

"For sure."

She walks off, her little basket swinging and I feel a tightness in my chest.

I'll miss *her* too. I don't know her very well, but I want to. She seems awesome, and *fuck,* it would be nice to have a kickass friend like that.

I love taking care of people, but damn, having someone else sashay up like that and just handle shit is amazing.

It's a lot like how I feel when Henry shows up and takes over.

I know that's not independent thinking and I don't want to *need* a man, but I can like it when it happens, can't I? That's not too terrible, is it?

April takes hold of the cart again. "'Bye, Crystal," she says, firmly, obviously ending the conversation.

If you can even call what just happened a conversation.

She pushes the cart around the other two women and this time they don't block our attempt to leave.

We leave the produce section and head for the checkouts.

April keeps walking straight ahead, but she says, "I didn't get all the salad ingredients." She blows out a breath. "And I really don't want to go back there."

I laugh. "Same."

April looks over at me. "But we should, right? Just

march back there and do our shopping? We shouldn't let them intimidate us."

I take a deep breath. Then nod. "Yeah. Probably. But, you know what?" I reach for the stack of plastic containers on the display table just before the registers. "I think some days you need to eat your vegetables. And some days it's totally okay to eat dessert first." I hand her a container of frosted brownies, then take one for myself. "And some days, you can have *just* brownies for dinner."

She looks down at the brownies and then nods. "Yeah. I think you're right."

I am. I'm sure of it. I hand the package of chicken and the few vegetables we did manage to gather to the woman running the register. "I won't be needing these after all," I tell her.

She scans my package of brownies and nods. "Some days are like that."

CHAPTER 13

WAIT 'TIL I TELL YE

PODCAST EPISODE 903 TRANSCRIPT

Lindsey: Welcome to this very special edition of *Wait 'Til I Tell Ye*. I know, I know, we're almost never on at this time of night.

Jen: But never fear! We are here for you whenever something big happens that you should know about!

Lindsey: That's right. And with this royal family, there's no telling when something exciting might happen.

Jen: <Laughs> Exactly! And I feel like we've been talking nonstop about them. We had Cian's wedding and Scarlett's sudden appearance. Then we had Declan showing up, shocking all of us.

Lindsey: His family included, according to our sources.

Jen: Well, considering it's literally been like seventeen years since he was here, I'd say shocked is the right word.

Lindsey: And then we find out that Declan and Astrid

also said wedding vows! Now, I assume the family knew *that* was coming, but we sure as hell didn't.

Jen: I am actually disappointed there are only four children and they're all now married because these past few months were so fun!

Lindsey: I agree! *But*, we get to keep talking about their new relationships, get to know the new princesses better, and then there will maybe be babies and stuff!

Jen: Not to mention all the cool stuff they're all doing. Like the topic of tonight's show!

Lindsey: Yes. Cian and Scarlett headed for the US last night and arrived in Portland today for their first big event together and there was a really fun crowd there with them.

Jen: There sure was! Since Declan, Astrid, and Alex all live there, not only did we have Cian with his big brother at a public event for the first time in forever <little happy squeal> but Jonah and Linnea traveled with Cian and Scarlett, so the three Olsen siblings were all there together as well!

Lindsey: Yeah, for a while, we were watching Louisiana since we had a little gathering of royals there after Fiona and everyone moved. Then Fiona fell in love. Then Colin. Then Torin met Abigail there. But now, it seems maybe Portland is where we will be getting juicy information from?

Jen: Oh boy, I hope so! I want to know *everything* about the newlyweds, Declan and Astrid. And we *never* hear enough about Alex! Do we have sources in Portland to keep us updated?

Lindsey: <laughs> Of course we do.

Jen: Excellent. But we didn't need a source for what we want to tell you about tonight because it was all pretty public. Cian and Scarlett showed up to the site where they are opening the first community through their foundation, Ruby's Way.

Lindsey: Yes, and we should note for anyone who hasn't read up on the Ruby's Way Foundation yet, that Cian and Scarlett named it after Scarlett's twin sister, Ruby.

Jen: Aw, I love that.

Lindsey: Everyone can go to the show notes and click the link for Ruby's Way to learn more. But basically, these are living spaces—some are apartment buildings, some are houses—that are provided at no cost to groups of single moms who come together and live as a community, helping one another with child care, meals, keeping their houses, laundry, shopping...just all of the everyday tasks that go into homemaking and raising kids that can be that much harder when you're doing it alone. These are single moms who are all in the same boat, coming together to support one another with friendship and companionship as well as literal hands-on help.

Jen: It was inspired by Princess Scarlett's own experience as a single mom, the way her sister was there to support her, and the way they built community with other people around them as they raised Princess Mariah. It's really cool.

Lindsey: It is. And to further entice you to click and read more, there are also a *ton* of photos from today that you are all going to *love*! Linnea sent those over to us personally and so they are up close and behind the scenes and all kinds of fun!

Jen: Princess Scarlett seems so happy! She did a really great job with her speech, and she seems so proud of this. As she should be.

Lindsey: Absolutely. And it's so wonderful to see Prince Cian really stepping up and embracing this role and using his outgoing personality and charm in such a wonderful way.

Jen: <laugh> And his money and connections.

Lindsey: Definitely that too!

Jen: But really, Cian is always so much fun to watch and follow. He's so happy and bright and charming, but there is this extra light about him now. He's clearly so in love and so...what's the word I'm trying to think of?

Lindsey: Content. I think that's how it seems to me. Like he has found his place.

Jen: <sighs> Oh, I really like that. Yes. And Scarlett seems to be taking to all of this pretty well. I know it's all new to her and it is probably a little overwhelming, but she seems to be handling it.

Lindsey: I agree. I think we've found ourselves another amazing princess, Cara. After all these years, watching and loving this royal family, but admittedly worrying a little when they were all restless and living in the US doing all kinds of different things that didn't always make sense, we wondered about the future of our country and our leadership. So it's amazing to see our princes and princesses finding their places, finding happiness, and settling into their roles.

Jen: I agree. I think they've found their true matches and that makes all the difference.

Lindsey: I am not the romantic of the two of us, but even I have to admit that this all feels really good.

Jen: You heard it, everyone. Even Lindsey's won over. So on that note, I think we wrap this up for tonight. Everybody, go look at the photos, and we will talk to you later.

Lindsey: Oh hey, real quick, did you find it interesting that Jonah and Linnea traveled to Portland with Cian and Scarlett? Of course, Linnea has been involved in helping them with the foundation, but it seems that Henry didn't go along to Portland.

Jen: I did notice that. I assume Jonah was there providing security. Maybe they just thought as long as they had Jonah, they didn't need Henry too?

Jen: Maybe. If any of you know anything about Henry's whereabouts, let us know. Or heck, comment and speculate! That's fun too!

Lindsey: <laughs> You want to start rumors?

Jen: Why not?

Linsey: Oh boy. And on that note, 'bye, everyone!

CHAPTER 14
RUBY

I sit in the parking lot of the baseball field, just staring at the dark scoreboard.

I'd decided to listen to the special edition podcast episode on my way home from dropping April off at Mandy and Will's.

I'm a huge fan of the show and have it set to send me notifications any time a new episode posts.

But I pulled over four blocks from home when I realized they were talking about Scarlett.

Okay, Scarlett and a bunch of other people.

But definitely Scarlett.

I thought it would cheer me up. I thought I'd laugh a little.

I didn't expect to feel like I couldn't take a deep breath.

I already had a weird bunch of emotions tumbling around inside me.

The truth is, I thought April and Elliot were going to be staying with me longer, and if I'm being honest, I was going to use them as a distraction from the fact that my sister has a new relationship that is more important to her than I am.

My niece also has a ton of new exciting things happening in her life that I am only on the fringe of.

Seeing how everyone embraced April today was heartwarming and amazing. But it also made me realize that I am not the only person that can help April through this time in her life. I may not even be the best one.

And I'm wondering why I don't just head to New Orleans.

At least there I would be able to focus on my next steps, my new chapter, the exciting things I have ahead of me.

But all of that comes with a bunch of complicated emotions, too. Leaving my sister and Mariah. Starting over somewhere alone for the first time ever. And leaving Henry.

Now, instead of feeling lighter, I'm ashamed by the sense of hurt and disappointment I feel that I am hearing about how great Scarlett's trip to Portland turned out from the podcast rather than from my sister or niece.

They've been busy. I'm sure Scarlett was nervous. She's so passionate about this project, but the last time she was a big public speaker, up in front of audiences, trying to sell them on ideas, it was for our father's church. I know that has left a bad taste in her mouth, and she has avoided the spotlight and public speaking for years.

But she didn't even call me for a pep talk. Or text me, *tell me I'm going to be fine.*

She didn't reach out to me before or after.

The event has been over for at least three hours now.

I'm glad it went well. *Of course,* I am. She needs to be good at this. The foundation means a lot to her, and it will do amazing work. She has to get out there and talk about it and not have flashbacks to her days of preaching and evangelizing.

But I did kind of think she might need a *you can do this* from me the first couple of times.

Still, this is *good*. I know that. This is her new life. Not only is she the wife of royalty, but she's married to a guy who is natural as a public figure and who has now seemingly embraced the fact that he can do a lot of good if he decides to be Prince Cian rather than just some random unimportant guy the way he has for the past decade or so hiding out in the United States.

But, clearly, besides being her biggest cheerleader—and I may have lost that designation to Cian as well—I'm not the one to help my sister navigate this next chapter of her life.

She's doing just fine without me.

I go to the show's website and start scrolling through the photos they referenced.

There are more than I expected. Jonah and Linnea look incredibly happy. Alex Olsen is *very* handsome. Declan and Astrid make an amazingly beautiful couple.

But it's the photos of Cian and Scarlett and Scarlett and Mariah that I linger over.

My sister looks gorgeous.

And it's not her hair or her makeup or what she's wearing. It's her smile.

My heart aches a little in my chest, but I feel my own smile as I study her face.

I don't remember the last time I saw Scarlett smile like that.

It was probably something to do with Mariah. Watching her up on stage at a school program or listening to her give an impassioned monologue about something important to her. She does that a lot.

My sister only looks like this when it has something to do with the love of her life.

That has always been Mariah.

Until now.

Now she has added something else. Or *someone* else.

My sister is completely, blissfully in love and happy.

And I am hit with a crazy mix of emotions.

The first is, and always will be, an equal measure of happiness.

This is what I always wanted for Scarlett. That look of contentment and happiness and the ability to laugh and relax and know that things are going to be okay.

I feel tears sting the backs of my eyes and blink rapidly.

Thank you, Cian.

My sister can finally just *be*. She can be happy, and she can rest. Of course, she'll be working with the foundation, taking care of Mariah, and embracing her new life. But her spirit can rest. She doesn't have to worry about money or material things. She doesn't have to worry if Mariah is safe. She won't be lonely or afraid.

I was always there and always did what I could, but now *I* don't have to worry about her and those things for her either.

So, along with the happiness is relief.

We made it.

Through all the tough times, through all the anxiety, through all the hard work, we're finally on the other side.

God, that feels good. It feels so good to take a deep breath and know that we don't have to dread getting bills in the mail, worry if Mariah will qualify for enough financial aid to go to college, or dream about an amazing vacation where we just sit on our asses, eat incredible food, sleep late, and have *no* responsibilities for a week.

Now Scarlett can do that any time.

Fuck, I love that.

But I'm also hit with an incredibly strong sense of sadness.

Scarlett isn't just mine anymore. I mean, I've shared her for sixteen years with Mariah, but that's different.

Now, someone else, a grown adult from outside our little circle of three, has come along and taken up space in her heart.

I have to actually give up the *majority* of her time, energy, and attention.

Those belong to Cian now.

So, directly on the heels of all of *that* is a strong wave of guilt.

I should feel nothing but happiness.

I should only want all of the best things for Scarlett.

But I do feel a little jealous, a little sad, and a little relieved all at the same time.

Scarlett doesn't need me anymore.

Mariah doesn't need me anymore.

April doesn't need me anymore. I'm not so sure she ever really did.

And that's all great. I'm so happy for them.

The only problem is, if I'm not taking care of someone, I don't really know who I am.

I put the car in drive and head toward my house.

It's time for me to go to New Orleans.

My sister will miss me, my niece will be sad, my friends will be surprised, but they will all be okay. They have other people, other things, to focus on.

But Henry Dean will actually miss me a lot.

And tonight, as selfish as it is, I need to be around someone like that.

CHAPTER 15
HENRY

I'm in the kitchen at the breakfast bar when Ruby comes in through the back door.

I'd started wondering where she was, but I'd refrained from texting. I was proud of myself for that.

But when I see her face, I swear internally. She's upset. *Bloody hell.*

I don't know what about exactly—not that it matters—but I wonder if she's heard from Scarlett.

"Hi," she says, setting a container of brownies on the counter.

Just a container of brownies.

Yeah. Upset.

"Hey." I give her a smile. "I just got a text from Elliot."

That kid will cheer her up.

"Elliot has your number? Wait, Elliot has a phone?" she asks.

I grin. "Will has my number. Elliot's using his phone."

I love that he texted me. He wanted to share what he's doing tonight and he thought of me. It's *not* a big deal but...

it is to me. I've convinced him that I'm someone who cares about him and what's going on with him. That matters.

Ruby smiles and the tension around my chest loosens a bit.

"Okay, that makes sense. What's he texting you about?" She shrugs out of her jacket, tossing it over the back of one of the kitchen chairs. She's wearing the black fitted v-neck tee with *I like Big Dick's* on the front in electric blue letters and I have to fight the urge to roll my eyes.

Honestly, the T-shirts are funny.

On anyone other than my…fuck it, *my woman*. She is. Whether we're saying that out loud or she wants to admit it or not, she is.

She comes around the breakfast bar and slides up on the stool next to me.

I turn to face her, my knees on either side of hers.

I turn my phone to show her the screen. It's a photo of Elliot. And a potbellied pig.

She grins. "Aw, that's cute. Elliot's excited to live with Porter, and April thinks it will be a great trial. He'll get a chance to be around an animal and help take care of it, but they won't have to commit to something they're fully in charge of. If Elliot does well, she's thinking about getting something when they move out on their own though."

"Mandy and Will actually have a pig as a pet?" I ask.

"Yep." Ruby looks up. "Their middle daughter, Riley, got him when she was in high school. Told them he was a 'teacup' pig, but teacup pigs are just a type of potbelly pig, actually ones that have been malnourished, so they stay small." She frowns. "Anyway, he wasn't truly a teacup pig, and he ended up growing full-sized. He's nearly two hundred pounds. She couldn't take him with her when she went to college, so now he's Mandy and Will's." She laughs. "He's also kind of mischievous."

"I told Cian that teacup pigs weren't actually tiny," I mutter, looking at the photo. Should I send the photo to Cian with *I told you so*? Or will that just encourage him?

"You and Cian talked about pigs?"

"Let's just say that I'm considering volunteering our dear prince as a pig sitter for Mandy and Will and hope that gets it out of his system."

Ruby laugh. "Mariah loves Porter."

I groan. "Don't tell me that."

"Cian definitely seems like the kind of guy to have a pet," Ruby muses. "He has a lot of energy. He probably needs a big rambunctious dog. Or a bunch of goats or something."

I nod. "You're right. He's been around animals forever because of Fiona. Of course, he's used to things like giraffes and lion cubs. Not just cats and dogs. And he had a bunch of goats to play with in Autre."

Thank God. Those goats are trouble, and Cian thought they were hilarious. His willingness to help round them up when they escaped the petting zoo and ended up in people's backyards, the motel's front lobby, and the funeral home's serenity garden probably kept them from becoming ground meat.

"You've never found a puppy hidden in the back of his closet?" Ruby asks with a grin.

I grab the container of brownies, pulling them toward me as I give her a *may I?* look.

She nods. "That's your dinner."

I smile. I'll make her something else. She's not eating just brownies for dinner. But it's been a day. I pop the container open and pull a thick brownie with gooey frosting out. "Cian never had to hide anything," I answer her question. "Thank God we went from the animal park in Florida to the animal park and petting zoo in Louisiana. He always had plenty of animals around. If he hadn't, I'm sure he would've filled the house with ridiculous shit. We would have had chinchillas or something. But, as it was, he got his fill of otters and alpacas and tigers. Even penguins in Autre."

I'd known Fiona O'Grady for years and lived with giraffes and emus in my backyard in Florida but I was still surprised to find a colony of endangered penguins in the tiny bayou town in Louisiana.

I feel Ruby's eyes on me as I bite into the brownie and lick frosting from my thumb.

I take my time swiping the chocolate from my finger with my tongue.

I don't care what she says, or tries to tell herself, the girl likes my tongue. And my thumb.

She clears her throat before she asks, "You like animals, right?"

We've never talked about either of us having pets, and I'm aware again of the other thing we haven't talked about. There's a lot about my past, my family, that she doesn't know. Things she probably should know.

"Of course," I say. "But taking care of a handful of Royals, who never follow a plan, was enough. I left all the animal wrangling to Fiona. And then Colin by default."

"You never helped?" she asks. "I know a lot about Princess Fiona and her animal rescues. She's done everything from breaking up puppy mills to rescuing endangered tigers from illegal trade in Texas. But you were around for all of that. You never got pulled in to help?"

"Oh, I helped."

First, it's nearly impossible to say no to Fiona O'Grady. She was born a princess after all. Second, she has a heart of gold. She asks for things like help rescuing abused and neglected animals. Who can say no that?

I hold out my right hand, flexing my fist and showing off the scar across the back of my knuckles. "Got a little too close to the wrong end of a tiger one time." I turn the hand over and show her a scar running up my forearm. "And an emu decided I looked tasty another time."

She gasps and grasps my hand, studying one scar then the other. "Oh my God, that is so cool."

I chuckle. "It's so cool that I'm *scarred*?"

She looks up at me as she runs her thumb across the scar. "I've seen these before, of course, but I assumed you got them fighting or rock climbing or something like that."

That makes sense. "I have few from that stuff too," I say, pointing to a scar on my wrist that came from a mountain in India.

She runs her finger over it too. "They're all cool," she says. "Your family—well, the O'Gradys—are fascinating. The things you've all done, the way you just all dive in to fix problems and save people and animals and do the hard work, is amazing. I know you joke about them being spoiled, but all of the princes and princesses have truly gotten their hands dirty with things that matter to them. And all of the bodyguards—their best friends—have been right there beside them."

I don't say anything. I just give a slight nod. It's true. But we don't do any of it to be "cool" or for praise. It's just all the right thing to do. I've never even punched anyone who didn't really deserve it.

Suddenly, Ruby leans over and presses a kiss to the back of my knuckles. "Very cool. And very sexy."

The touch of her lips to my skin sends heat sizzling up my arm. My gaze drops to her mouth again. "I know what you mean. All day long in that bar, I've wanted to grab you and kiss you. Your big heart and natural inclination to build community is sexy as fuck, Ruby."

She is so not the woman I ever expected to fall in love with.

I never wanted to fall in love at all. But if I had entertained the notion, I would have guessed I would have been drawn to a woman with a stable, almost boring family and past, someone who did 'normal' things like dinner with her grandparents, and liked to bake and, I don't know, knit? Someone who would counter my nightmare family story, someone who could balance the chaos that comes with my life and job.

But no, it's Ruby.

A woman whose backstory is a hodgepodge of places and people and who attracts chaos because people in need find her like little floating metal shavings to a powerful magnet.

She gives them a place to stick. She grounds them.

She makes me feel like a powerful magnet, too.

God, I love her so much.

It's not just physical between us.

Which makes it far more dangerous to my heart.

"You did grab me and kiss me," she reminds me.

I sure fucking did. "I want it on record that I showed extreme restraint today. The fact that you left that bar with all the clothes on that you came in with is a testament to that."

She looks like she's fighting a smile, but she loses the battle. "Duly noted."

She doesn't even bother to joke that she wouldn't have let that happen.

She would have. We both know it.

She lets my hand go to reach for a brownie of her own.

"So April does plan to move out?" I ask. "You said she's thinking about a pet when they move out."

She chews her bite of brownie, swallows, and nods, "Yes. Of course."

"How long have they talked about her staying with Mandy and Will?"

It better be until several months after the divorce from Christopher is finalized. I don't want them out on their own during any legal battles and the emotional toll that could take. I don't want April to waver for one damned second. I do think that Mandy and Will can help her stay strong through it all, though.

Ruby seems to read what I'm thinking.

"It will be a while. For sure until the divorce is final, there's a solid custody plan in place and it's been working for a while," she assures me. "And, if Mandy and Will have their way, until Elliot graduates from high school."

I give a short laugh. "Really?"

Ruby shrugs. "Maybe not that. But they won't be in a hurry for them to leave. They don't love being empty-nesters. They'll be good for April and Elliot. And vice versa."

I watch her closely as I ask, "So you're not worried about them at all?"

She takes a breath and then shakes her head. "No. I mean, yes. Kind of. But every time I think I should be, or something occurs to me to worry about, something happens, and I realize they're okay." She pauses, then says, "They might need help, but they don't need *me*." She gives me a small smile. "And that feels a little weird, and I don't like it, but it's true. Even at the grocery store..."

I don't like the way she trails off. I lean in. "What happened?"

"We just ran into some women who were giving April a hard time about leaving Christopher. Defending him. And... she handled it. She was fine. Then, before I could say a word, someone else was there, sticking up for her and putting them in their place." Ruby lifts a shoulder. "She didn't need me at all."

I'm quiet for a moment. I know exactly what she's feeling. I've felt it myself. "And you were so damned proud of her and happy for her because you truly want her to be happy and confident and independent." I pause. "And you were also a little relieved because you don't have to worry as much." I take a breath. "But at the same time, you felt a little sense of loss because that's your job, and if she doesn't need that, then does she really need you at all?"

She stares at me. Then nods slowly. "Yeah. All of that."

"That's how I feel every time I watch Cian and Scarlett together," I admit. "That pride and happiness and relief and sense of loss were so fucking strong when I watched them say their vows."

I don't feel bad confessing that to Ruby. No one else in the world would understand all of that. I would never tell all of that to anyone else. I know it makes me sound like an asshole to not be fully happy for my best friend on his wedding day.

But Ruby nods again. "Yeah. All of that, too."

"I felt kind of unnecessary all day today," I say.

"Same." She smiles. "At least you brought the cinnamon rolls."

I chuckle. "I also got a really challenging part of the jigsaw puzzle put together."

"Right." She sighs. "I didn't do much at all."

I lean in, my elbow on the breakfast bar beside her. "You know that's not true. Even if you didn't do anything directly in the moment, you are a huge reason for everything today. For that place and that group of people even being there. For it being a place April feels comfortable and safe. April had the courage to leave last night because she knew she had a place to go. Your house, then Dick's today."

Still, Ruby shrugs. "I like being needed all the time."

"I know."

I get it. We're the same.

"I feel that way sometimes." I shrug. "Look at the group I hang out with. There are lots of instances when I'm not needed or where I'm the least important person in the situation. Not only are there lots of other people with power and money, there are other bodyguards who have the same training and skills I do."

She tips her head. "Hmmm...you know, I never thought about it, but that's got to be hard on you. Not always being the most handsome, or richest, or most charming, or most talented guy in the room..."

I narrow my eyes and drop my voice low. "Don't even try that. You don't even notice other men when I'm around."

I can tell she's fighting a little smile and I know she's feeling a little better if she can tease me.

"To be fair, until Scarlett's wedding, I was comparing you to men in Emerald, Ohio. That trip to Cara was the first time I'd met Jonah. And Torin. And Colin. And Declan..."

I grasp the edges of her stool, and tug her between my knees. "Let me tell you something right now, Gem."

She swallows hard, her wide-eyed gaze on mine. "What?" she nearly whispers.

"If you need to be needed, there isn't another person on this planet who needs you the way I do."

Her pretty mouth falls open slightly.

I lift my hand and cup her face, dragging my thumb over her bottom lip. "You consume all of my thoughts," I tell her. "I want you every second of every day. I wish like hell I could move on, but I already know for a fact that that's impossible. *I* need you. If you need to be needed by someone, you don't have to look any further than right in front of you."

She stares at me for three beats. Then she says simply, "Show me."

Those are the only two words I need.

Ruby needs to feel needed? She needs to be important to someone? She needs to be the center of someone's universe?

I am *that* fucking guy.

CHAPTER 16
HENRY

I scoop my hands under her ass, lift her from the stool, and pull her forward as I stand from my seat. She wraps her arms and legs around me, and I stride to the only empty wall in the room.

I press her against the space next to the fridge, making sure she feels how hard I am already.

"I need you more than I need air," I tell her. "I need your taste." I kiss her deeply, sliding my tongue over hers, loving the way she meets me stroke for stroke. I lick over every inch of her mouth. Then I pull back. "I need to lick you, kiss you, fuck you, own you. I need your cries, your moans, your gasps. I need to hear my name from this gorgeous mouth. I need you to come. I need you to shatter. And I *need* to make you happy."

"Yes."

That's all she says. That's all she has to say.

I put her feet on the floor, then drop to my knees in front of her. I slide my hands up her thighs, my fingers slipping under the hem of that fucking T-shirt, inching it up her flat, smooth stomach. "I need you happy. I need you mindless. I need you overwhelmed. I need you spent."

Her head falls back against the wall behind her, and her eyes slide shut. But her hand reaches out, gliding into my hair and gripping.

"I need you so fucking much," I say, leaning in and putting my face against her stomach. I breathe deeply, the scent of her soap mingling with scents from the bar and the definite scent of her arousal already obvious.

"I need to please you," I tell her. "I need you to open this sweet body up so I can get at every inch and make you scream."

She takes a shuddering breath, and her fingers curl against my scalp.

I kiss up her stomach as I strip her shirt up and over her head. I toss it, my hands immediately going to the clasp on her bra as I kiss her deeply again. When her bra is gone, I fill my hands with her gorgeous tits.

"I've missed you," I tell her. "The feel of you—your skin, these tits, these nipples." I pluck at her nipples, eliciting a gasp, then a groan.

I lower my head, licking, then sucking, and making her arch into me.

I kiss back down her stomach, continuing to tease those delicious points with one hand as I tuck my other hand in the waistband of her black trousers, tugging one side down, then moving to the other, only to find her helping me out. We push them down her legs until she can step out of them and kick them to the side.

I sink to my knees and lean in, putting my nose against her mound and breathing deeply. Thin silk still separates me from her pussy. I pull it to the side and just look at the gorgeous sight in front of me. Pink, glistening, her clit plump and needy. I groan and she grips my hair tighter.

I give her a little lick as I grasp the white silk with both hands and jerk, ripping them.

"Henry! I liked those panties!"

"You need to wear panties less often anyway," I tell her unapologetically, leaning in to lick her clit again.

She moans and bucks her hips forward. "You have to buy me more," she tells me breathlessly.

"I'll get you your own credit card on my account."

"Don't be ridic—"

I suck her clit hard before she can finish that sentence.

She cries out my name and I trust that ends her protest over spending my money. Especially on panties.

I run my hands from her ankles to her ass and back down.

"I fucking need you, Gem. In every way. But right now, I need your legs spread open and my face in this sweet cunt."

She doesn't say anything, but she lifts one leg.

"That's my girl," I praise as I grasp her thigh and hook it over my shoulder.

I spread her open with my thumbs and then drag my tongue from her slit up to her clit in a long, firm lick before sucking hard.

The way she cries my name is the most beautiful sound in the world.

I lick, suck, and slide two fingers deep to fuck her to a fast, hard orgasm.

"Henry! Yes! Oh, God!"

I stand, keeping my fingers buried inside her. I pump them lazily as she comes down from that first climax. I kiss her deeply, swirling my tongue around hers, making sure she tastes all the sweetness I just tasted.

Her arms go around my neck and I slide my fingers out, cupping her ass with both hands. "Need to fuck you, Gem."

"Yes, please," she says, still panting.

I lift her and her legs wrap around my waist. I reach between us to shove my trousers out of the way. Then I sink deep into her with one thrust.

We stopped using condoms a long time ago. We've both tested negative and been monogamous despite the tension between us. She's got an IUD. So I've been fucking this woman bare, with nothing between us—except for our very complicated damned lives—for months.

And it feels like heaven every fucking time.

We both take a shaky deep breath as I slide deep, pull out, then slide in again.

"Yes, *God*, I've missed this. I've missed you so much," she says breathlessly, her fingers digging into my shoulders.

It's a tight fit anyway, and then she clenches her inner muscles around my shaft, making me suck in a quick breath. "Fuck, Gem."

She moves her hips, circling her pelvis on me. I do so love how this woman knows how to work a pole. Her core strength is incredible.

I thrust harder. "I should have bent you over the chair." I squeeze her ass. "Or made you ride me."

Her head comes up and she nods eagerly. "Let me ride you."

Fuck. I love when she does the lap dance thing for me. I don't care what Ruby's done in her past, and I would never try to tell her what she can do in the future—okay, I would, but I would also expect massive push-back and would not at all be surprised if she told me to keep my fucking opinions to myself—but I love the fact that she's given up stripping.

She's gorgeous, and I know she made very good money. For very good reason. She knows how to use this body. But I would now have to kill any man who sees her naked or thinks he can pay to touch so much as the bottom of her muddy shoe.

I grip her ass and carry her over to the kitchen table. I kick one of the chairs out and sink onto the seat, still buried deep. Now she's straddling me, completely naked, while I've only got my clothes pushed out of the way.

And she's totally in charge now.

She gets a sly look on her face and I see when she shifts into stripper mode. There's no question that the women know they hold all the power when they're taking off their clothes for those poor schmucks who can be manipulated by their lust.

I'm one of those schmucks right now. And it's not just my lust. I'm in love with this woman from head to toe, and inside out. She's amazing, gorgeous, and too good for me in every way.

The fact that she deigns to get naked for me, let me see her, touch her, please her, is incredible. I appreciate that she's taking pity on me.

She lifts herself, sliding up and down my cock. Then she lifts herself off my lap.

"Mr. Dean, I understand you want a private performance tonight?" She stands between my knees, running her hands over her body. She cups her breasts, fingers her nipples, runs her hands down her stomach, over her mound, down the front of her inner thighs, then back up. Her index finger brushes lightly over her pussy and then she lifts her finger to her mouth, sliding the digit over her lower lip. "Is that right?"

"That is right, Ruby," I say, working to keep my voice steady. "I'm willing to pay whatever you say."

"Oh, I'm going to make you pay," she says, that wicked glint in her eye making my cock pulse. "Don't you worry about that."

"I expect an incredible performance," I tell her.

"Of course." She gives me an arched brow laced with mock insult. "But this is a special performance."

"Is it?"

She nods, running her hands down the front of her body again. "It's interactive."

I let my grin spread slowly. "Sounds expensive."

"Very."

"How much?"

"Two orgasms," she says. Then she smiles. "Two *more* orgasms."

"I'll *happily* pay that price."

"And you can only touch me when and where I say," she tells me as I reach out.

Brat. She knows that will be the most difficult part.

I let my hand drop back to my lap. Then I think better of it. I wrap my hand around my cock and give myself a stroke. "Okay."

She shakes her head. "Just don't make yourself come. That's all *mine*."

I stroke myself harder. "You didn't say that. You said two orgasms. I can make you come even if I've already spilled all over my own hand."

That makes her catch her breath and her eyes are glued to my hand and my cock.

"But..."

"Say it, Gem," I tell her. "Just tell me what you want."

"I want you to come inside me."

Bloody hell. That's what I wanted her to say, what I expected, but damn it nearly makes me lose it hearing it.

I take my hand away and hold it up. "It's all yours."

She meets my eyes and lets her façade drop for a moment. "I want to play, but I don't know how long I can wait. I need you inside me, Henry."

She is everything I will ever want or need. "Play as long as you need to. I'm right here. This is all up to you. But you do love to pretend to be in charge."

That makes a spark of competition flare in her eyes. "Pretend to be in charge?" she repeats.

I lift a shoulder. "We both know that I play you like a fine instrument."

"Uh huh." She does a little shimmy, then crosses her legs and executes a graceful turn. Then bends.

Fuck me.

She hugs her legs and peeks at me. "A fine instrument?"

"Yep. A *very* fine instrument." I lean forward. "Your pussy is so pretty like this. Pink and wet from your first orgasm and from being stretched by my cock for just a little bit before you pulled off and decided to torture me." I reach up but don't touch her. "Let me touch you, Gem."

But she shakes her head. She turns again, stretching upright in one fluid motion. Her arms go overhead, her back arching, showing off her gorgeous body. Then she parts her legs, pulls one up, nearly to her ear, exposing her pussy again before spinning on the other foot.

Then she drops to the floor. She doesn't have a pole here, but that doesn't stop her. She goes through a routine that clearly is familiar, arching her back, rolling to her stomach, spreading her legs, bracing with her arms, pushing up, bending, arching, rolling until I'm nearly crazy.

She seems to know when I've reached my limit because

she stretches to her feet directly in front of me. She places one foot on the floor beside my chair, then props the other foot on the seat between my knees.

She takes one of my hands and runs it up her leg until my palm is against her inner thigh. "Touch me, Henry."

"I am touching you."

"More."

"Tell me what you want, Gem." My tone is firm. She's been winding me up, on purpose, and I'm not playing games. "Tell me where to put my hand, my fingers, my mouth, my tongue. Exactly."

"In my pussy."

"What do you want in your pussy?"

"Your fingers."

"How many?"

"Two."

My hand glides up her leg, two fingers sliding into her very wet, hot pussy. "Did you always get so wet when you danced?" I ask.

She shakes her head as her pussy grips my fingers. "No. God." She laughs. "Absolutely not. Only for you. It was so hot having you watch me."

I pull my fingers out and then thrust again. "You are the most beautiful thing I've ever seen."

She lifts her hands to cup her breasts, teasing her nipples as I finger fuck her.

"My clit too, please," she says, twisting her nipples hard.

"Why don't you put one of those nipples in my mouth and play with your own clit?" I ask.

"Thought I was in charge," she says, even as she leans closer so I can suck her nipple into my mouth.

"Sure, unless I have a better idea," I say, licking over the tip as her fingers find her clit.

She starts circling, and I slide a third finger into her pussy, thrusting harder and faster.

"God, yes, Henry." She pushes down against my hand.

"You spread out over me like this is so fucking hot and dirty," I praise. "Look at your pretty cunt filled up, your fingers working that clit, nipples hard. You're looking pretty needy yourself right now, Gem."

She nods. "I need to come, Henry."

"Come then." I curl my fingers against her G-spot.

And she does. Hard. Loudly. Crying out my name. Her pussy clamps around my fingers, and her legs wobble a little.

I pull her into my lap. My cock is aching. But I kiss her rather than just pulling onto my length and fucking her.

I let her mouth go when her shivers stop.

But then I lift my sticky fingers to her mouth. "Suck my fingers clean."

Her eyes widen slightly, but it's with lust. She opens, and I slide my fingers into her hot mouth. She sucks, then runs her tongue over each digit.

"Good girl," I say gruffly, taking the hand and wrapping it around my cock. "Now let me have your pussy, or I'm going to come all over your stomach, and you'll have to wait until I can recover to have me fill you up."

"No. Mine." She shifts, takes my cock in hand, and positions it so she can sink down onto it.

God, I love my dirty, sweet girl.

We both groan and I grip the back of her neck as I bring her in for a deep, long, hot kiss.

She starts moving up and down my length. I grip her

hip and tear my mouth from hers. "Easy. I'm wound very tight. If you want to come again, you need to go easy here."

"I'm on the edge," she tells me. "God, giving in after trying to resist you, dancing for you, and just...everything. *Everything*, Henry. I swear I can't get enough."

She keeps moving up and down and who am I to fight it? I take her hips in both hands and just say, "Take what you need, love."

She moves faster and faster and I feel my climax building.

"Gem," I say through gritted teeth.

She nods. "I know. I'm almost there."

"I want you to—"

And then, holy shit, she comes again.

There have been many nights where I've made sure she's had multiple orgasms. I love making this woman come. But damn, this feels easier than usual. Not that I'm complaining. But is she really going to make us live without this?

That thought makes me grip her hips and pound up into her in an almost punishing rhythm.

My orgasm rips through me and I'm roaring her name and emptying myself into her, before wrapping my arms around her and crushing her to my chest, holding her tight.

She slumps against me, holding me just as tight. As if she can't imagine ever letting even an inch of space between us.

If only it could be that simple.

We stay like that for nearly ten minutes. I'm definitely not going to be the one that breaks this connection.

Finally though, she stirs in my arms and sits up.

She pushes her hair back from her face and says, "Oh, no."

I sigh. "Seriously? You're already regretting it?"

She shakes her head. "Not regretting. Just realizing that I'm probably going to ask you to come to New Orleans to visit me."

My heart gives a hard kick against my ribs. "Done."

"Like once or twice a month, Henry. I don't think I can live without orgasms. And I don't want them from anyone else."

I growl. Loudly. "You're *not* getting orgasms from anyone else. I will come to New Orleans any time you need me."

There's a beat of hesitation. During which I swear a million things are said. Like 'I need you all the time', and 'you'll come unless Cian needs you', and 'if it's like this between us, why can't we just be together?', and 'maybe I should just stay here'.

And even if all of those words and questions are only in my head, Ruby and I need to talk.

"Why don't you go take a shower, and I'll make us some real food? Brownies are not dinner, Gem," I say before she can point to the plastic container. "And...I'll tell you about my mom and dad and brother."

Her eyes widen with interest.

We haven't talked about my family and my past. Not because I didn't want to. It just honestly didn't come up.

Now it has. Even if she doesn't know it. Or how it connects to Cian and the O'Gradys and my job.

"Okay." She hesitates, then kisses me quickly before climbing off my lap, gathering her clothes, and heading toward the stairs.

"Hey, Gem?" I call.

"Yeah?"

"If I installed a stripper pole, would you do those routines for me too?"

She pops her head back into the kitchen. She grins. "I have a pole. I work out with it all the time. It's great for my core. My abs. And my pelvic floor."

I sit up straighter. "Where?"

"In the rec room in our basement."

"In this house?"

"Yeah."

"Why didn't I know this until now?"

She shrugs. "You probably need to stop pissing me off. I might know all kinds of fun things you'd be interested in."

Then she turns and sashays her gorgeous naked ass up the stairs.

CHAPTER 17

RUBY

He made me chicken quesadillas.

I didn't even know we had the ingredients for chicken quesadillas.

I was expecting grilled cheese. Maybe scrambled eggs. That's what I would have probably made. I mean, I *can* cook. I just don't very often.

And honestly, it is a universal truth that food other people make for you always tastes better than food you have to make for yourself.

"These are *so* good," I say for the fourth time.

Henry chuckles. "Your standards are too low." He pauses, then says, "Maybe I should be glad about that."

I roll my eyes as I chew. I swallow and say, "Right. My low standards that include *only* fucking gorgeous, smart, over-protective bodyguards who love to throw money around and have sexy British accents and huge cocks."

He chokes on his bite and reaches for his iced tea. When he's swallowed, he frowns at me. "There is exactly *one* man who fits that description in the entire world, for your information."

I nod, taking another bite. "I'm aware."

He seems satisfied with that answer, but he's still watching me with narrowed eyes.

"What?" I ask.

"You have to eat your vegetables too."

He cut up a couple of bell peppers and arranged them in a colorful fan on my plate. I roll my eyes and pick one up, biting into it. "You know, you seem to think my body is in perfectly fine shape," I say.

"It's in amazing shape," he agrees. "And I'd like to keep you around for the next eighty or ninety years in good shape."

I freeze with a sliver of pepper halfway to my mouth.

That sounded very...relationship-y.

Did I screw up? Sex was inevitable between us. It just was. But Henry cannot expect that it means I'm staying here in Emerald now.

And if he starts talking about that, asking me about it, even begging me... I might say yes. And I fucking *hate that*. I want to go to law school.

In fact, I think I *need* to go to law school.

I need to help people. That's who I am. And today showed me clearly that Emerald, Ohio, doesn't need me. I need a bigger place, a place with more people, a place where people don't form little community centers inside bars.

Of course, anyone could form a community inside any place. It was just about bringing people together. There are people like Ada, Will, April, and Dan everywhere. Just because they're in a bigger city doesn't mean that inside that city there aren't little communities...

But no. I force myself to stay on track. I need to go out

and make a difference. Emerald and the people here will be okay without me. I need to find a place that also needs me.

"Henry," I start. "Today was awesome. And the idea of not—"

"I want to tell you about how I came to work for Cian."

I frown, my train of thought derailed. "Okay. Why?"

"You need to know why I'm so loyal to him."

I shake my head. "He's your best friend. He's basically your brother. You love him. You don't have to explain that to me, Henry. I get it."

But he takes a breath and moves his chair closer to mine. "I need to explain why I keep saying that I have to choose him over you. It's more than just my feelings for him."

I sit up a little straighter, sensing that this is serious. "Are you okay?" I ask him. A thought occurs and I frown. "Are they somehow forcing you to stay with him? Coercing you? Because I will..."

I'm not sure what I can do. I know self-defense, and I *would* shoot someone who threatened someone I love, but I don't have a gun, or extreme survival skills, or a crazy network of resources that could outrun or outsmart the royal family.

"I'll take you somewhere," I finally say. "Hide you. I know people who can make fake IDs and..." I frown. "That's about it. But I have a lot of influence over Scarlett, and she has a lot of influence over Cian, and we will use it to help you."

Henry's looking at me with a mix of wonder and amusement. "You'd convince your sister to cut Cian off to save me?"

"He's *really* crazy about her. I think the threat of never

seeing her naked again could get him to do almost anything," I say.

Henry smiles and nods. "I think you're right. Living with him in those months they were apart was awful. Now? He'll never let her go again."

I nod resolutely. "Okay. I'll get Scarlett to get Cian to help you."

"What if he's in on it?" Henry asks, clearly amused now.

I feel the tension start seeping out of me. I shrug. "Poison? Suffocation?"

His eyebrow arches. "First, your sister would be very upset if you killed her husband. She's pretty crazy about him, too. Second, suffocation is a very aggressive way to kill someone. I don't think you've got that in you, Gem."

"First," I counter. "Scarlett would be a lot less crazy about him if he's actually a bad guy and he's forcing you to work for him with blackmail or something. Second, I've got it in me if you need me to have it in me."

Something flickers in his eyes. Heat? Yes, but also something that looks like gratitude? But that doesn't make sense.

"Third," Henry says. "You're telling Prince Cian O'Grady's bodyguard that you are willing to do him harm."

I narrow my eyes. "Yeah, I am. What are you gonna do about it?"

Henry's smile is slow and has a touch of the wickedness that makes my panties wet every time. Henry Dean is the only man to ever do that to me with a simple smile.

"I'm not sure," he admits. "But I think it would be difficult to avenge my friend because we'd both enjoy all the things that came to mind far too much."

I smile and lean in. "Well, for the record, I'd do whatever I could to save you. Say the word."

He takes a deep breath. "You're just determined to make it so I can never get over you, aren't you?"

That makes my smile fade. But the wetness in my panties becomes an even bigger issue.

I don't want him to get over me.

I don't want to get over him.

This is going to be a big problem, but there's really no way around it now.

Finally, he shakes his head. "No, Gem, I'm with Cian voluntarily. But it's more than just because he and I are good friends. I need you to know that I'm not choosing him because of something like I love to play video games with him or because I love the private jet thing."

"But you do love to play video games with him, and that private jet is amazing." I feel this urge to keep things light. I can sense that whatever he's going to tell me is *not*.

"I do, and it is," he agrees. "But I can play with him online wherever I am. And I think he'd let me borrow the jet pretty much any time."

He's right. "So what's it about?" I guess I'm ready to hear it.

"It has to do with my family. My parents. And Alfred Olsen."

We've never talked about his family. Honestly, when we did talk about our pasts and histories, we spent a lot of time on mine because my family situation, my father being the pastor of the megachurch that seems to rule over half the town, and my single-mom sister Henry's best friend was in love with, was all central to why Henry and I even met.

But I want to know everything about Henry, so I lean in. "Alfred Olsen? Linnea, Astrid, and Alex's grandfather?"

Henry nods. "He was also King Diarmuid's best friend and one of his closest advisors. In fact, there were many times that without Alfred's level-headedness and his general optimism and compassion, Diarmuid would've definitely made different decisions."

"Like what?"

I've never tried to hide my fascination with the royal family. Once we found out that my sister actually had a one-night stand with a real prince, it was impossible not to get caught up in all of the stories, history, and gossip around them. The podcast fed that fascination and, of course, every little bit of information Henry would share.

It's still bizarre to me that we know people who are actual royalty. Sure, Cara is a small country with very little international power or influence, but still, their mind-blowing wealth, their quirky history, their charming country…it's all enthralling. Even if it's much different from the movies and novels, there is still a fun fantasy-adventure feel to the whole thing.

"I want to hear it all," I tell him.

"Alfred and Diarmuid met when they were young men. Before Diarmuid was king. Alfred came from an influential, wealthy family in Denmark, even before Diarmuid actually made him a Duke. Diarmuid took over the throne at thirty-nine after his father suddenly died. He knew he'd be king someday, but he wasn't fully prepared. Alfred helped him through a lot in those early days. Along with Queen Roisin and Diarmuid's friend Oisin, Alfred helped Diarmuid become the king he is.

"But Alfred was often frustrated with the fact that Diarmuid wanted to keep Cara quiet, under the radar, and more or less cut off from the rest of the world. Cara relies almost entirely upon their trade relationship with Denmark.

Denmark is their only true ally, and Alfred knew it wasn't good for Cara to be at the mercy of the whims of the government there. He wanted Cara to expand its friendships and kind of come out of its shell.

"But Diarmuid was afraid they were too small for other countries to care about? That maybe someone would try to take them over or something? That they needed that friendship with a larger, richer country to protect them?" I ask. "That makes sense to me."

"Yes. And that does make sense. But it also kept him indentured to Denmark and whoever was in power there."

"Okay. I guess that could also be bad. It's like when Rachel Goosman told me I couldn't be friends with anyone but her in second grade. Then when she was a shithead, I didn't have anyone on my side, or anyone else to turn to." I scowl remembering it. "And *only* Rachel came to my Halloween party. Scarlett didn't even stay home for it, because she hated Rachel. A party with just two people is *far* less fun than parties with a bunch of people."

Henry is looking at me with both brows arched.

I shrug. "It's not a terrible metaphor."

He laughs. "I guess not. What happened to Rachel?"

"She moved away, actually."

He laughs again. "Well, then the analogy falls apart a bit. Denmark isn't going anywhere. And they've always had lots of 'friends'. It was only Cara that was cutting itself off. It still does to some extent. Though Torin is working to change that."

"So Alfred didn't change Diarmuid's mind? The king didn't mind having lame Halloween parties?"

"Pretty much. So, Alfred decided to make a plan B. When it came time for Declan to start preparing to take the throne, Alfred encouraged him to leave Cara instead."

My eyes widen. "Wait. Declan abdicated because of Alfred?"

I know from my study of the country and the O'Grady family that all of the grandchildren abdicated the throne and left the country, but Declan actually left almost five years before the others did. And when he returned for Cian's wedding—which also turned into *his* wedding—that was the first time he'd been back to the island since he'd abdicated.

Henry nods. "Diarmuid didn't know that for a few years, and when he found out, he didn't speak to Alfred for nearly six months, but yes, Alfred encouraged Declan to leave and invested in all of his startups. He felt strongly that someone in the family needed to be divorced from the throne, loyal to the country and family in their heart, but independent of their power and money."

"Why did he choose Declan? He was firstborn, so he should have been king. Alfred could have just convinced Declan to be the king he thought Diarmuid should be, right?" I ask.

"Because Declan has the right personality to go out and kickass in business and politics in the US. Torin is the right one to lead the country. Alfred saw that in them even before Torin abdicated."

"Did he panic when Torin left Cara?"

"He expected it. It made him happy. It meant Torin would have experiences that would make him an even better king. Because he also knew, somehow, that eventually Torin would return to Cara. It was hard to keep Declan in Portland though."

"No way. Declan thought about going back to Cara?"

"Yep. Alfred practically had to chain him to a chair."

"What did he do to keep him from going back?"

Henry grins. "He hired Iris."

Oh, I kind of love this. "Iris kept Declan in the US?"

"Yep. They—she and Alfred—convinced Declan that everything was going according to plan and it would be fine. That Declan's role was to build wealth, power, and connections outside of the royal family so they had that additional layer of networking and influence."

"Wow."

He nods. "We always called Alfred the Boss. He had the vision and the heart the family needed. He knew the royal family and his own grandchildren could, and would, use their privilege and resources to do good things in the world, if they were given the support and the occasional nudge in the right direction. But he *really* wanted to get them out of Cara to make that happen. He loved the country, but it was so small, and he wanted it connected to the rest of the world. The opposite, really, of what Diarmuid wanted. Until after Alfred died." Henry sighs. "I think losing Alfred made Diarmuid realize that he'd been right about so many things. Then seeing all of the grandchildren actually out in the world doing great things, was the final proof."

"Now that Alfred is gone, who is managing things in the US? Helping Iris?"

Henry smiles mysteriously. "No one."

"What?"

"Everyone thinks there's a new Boss, someone Alfred appointed to take over for him, someone pulling the strings. But...it's Iris."

"Iris is the big overall boss?"

"Yep."

I only vaguely remember the other woman. But my impression of her was someone who was confident, take charge, and mildly irritated with...everything and everyone.

"I'm impressed."

"Alfred loved Iris. He trusted her with everything."

"And he was practically a prophet," I say. "Everything is turning out the way he planned."

Henry laughs at that. "Uh, no. Nothing is going according to plan. Everyone has gone rogue."

"What?"

He nods. "It's kind of a mess. Linnea and Torin were supposed to get married and produce the heir. Alfred had ideas for the work and causes everyone would be best at. Everyone is...adjacent to those ideas." He grins.

"So Alfred thought the O'Gradys and Olsens needed to be bonded by blood? So there would be a next generation of amazing people doing good works in the world too?"

Henry pauses, then shakes his head. "That was purely emotional. Alfred and Diarmuid wanted their families to be one big, united family. They felt arranged marriages between their grandchildren was an obvious solution."

I laugh. "If only arranged marriages weren't so last century."

Henry gives me a half smile. "For two men who were into making deals and networking, and even manipulating when necessary, for the greater good, it still made sense regardless of the date on the calendar."

I guess that makes a kind of sense. I'm more convinced after seeing that photo of Declan and Astrid. If they actually have a love match and true passion between them, that's amazing.

"Anyway, I owe Alfred Olsen my life."

Whoa. That makes me focus fully on the man in front of me again. I lean in. "Literally?" With this group, it wouldn't surprise me if Alfred pulled Henry off the edge of a cliff or scooped him out of the ocean or something equally dramatic.

Henry nods. "Yes. And figuratively."

"How did that happen? How did you meet Alfred?"

"My family was also very wealthy. Alfred and my father had several people in common. They were in a similar social and business circle. So when my family situation... got complicated, Alfred found out about it and intervened."

"What happened?"

Henry takes a deep breath and turns his palm over. I slip my hand into it, and he intertwines our fingers. He stares down at the tabletop as he begins talking.

"When I was fourteen, I was at home alone with my mother. My father was at work, my brother was off with friends. It was our country home, so we had fewer servants, and, I don't know, they just weren't there that afternoon." He takes another deep breath. "There were some branches that were brushing against a bedroom window on the upper level of our house. This house wasn't as big as our regular house, but it was still enormous. Mom wanted to cut those branches back before we had guests come stay, believing that the branches scratching against the window would be a nuisance. She couldn't find the gardener, so she hauled a ladder out herself and climbed up. I was in the house but didn't know what she was doing. She didn't tell me or ask me to help. I went looking for her later and—" He stops and squeezes his eyes shut. I dread what he's about to say, but I put my other hand on top of his, sandwiching his between mine.

"She had fallen from the ladder and hit her head on the stone path." His grip on my hand tightens. "She was dead. Lying there in the grass of our side yard."

Oh, God.

I can't breathe.

I stare at him.

He'd found his mother dead? As a child? When he was home alone?

That's so horrible. I don't want to think about it, but this is Henry. I can't shy away from this. This is his past. His truth.

My eyes sting. My heart breaks for the little boy that he was, who had to find his mother that way. For the man who is still, clearly, so broken by it. For the sudden, awful loss that has been a part of his life for so long.

"My God, Henry," I choke out. "I'm so sorry."

He swallows hard and keeps going. "My father was beside himself. He was never an emotional man. That was the first time I ever saw him show any emotion other than anger, or boredom, honestly. But his grief was… indescribable. I'll never forget the look on his face. Or the look when he turned toward me and said, "This is all your fault.""

I gasp. "Henry, *no*. How could he blame you for that?"

He's not looking at me, and I'm torn between wanting him to focus on something other than the image of his father's face and not wanting to see the crushing pain in his eyes.

"I could've climbed the ladder for her," he says, his voice ragged. "Or I could have insisted she find the gardener. Or gone to find him myself. Or insisted that she wait. Or I could've at least been there when she fell. Maybe, if I'd been there, I could have called for help. We could've saved her."

Obviously, he's been haunted by these thoughts for years, and I have to wonder if he's actually heard these words from his father. I grip his hand tightly. "Henry, you didn't even know what she was doing. It's not like you refused to help her. And even if you had, it's not your fault that she fell. It was an *accident*."

He doesn't respond to that. "My father stopped speaking to me after that," he says. "He couldn't stand to be in the same room with me. He told the family counselor who came to the house that I was a reminder of her and what had happened, and he would never forgive me."

Jesus. I hate Henry's father. So, so much.

I wonder if King Diarmuid could do something to him.

Or maybe Jonah or Colin. They're highly trained body-guards. Surely, they know some good, appropriately horrible torture techniques.

Or Iris.

She's the boss now.

"Henry."

He keeps going. "After that, my younger brother, at only thirteen, got into drugs. Six months later, he got high at a party and drove himself and a friend home. He smashed the car into a brick wall, and he and his friend were badly injured. They were in the hospital in intensive care for a month. The friend's family sued my father for ten million dollars. They won."

Oh God. This just keeps getting worse. I rub my hand over my chest, where my heart is literally aching. Tears prick my eyes. "Henry. God."

"I want to tell you. You need to know how this all happened."

I meet his eyes. There are so many emotions there that I want to look away. But I can't. This is a huge, impactful part of the life of the man I love's life. I need to know it. And no matter how painful it is for me, it's a hundred times worse for him. If telling me helps him in any way, I will listen and take this in.

I nod. "Go on."

"My father also blamed me for my brother. He said I should've realized my brother was so upset. I should've gone to the party with him, I should've realized he was using drugs, I should not have let him take the car, I should have picked him up from the party, there was a whole list of things I should've done.

"So, before my brother even came home from the hospital, my father sent me to boarding school. Honestly, at the time, I thought maybe it was best. I didn't want to be around my father either. So I didn't argue or fight it. I just packed my bags, and our driver, Steven, drove me to school and dropped me off at the front door." He pauses. "I never went home again."

I stare at him. "What? You *never* went home again?"

He meets my gaze directly. "I never saw my father again after I left my house that day. He never came to see me, and I never went home. He died six years ago of a brain aneurysm. My brother and I reconnected at his funeral, and we've been very slowly rebuilding our relationship, but it's not easy. And—" He takes another deep breath, then blows it out, as if blowing out the painful words and memories. "My life has been very good anyway. I've missed my brother, but I never missed my father. It makes me feel terrible to say that, but it's true. He was a cold man before, and after all of that happened, the way he blamed me and then just threw me away, I realize now that he was not a good father. I've accepted that, and while I haven't forgiven him, I have let it stop influencing me."

I nod. I think that's good. His father didn't deserve to know this amazing man. He sent Henry away. That was his choice. "Fuck him," I say simply.

Henry nods. "He tried to reach out once after he found out I was working for the royal family."

"I'll bet he did." I'm not sorry I'll never meet the man.

"It felt really good to say, through the palace, that I had nothing to say to him, and I didn't want to hear from him ever again. And I never did."

I squeeze his hand. "Did you meet Cian at boarding school or something?" I think about how he is when he's with the O'Gradys—happy, comfortable, clearly relaxed, and fully accepted.

Damn, I love them.

They've made my sister feel all of those things, too. And they helped heal the man I love. I will always be a loyal royal fan-girl.

Henry shakes his head. "No. I was at boarding school for two mostly uneventful years. I'd go home with friends for the holidays. I spent summers taking additional classes or working."

Oh fuck. I hadn't even thought about him being alone on holidays.

I hate his father even more now.

"Then, one day, I was pulled out of class because this man, Alfred Olsen, wanted to meet with me."

"How did Alfred find you?"

"There were a couple of events, I believe one was a Christmas party, where Alfred expected my father to have his children with him. When he didn't for the second or third time, Alfred started asking around. He immediately came to the boarding school when he found out where I was. He told me that I had been selected for a special program and transferred me to another school. It was a school that Alfred helped fund, of course, and was for people who were tapped for special assignments."

"Assignments?"

"It was much like the Secret Service or the CIA. Specially trained, secretive, select. But specifically to be bodyguards for very important people. I learned martial arts, marksmanship, archery, all about every available kind of technology and several that weren't available yet. I learned to skydive, deep sea dive, and wilderness survival. Anything and everything I would need to become specialized security for dignitaries."

"At age sixteen?" I ask, amazed.

He nods. "My first job was a short-term assignment accompanying a U.N. ambassador's son on a skiing trip."

"Oh. Like what you did for Cian," I say. "You protected people around your age so you could blend in, seem like just one of the guys."

"Exactly. I continued going to school, receiving special training, but then would be pulled out for various assignments."

"All because Alfred didn't like how your father treated you," I say.

"That's how I got on his radar," Henry agrees. "But he did his research. Talked to professors, people who knew me, decided I was exactly the kind of person he wanted to bring into the O'Grady inner circle."

"So he was recruiting you from the beginning."

"Essentially. And then Fiona, Torin, and Cian abdicated and headed to the US. I got tapped to be Cian's bodyguard a little sooner than they'd expected. But it worked out."

I squeeze his hand. "It really did." If I think of all the ways we could have missed ever meeting one another, I'm nearly overwhelmed that he's sitting in my kitchen right now.

He's from a wealthy British family. Was specially

trained to be the bodyguard to a prince from a little island country. Then landed in Florida and then Louisiana.

How he ever ended up walking into my bar in Emerald, Ohio, is a miracle.

"So Alfred not only saved me from boarding school, he… gave me a purpose. Showed me I was not worthless. He kept me from just being thrown away. He gave me a place to belong. A family." Henry has to clear his throat. "I'm a protector, just like you. And just like you, I'm lost when I don't have someone to take care of. Alfred saw that in me, and he gave me exactly what I needed."

"Yes, times about a thousand," I say with a smile. "You take a protector and a caregiver and make them into the bodyguard of a prince, I'd say that's pretty visionary."

"Alfred knew that each of the O'Grady and Olsen kids would do something amazing with their lives and their power. Alfred picked very specific people for each of them and gave us the assignment to not only be their protector and their friend but to truly help them find and reach their potential. As I've gotten to know Cian over the years, I've been more and more flattered by that. Cian really does have the ability to do amazing things. The fact that Alfred thought I could be a part of that is humbling. Our whole team feels that way."

I am having a hard time taking a deep breath. What I'm feeling at the moment is something I've felt before. For my niece and sister. Only the people I love with all my heart. It's that combination of pride and happiness, knowing that they have found something that truly completes them, fulfills them, and shows them everything they are capable of.

And the realization that I have to let them go in order for them to have that thing.

"I am so grateful that Alfred Olsen saw that in you and helped you see it," I say sincerely.

Henry studies my face, his eyes searching mine. "Thank you."

"And I understand that you can't leave Cian because you feel like Alfred gave you this assignment, and you owe it to him to stay with Cian. And the family. And your team. You are all in this together, right? You'd never leave Jonah and Iris either."

Henry swallows hard. "Before his dementia got really bad, Alfred realized what was happening. He met with each of us, the bodyguards, about going forward. When we talked, he said that I had done so well. He said he knew he could leave Cian and the O'Gradys in my hands because I would always do everything I could to make sure they were safe and happy, no matter what. We all feel that way."

I wet my lips. "It's that 'no matter what' that's got you, right? No matter if it's hard on you, or if you have to give something up."

He just nods.

Well...fuck.

I'm never going to feel this way about anyone else. And he's staying here in Emerald, Ohio.

So...

I lean in and press my lips to his. "Thank you for telling me. I get it."

He cups the back of my head, resting our foreheads together. "I knew you would. But I know it sucks."

"I don't know, it definitely proves that I have *amazing* taste in men. When I finally, fully fell in love with someone, I fell for the best man in the whole world."

He pulls me in for a deep kiss. It's slow and sweet, but

it's all-consuming. He tastes me fully, making sure I feel every stroke, every press, every emotion.

I'm about to climb into his lap and start stripping my clothes off when my phone starts ringing, and Henry's dings with three texts in a row.

We pull apart.

We stare at each other for a long moment.

But then, because we are who we are, we, of course, both reach for our phones.

Someone might need us.

CHAPTER 18

HENRY

"It's Scarlett," Ruby says, looking at her phone.

"Go. Talk to her. I know you want to hear how things are going."

She gives me a little smile. "Things are going great. I listened to the podcast."

I know things are going great. I heard from Jonah just before Ruby got home. But I didn't tell her. That would have been rubbing it in that Scarlett and Mariah were fine without her. I knew that would be hard.

"You still want to hear it from Scarlett. Hear how she feels about it." I know hearing Cian's version of events is always different.

She nods. "Yeah."

"Go talk to her. I have a couple of messages to return. I'll clean up the kitchen."

"Okay. I..."

I wait.

She sighs as if she knows she shouldn't say it, but then she smiles and says, "I love you."

I smile. "I love you, too."

That complicates everything. It makes all of this harder. But it's still true.

I'm glad I told her about Alfred. I'm glad she knows my whole history.

She heads upstairs to talk to Scarlett, and I open my text.

From April.

April: *Elliot and I are going to spend the night at Mandy and Will's.*

Me: *Ruby would really like to see you and hear how things went at dinner.*

I know that April is already getting her life together and moving on from Christopher, which is not only impressive, it's healthy. I don't want to block that. But Ruby needs a little slower separation. She deserves to hear and see April and Elliot doing well and being happy, at least. Not just seeing it in texts.

April: *I will fill her in tomorrow.*

Screw this. I dial her number.

April answers immediately. "Hello?"

"Why the rush to stay over there? Don't you at least need Elliot's pajamas? A few toys? Toothbrushes? How about Ruby and I bring some things over?"

"It's not a rush. And all of that would be great. I just—"

"Hey, Henry."

Suddenly I'm talking to Will.

"Uh, hey."

"So I think it's better if April and Elliot stay here tonight. We had to handle something with Christopher and he knows where everything stands now."

I stand immediately. "What? Christopher came over?"

"He did. I assume he felt safer approaching her here than at Ruby's after meeting you."

Well, that's good. He definitely shouldn't feel safe approaching her when I'm around. "Is he still there?" I'm already moving toward the door. I obviously need to make things even *more* clear with Christopher.

"No, no. He left pretty quick. Well, after John got here."

I stop at the door. "Is John your cop friend?"

"No. I was gonna call him but then I remembered I know someone even better for dealing with Christopher."

This I have to hear. "Who's that?"

"John."

I roll my eyes. "Will, who is John?"

"John and I went to high school together. We were on the baseball team together. Went to State our junior year. We had a bit of a falling out after senior year. I stole his girl." Will chuckles. "But he and Mandy weren't a good fit."

Fantastic. Will stole Mandy from John thirty-some years ago. What this has to do with Christopher, I don't know, but I assume Will will get to it tonight eventually.

"Mandy felt bad and set him up with her friend Rhonda. And they fell madly in love. So, obviously, John forgave me and we're all good."

I wait. Surely there's more. But he doesn't go on. "Will? What does that have to do with Christopher?"

"Well, if John hadn't gotten together with Rhonda, they wouldn't have had Sally. And Sally wouldn't have had Christopher."

I blow out a breath. "John is Christopher's grandfather?"

"Yep. And I called him up and said his grandson was on my porch acting like an ass. John drove right over and had a talk with him. He and Christopher left, and John said Christopher won't be back."

"You believe that?"

"That Christopher will listen to his grandfather? For sure. If he doesn't, John will tell Rhonda. Christopher does *not* want that to happen."

I shake my head. Okay, then. And they still have the cop friend as backup, I guess.

"That still doesn't explain why April and Elliot can't come back to Ruby's tonight."'

"Well, Elliot fell asleep on the bed in his new room already. Porter's in there with him. And April's just—"

"Hi, it's me again." April comes back on the line.

"I'm sorry. We're just settled here, and now that Christopher's been over here but John stepped in for us, it feels good here, and, I don't know, Ruby was just so awesome to take us in, but we were completely crashing into her life. I'll come over after work tomorrow and grab all of our stuff."

"She doesn't mind at all, April," I say sincerely. "She loves helping out."

"I know. I really do. But it's temporary with her. She can't take us on for good. She agreed that first night spur of the moment, and I'll always be grateful."

I sigh. Fine. She's right. "I'll bring some stuff over to you."

"Thanks, Henry. We really appreciate you, too."

We disconnect. I head upstairs to grab a few necessities for April and Elliot. Along with a few not-so-necessities. Like flannel pajamas and toy airplanes.

I can hear Ruby's voice behind the door of Mariah's bedroom. She's still on the phone with Scarlett. I'll leave a note on the kitchen counter.

I gather the things I need and head back downstairs, but even after I drop everything off, I'm antsy. I want to do more.

I need to do more.

I need to make sure Christopher understands who else April has on her side.

I can't go to his place. I want to, but I'll just be picking a fight. The way Will handled it makes sense.

Still, I'm in the driveway and I can't resist pulling up Christopher's phone number. Right after I pull up his bank account information.

I do a little typing.

Then I call Christopher.

"Hello?"

"You should not have gone to see April tonight. Did you follow her? That's pathetic."

"This is none of your business."

"You're wrong about that. I am April and Elliot's friend. And you're bothering them. This is very much my business."

"You need to stay out of it. It's fine. We're fine."

"Christopher, I need you to check your bank account."

"My bank account?"

"Yes, I assume you have a mobile app for your bank?" I ask, knowing he does.

"Yes."

"Check your account."

"Man, why don't you just fuck off."

"Okay. I hope you don't have any automatic withdrawals coming out soon. And, um, don't stop for coffee or breakfast in the morning." I hang up.

Two minutes later, my phone rings. "Hello?"

"You fucking stole all my money?" he shouts into my ear.

"No. I proved to you that I can get to your money."

"You *took all of my money*! There's three dollars in my account!"

"Yeah, it looks like you bought a boat," I say. "Not a great idea, Christopher. That took everything you had."

"You *asshole*! I'm calling the cops."

I keep my voice calm as I say, "You won't be able to prove anything." I hit a few more buttons on my phone, then say, "Check your account again."

"You are a son of a bitch! I will find a way to prove this! I have this call! This will be on my call records!"

"Even if it did show up, which it won't, that won't prove anything. I called you to tell you to leave April and Elliot the fuck alone. You called me back to yell at me further after I hung up. What's that got to do with you buying a boat, Chris?"

"You are a—"

"Look at your account again," I say firmly, my voice low and menacing now.

There is silence on his end for a few seconds, then he says, "You put it back."

"Yes. I'm not going to take your money and ruin your credit unless I have to. I'm also not going to do any of the dozen or so other things I can do from the comfort of my bed, with just my phone, to make you miserable. And then there are the dozens of things I can do to you *in person* if I must. Don't make me do those things, Christopher. Leave April and Elliot the fuck alone. I mean it."

He's quiet again for several long seconds. Then he says, "I want her back."

"Too bad."

"I can do better."

"No."

"I just—"

"You had your chance. For some reason, that sweet, wonderful woman fell for you. Or thought she did. You had a chance to be a good guy, a good husband. You blew it. Let her go."

"I love her."

"Then let her go, Christopher. No matter how much you love her, you don't get to decide what makes her happy. She decides that. You just get to hope and pray that you're a part of it. You just try every fucking day, with everything you've got, to deserve her. And you already fucked that up. So, leave her alone now. April decides what she wants and needs, not you."

He's quiet for a second. Then he says, "My grandpa basically told me the same thing."

I nod. "Hopefully, he added that he'd kick your ass if you didn't back the fuck off."

"He said he'd write me out of his will if I embarrassed him in front of old friends of his again," Christopher says. "Then he said he'd tell my grandma. She'd kick my ass."

"Good," I say bluntly.

And I really do understand how his family was more effective in getting him to back off tonight than I was last night. I would do anything to keep King Diarmuid, or Ellie and Leo Landry, or... any of the O'Gradys or Landrys happy and proud to call me one of theirs.

"Don't make me see you," I say to Christopher.

"When can I see Elliot?" he asks. "He's my kid. I have rights."

"You're going to let the judge figure all of that out and you're going to do whatever she or he tells you."

"Fine." He sounds miserable.

I'm glad.

"Good answer." Then I hang up on him.

I head into the house, put all the dirty dishes in the sink for the morning, shut off the lights, and head upstairs.

Mariah's bedroom door is still shut. I don't hear Ruby's voice on the other side, but maybe she decided to sleep in there.

I don't like that. At all. But I'm not going to push her. Tonight was big. Sex. Finally telling her about Alfred. Maybe she needs some space.

But after I brush my teeth, clean up in the bathroom, and slip between the sheets in her bedroom, I hear the door open.

"Hey."

"Hey," I say, rolling toward her.

"Where are April and Elliot?"

"Staying at Mandy and Will's tonight."

"Are they okay?"

"Yep. Everyone is good."

She seems to accept that. She steps closer to the bed.

"How're Scarlett and Mariah?" I ask.

"Really good. They love Portland. They love Astrid and Iris. They're so proud of the foundation." She sighs. "They are happy. So happy, so accepted, so secure. It's everything I ever wanted for them."

"I'm glad."

"Me too." Her smile is genuine and the tightness around my chest loosens a little.

Then she kneels on the mattress. "Can I sleep in here? Mariah's pillows suck."

She took one of her own in there, but I'll let her use any excuse she needs to be in here with me. I lift the duvet, and she slides in next to me. I put an arm around her, cover us, and take a deep, contented breath. "Don't try to seduce me, though," I tell her with a yawn. "I need some sleep, and I have to get up early to deliver cinnamon rolls."

She laughs and snuggles closer. "Okay, good. That means I can sleep in like usual. Early mornings are bullshit."

I settle my hand on her ass and cuddle her close.

Yeah, early mornings are bullshit.

Those and about twenty other things I can think of right off the top of my head.

But falling asleep with Ruby Gale in my arms is definitely not one of them.

However, realizing I don't get to do this every night for the rest of my life is absolutely on that list.

CHAPTER 19

RUBY

I hear the shower turn on in the bathroom and roll over to my back with a huge smile.

I take a deep breath and look up at my ceiling.

I do really like sleeping in my own bed—my pillows are absolutely superior to Mariah's and I should have taken more than one that first night—and I really, *really* like sleeping in my own bed with Henry next to me.

I also like sleeping when everyone is great. Scarlett is great. Cian is great. Mariah is great. April and Elliot are great.

I have no one to worry about.

Sure, that makes me feel like I'm floating without a real destination or plan at the moment, but I'm also *floating* which is a nice feeling.

Once I get to New Orleans, I'll have a plan again.

A glance at the clock tells me that Henry either realized or got a text telling him that he didn't need to pick up cinnamon rolls and deliver them to the bar this morning. April stayed over at Mandy's. Will always goes and picks up

Charles, so Mandy probably gave April a ride to Dick's with the cinnamon rolls sitting on the seat between them.

I stretch and contemplate joining Henry in the shower.

I only contemplate it for about a minute. Why would I not do that?

I get up and pad to the bathroom door. It's not latched and just as I reach out to push it open, I hear the unmistakable sound of a low, husky male groan.

That doesn't sound like a groan of pain or illness. I've heard that groan before.

I quietly nudge the door open another inch. I hear the groan again and then my name.

"Ruby. *Fuck*."

Oh, I know exactly what's going on.

And while it is very hot, I can't believe he's doing that without me.

I push the door open further and slip inside.

Steam makes the air a little hazy, but even without that, I wouldn't be able to see him.

Unfortunately, we live in an older house that has not been renovated in the past twenty years. If only we'd had the money to put in an all-glass panel shower. Because *this* would be a very nice sight.

As it is, Henry is on the other side of a plastic shower curtain covered with seahorses, and I can't see anything.

But I have a very good imagination, and I have committed every inch of this man to memory.

I lift myself up onto the bathroom counter as he groans my name again. I'm only wearing a long T-shirt and panties, so the countertop is cold against my ass and bare thighs, but I don't care. I cross my legs, brace my hands on the counter, and grin.

"Ruby. Fuck, just like that. That's my girl."

Sounds like I'm doing a great job.

"Yes, *yes*."

I'm imagining him with one hand braced against the shower wall, water sliding over all of those sculpted muscles, head hanging, his big right hand wrapped around his thick cock, pumping the length rapidly.

Is he imagining me giving him a blow job, or is he fucking me in this fantasy?

My thighs clench in response to both images.

He groans again, and I uncross my legs. I move my hand between my thighs, over the silk of my panties, pressing against my clit.

Why should he be the only one having fun? He could've invited me into the shower with him. Or he could've stayed in the bedroom and woken me up. Or he could've just waited until I woke up, and we could've done this in the bedroom. Or he could've carried me into the shower.

He's the one who decided to go solo. So...

I slip my hand inside my panties, my middle finger sliding over my clit. I pause and circle, imagining it's Henry's tongue. I slide my fingers lower, teasing my entrance, then sliding first one finger, then another inside.

I'm so wet from just listening to him and imagining what he's doing.

I can definitely get myself off right here and now while he's doing the same on the other side of the shower curtain.

I let my head fall back, and I slip my other hand under my shirt and up to cup one breast.

Suddenly, the shower curtain slides open.

"What are you doing, Gem?"

I gasp and jerk both hands away from my body guiltily.

Then I frown. Why should I stop? I'm not doing

anything wrong. Besides, he's seen me do this before. "What am *I* doing? You started it."

"Were you just masturbating on the bathroom counter?" he asks.

I let my gaze track over his wet, naked form. He didn't finish. His cock is hard, huge, almost angry-looking.

"I was," I admit. "While listening to *you* masturbate in the shower."

"You just walk into the bathroom when other people are showering?"

"Your groaning and calling my name made me curious. I thought maybe you were sick."

Finally, he gives a short laugh. "You came in here because you were *concerned*?"

I give him a little smile. "No. I've heard you say my name like that before. I was pretty sure what was going on."

"Why didn't you just get in the shower with me?"

"Why didn't you wake me up and bring me in here with you?" I counter.

"I didn't intend to jerk off in here. But then I started thinking about last night."

"And you have such little control, you just couldn't wait?"

He grins. "Something like that."

I push myself off the counter and pad across the floor to stand in front of him. "Or were you hoping I would hear you?"

He reaches out, grabs the front of my T-shirt, and tugs.

I laugh and step over the side of the tub. The water drenches my shirt and hair immediately.

"Maybe something like that." He leans over. "Took you long enough. I almost finished without you."

He strips my shirt off, something he could've done

before he pulled me into the shower, by the way, then grabs the side of my panties.

I realize he's going to just rip them and I grab his wrists. "There's another way to take panties off!"

"Told you that you wear panties too often," he says.

I laugh and push them down my legs. I have to wiggle and bend to drag the wet silk off.

As I'm bent, pulling them over my ankles, I find myself on level with his gorgeous cock.

So I go to my knees.

"Gem," he says, a note of warning in his voice.

I look up at him, the warm water sliding down my back, rivulets running down my face. "What?" I reach out and take his cock in hand. "Were you fucking me in your fantasy? It wasn't a blow job?"

His hand goes to my head and tangles in my wet hair. He brings me forward, and I happily swirl my tongue over the head of his cock before sucking just an inch inside my mouth.

"My fist was your hot, gorgeous, sassy, smart mouth," he says, his voice husky.

I look up at him from under my lashes. "I was hoping so."

I love giving Henry blow jobs. Having that kind of power over this man is my very favorite thing in this entire world.

I suck him further into my mouth, relaxing so that he can hit the back of my throat immediately.

He groans, and yes, that's exactly the sound I heard.

I work him with my mouth and my hand, making sure every inch of his cock and balls get attention.

It's sloppy, wet, hot, and so fucking good.

When he tries to pull back, with an, "I'm gonna come,

Gem," I reach around and grasp his ass, keeping him right where he is.

He doesn't fight me. He knows that I know what I want.

He pumps into my mouth, then comes with a growl that makes my pussy clench with need.

I pull back and look up at him, opening my mouth to ask if it was as good as his imagination, but he's already pulling me to my feet, lifting me, and stepping out of the shower. He sets me back on the counter where I was. We're both dripping all over the floor and the counter, but he doesn't care. He kneels in front of me, spreads my legs, and leans in, licking me with a long firm lick, then gives my clit a hard suck.

He eats at me as if he's starving, and I can't do anything but hold onto the edge of the counter and his hair.

It only takes a few minutes for him to send me careening over the cliff of a hard, hot orgasm.

I cry his name loudly, and then he kisses his way up my body, finally taking my mouth in a hot, yet so sweet kiss.

When he pulls back, both of us still breathing a little hard, he smiles down at me. "Good morning."

I laugh. "Good morning."

"I was thinking, everyone at Dick's is doing fine. I don't think they need us for a little bit. What do you say to going to breakfast at the coffee shop downtown?"

I'm surprised, but I instantly catch on. "You want to go to the coffee shop where Charles, Will, Ben, and Dan refuse to go?"

"Yep."

I shrug. He's curious. I get it. It's probably best to experience what I've described to him. "Okay."

"You up for it?"

Seeing our father and his followers around town has

always been hard on Scarlett. She has more direct experience and memories with them. For me, they're just people. Well, seeing our father always infuriates me, because I can't help but think of how he treated Scarlett and our mother, of course. But I nod. "Yes, but their coffee and cinnamon rolls have nothing on Dick's."

"I have a feeling I'll have the same opinion about the servers and the general clientele."

And how am I supposed to not be crazy about him when he's already fallen for my bunch of loveable oddballs at Big Dick's?

CHAPTER 20
HENRY

Downtown Emerald is charming. It looks like the quintessential small midwestern town.

But I agree with Cian that they completely missed the chance to really lean into the "Emerald City" theme complete with a main street of yellow bricks.

However, the Emerald City in *The Wonderful Wizard of Oz* isn't really green. Everyone is simply told to wear green-tinted glasses. It turns out, in reality, the city is no greener than any other city. It's all an illusion. Everyone is deceived by their 'wonderful wizard'. And I think I know exactly who is tricking who into what here in Emerald, Ohio.

As we drive toward the coffee shop, which is situated directly in the middle of Main Street, Ruby looks over at me.

"Why are you interested in the coffee shop? Really?" Ruby asks as we drive.

"Need to be sure my products and prices at Dick's are comparable."

"Uh huh. They're not. Your products are superior and far cheaper."

"So I can raise the prices and buy cheaper, crappier coffee?" I ask.

She laughs. "No."

I wouldn't do that, of course. And the coffee beans and menu board have nothing to do with our trip downtown this morning.

I glance over. I know Ruby doesn't have as contentious a history with their father and his church as Scarlett does, but his rejection of them as children is still a part of her story and his overwhelming presence in this town and influence over its people still affects her.

"Actually, I want to check the coffee shop out because of Will and the guys."

"They asked you to do this?"

I shake my head. "No. They just got me thinking. They're from here. Grew up here. Raised their families here. Worked here. But they're not comfortable coming downtown and hanging out at the local coffee shop. I figure the guys who are hanging out in there this time of day, a weekday mid-morning, are probably about their age, right?"

"They are."

"So our guys probably know them. Maybe even grew up with them. But they ran our guys out of a place in their own hometown? I don't like that."

"You're going to confront these guys at the coffee shop? Tell them that they have to accept Will and Dan and Charles and Ben?" She's smiling, clearly amused. "Our guys don't want that, Henry. They've chosen Dan's place. He's made it into what it is for them."

"I understand. They've built their own little clubhouse to avoid all the stuff down here. And that's their right. It's just that..."

I think about how I want to explain this. I don't know if it's really for the best. I've known them one day. I'm feeling protective of them after a few hours with them. I realize this is typical of my over-the-top ways. But...I don't care.

"I realize this comes from me having a place where I belonged and felt secure to being thrown out of that little bubble, and having no one, and then being taken into another bubble where it's been literally my *job* to keep the bubble intact—only certain people in or out." I take a breath. "But it seems strange to me that these men and women have spent their lives here, have people they can call when they really need help, the way Will said he could ask his neighbor for help, and his neighbor's brother, and the way he called Christopher's grandfather last night—"

"Wait, what?" Ruby pivots toward me in her seat. "What about Christopher's grandfather?"

I sigh. Shit. I wasn't going to worry her by telling her Christopher showed up at Will and Mandy's last night. "Christopher went over to talk to April. But Will called his grandfather. He came over, talked Christopher down, and he left."

Ruby is frowning but doesn't say anything.

"Anyway, it's clear these guys still have connections in this town. People who like and respect them. People they can reach out to and trust. That bigger community is there. They've just cut themselves off because of some bullshit with your dad's church. I don't like that. I just want to see if there's any way to make all these separate circles into more of a Venn diagram. Find some overlap."

Ruby is quiet for a moment, before she says, "My father likes it that way."

"What way?"

"Everyone in separate, non-overlapping circles. It's

what happened when Scarlet wanted to get closer to him and get to know him. He told her that she had to become a part of the church. And that meant cutting off everyone else. She moved in with him. She stopped seeing her other friends. Including me. She spent time with church kids only. He does that on purpose. He wants them surrounded by people who think the same way they do, he wants them to only hear the ideas that he approves of." She's quiet for a moment. "It's how you control people. Make them feel like they belong to the 'right' group and that everyone else is wrong. And keep them apart."

I nod. "I suspected that. Humans naturally want to belong to groups. They want to be accepted. Many times, the church is that place. They preach acceptance and love, and people are attracted to that, of course. That acceptance and belief that you're on the right side and everyone else is wrong or trying to harm you is what makes it hard to leave."

"Right. And you fear that if you leave, the 'other side' will reject you, and you'll be all alone. No one wants that."

"But I don't like that our guys have a history in this town, that this is their home, but they can't really *live* here, and feel cut off and unwelcome. That's ridiculous."

She grins. "I love that you think of them as 'our' guys."

I look over and she's smiling. "I already feel that way about them."

"See? I didn't really build that community. Maybe I came up with getting an espresso machine and bringing in cinnamon rolls, but they made the *community* part of it happen."

I reach over and take her hand, linking our fingers. "I don't like the idea of them feeling like outcasts at that bar."

"You want them to come down to the coffee shop instead?"

"Not necessarily. Maybe we can give these other guys another place to go."

"You're going to invite new guys to the clubhouse?"

"We'll see if they're worthy." I mean that. "But most card games are more fun with more people. That jigsaw puzzle would be getting put together faster. There would be new stories to hear. And the gossip would be juicier with more people telling it."

She squeezes my hand, grinning. "In that case, Mandy's going to have to start baking more cinnamon rolls."

I pull into a spot right along the curb. We walk toward the front doors of the coffee shop, holding hands.

"Who knows?" I say. "Maybe one of these other guys' wives is an incredible baker, too. Or one of these guys could bake. Maybe we can expand the menu."

She nods. "Charles has been asking for something with lemon or raspberry."

I laugh. "I'll see what I can do."

I reach for the door to the coffee shop, but it swings out before I can pull it open, and a tall man in his late fifties with salt and pepper hair steps out. He's in a navy suit despite the casual atmosphere of the coffee shop. And really, all of downtown Emerald.

He draws up short, clearly startled. But not just startled in general. He's clearly specifically surprised to see Ruby.

I feel rather than hear her sigh.

"Hi, Dad," she says flatly.

His brows slam together. "Don't call me that."

"Believe me, it's a lot nicer than the things I call you in my head," she tells him, her tone almost bored sounding.

"What are you doing here?" he asks her as if this is his front porch and not a public establishment.

I move in closer to her and open my mouth, but Ruby says, "Oh, you know, just spreading my bastard, heathen aura around town. As always." Then she yanks harder on the door, opening it wider and stepping forward, clearly intending to walk into the shop.

He steps out of her way as if worried she might accidentally touch him.

"You think you're cute, but you reap what you sow," he tells her. "Your attitude and disregard for decency will be your downfall."

Ruby actually laughs at that, and I can tell she's sincerely amused. "Well, geez, if I have a disregard for decency, it looks like I *did* inherit something from you after all."

He glares at her. She lifts her middle finger to him.

I cough.

I've never seen Ruby interact with her father. I've also never seen someone flip off a pastor to their face.

She turns and walks the rest of the way into the coffee shop.

His eyes come to mine finally. He opens his mouth, but I say, in my most menacing voice, "You have nothing to say to me that I want to hear. And it really is in your best interest to remain silent. In fact, I would warn you to make what you just said the last thing you *ever* say to Ruby."

I step past him, dismissing him completely.

If I thought for a moment Ruby was actually upset about their encounter, I would have had more words for him. As it is, it's me who needs to make this man miserable, not Ruby. She's clearly over him and fine.

I'm not.

I want that man to suffer.

I pull my phone from my pocket and type out a quick text to Iris.

Remember when I asked you to look into Ruby and Scarlett's father for illegal activity? I need a status update.

I had started looking into him when Ruby found out he was behind influencing Emerald's mayor to turn down a large state grant that would have provided resources for single parents in town. The same grant had been awarded to several communities in the state, including the neighboring town of Melton.

It is no secret to anyone in Emerald that the good pastor thinks single parents—single moms in particular—should have to support their families alone, even if it's a struggle, as part of their penance for having sex and children outside of marriage. He doesn't want programs to help them, proclaiming public support systems encourage their immoral behavior because then there are no negative consequences to their actions.

The man is a complete jackass.

He's clearly morally bankrupt and obviously leading a church for power rather than because of any true *righteous* belief system.

That's a huge red flag. There is surely illegal activity surrounding him.

I want to know what it is.

I join Ruby in line to order coffee and eye the cinnamon rolls in the bakery case. They don't even look as good as Mandy's. I'm still getting one so I can taste-test them, though.

A return text vibrates my phone, and I glance down.

It's from Iris, and it's simple. *Call me.*

Nope. I'm not going to do that. I'm sure Iris has several

things she would like to say to me about leaving Cara without notifying her, sending Jonah with Cian and Scarlett, and coming to Ohio where there are no O'Gradys or Olsens to protect.

I don't feel like getting into any of that with her right now.

Or probably ever.

"Are you okay?" Ruby asks.

I look up at her. "Shouldn't I be asking you that?"

"You know I'm fine. That guy and his opinion stopped mattering to me a long time ago. In fact, if he did like me, I'd be worried."

I appreciate that. I would feel similarly about my father if I ever had to interact with him. Being someone that our fathers like and respect is not a compliment.

"I'm fine," I tell her. "But full transparency, I'm looking into your father. And if I find anything to act on, I intend to."

"Anything illegal, you mean?"

"Yes. Though if I can find a way to act on anything immoral, I'll do that too."

"More immoral than leading an entire cult that fifty percent of this town follows?"

"Say the word, and I'll burn it to the ground," I tell her, not kidding. "But also, not half this town."

She looks up at me. "That church has always divided this town."

Oh, of that I have no doubt. "I know it feels like half the town and the people who follow his church are loud and obnoxious, so it seems there are more of them than there are. But only about thirty percent of the church-going people in this town attend his church. There are plenty that go to other churches or follow other religions. And then there are plenty of people who are not churchgoers at all. He doesn't even have a majority."

She studies me, thinking that over. "That's good to know. They do seem like a lot, though."

"Your father does that on purpose, too. And I'm sure he'd love it to be half the town. Or more. Your father is a greedy, power-hungry narcissist."

She nods. "Thanks. I need to remember all of that."

It's our turn to order, so we get a cinnamon roll, a pecan roll, a caramel vanilla latte, and a hazelnut cappuccino. If I'm going to tell people here that the coffee and pastries at Dick's are better, I need to know for sure.

After we pick up our order, I survey the room and note the table with four older gentlemen situated right in the center of the room.

"Is that them?" I ask Ruby.

She nods. "Yup. I'm guessing my father just left them. They're probably doing a Live Right Bible study session right now."

"Okay then." I lead her toward the table next to the guys.

Sure enough, they have two Bibles lying open on the table, and each of them holds a smaller booklet and a pen.

One of them is reading from the booklet, but I notice the two of the men keep glancing at the television above the bookcase. The same game show that the guys at Dick's watch every morning is on. It's turned too low to hear, and the closed captions are scrolling across the bottom.

I overhear something about it being everyone's obligation to model the behavior of Christ, but I tune them out as I pull out a chair for Ruby and then settle next to her.

"I want to ask you about how we're going to run Ruby's Way here in Emerald," I tell her, my voice low.

She has her cup lifted to her mouth for a sip, and she cocks one eyebrow.

"I have an idea, and I want to be sure that it's something you and Scarlett would like."

Ruby swallows and sets her cup down. "We're going to talk about that here?"

I incline my head toward the gentlemen. "They come here to talk with the intention of being overheard. The idea is for those around them to be influenced by what they say, right?"

She nods. "Quiet preaching. Leading by example. Kind of."

"We both know that Ruby's Way is going to be leading by a much better example. If we talk about our plans here and people overhear us and like what we say, that wouldn't be so bad, would it?"

She catches on immediately. "It's not a terrible way to get a message out, honestly."

"Less annoying than being on a soapbox on a street corner screaming into a bullhorn."

"And cheaper than a billboard."

I chuckle. Then I raise my voice slightly to say, "So I want to run some ideas past you because you and Scarlett get to approve it all."

She looks surprised but pleased. She lifts her cup for another sip.

"Here's what I'm thinking," I continue. "Since your father and the mayor declined the grant from the state to support families here in Emerald, Ruby's Way is going to step in and supply those funds. One million a year for housing, childcare, education, work training—and we're open to other ideas."

She nods. "That's amazing."

"But," I go on. "I want there to be a Board, made up of Emerald citizens, that meets at least twice a year and proposes programs and ideas where the money can be used for the community at large too, especially for families who are struggling. Single parents aren't the only ones who do, though they will have priority."

"You're in charge of this? Not Cian?"

"Cian just wants Scarlett to be happy and to help people. He's fine if I have specific ideas about how to run things here."

"Okay. Well, I think that sounds good."

"And," I lean in. "This is important."

"Okay."

"No one from your father's church will be allowed to be on that Board. That is not negotiable."

Her eyes widen.

"They have proven by their affiliation that they don't care about helping others in a way that meets my standards. If they choose to be affiliated with a group that chooses that kind of leadership, I don't trust that they'll make good choices for people in this town, especially those outside of that group. Also no one who is a member of that church will be awarded any money or resources from Ruby's Way. If they aren't willing to help others, then they can take care of their own."

"Wow."

"Of course, if they want to leave the church and come to us, we'll give them a second chance. We all really like those—"

She smiles.

"And we'll help, then, of course. Because that's the right thing to do."

Ruby wets her lips. And nods.

"I'm right to leave them out of this," I say.

She nods. "You are."

"So what do you think?"

"I think this sounds amazing and will have a big, positive impact on a lot of people."

"Do you think Scarlett will agree?"

"I do." She's just staring at me.

I lean in. "What is it, Gem?"

"Is all of that real, or is that just for show?" Her voice is quiet, and she glances toward the table of church guys.

"Of course, it's real. I did want to tell you, *ask* you, about all of that. Doing it here at the coffee shop is just convenient for other reasons."

"Well, Scarlett will love it." She pauses. "I love it."

"You would be proud to have your name on this?"

"Very proud"

"And this makes you happy?"

"So happy." She gives me a bright, sweet smile.

"Then it's a done deal. That's all I want."

She reaches out and squeezes my hand. "Don't look now." She leans close as if she's imparting an intimate secret. "The guys are listening."

I take the opportunity to kiss her cheek before I lean back. I tip back the rest of my coffee, acting casual. Then I say, louder again, "This was good, but Dick's is definitely better."

"Oh, I know," Ruby agrees. "I don't think I can ever eat a cinnamon roll again after having the ones out at Dick's." She pushes her unfinished roll away. "In fact, would it be crazy to go out there now and have one?"

I grin. "If they're not all gone."

We get to our feet and start cleaning up our garbage.

I nonchalantly glance toward the men at the next table.

They're looking at us, so I smile and ask, "Have you guys had the cinnamon rolls at Big Dick's?"

One of them scoffs. "The bar?"

"Well, it's not a bar till six at night. During the day, there is coffee and rolls. Sandwiches and burgers at lunch. It's pretty fun. They've got card games going, too." I gesture toward the television. "The guys out there love this show. They actually watch this one and the next two every single day."

They all look predictably surprised, and I am stupidly pleased.

"Do they listen to it with the sound on?" one of them mutters.

I still answer. "Oh, absolutely. They really get into it. You probably know the guys who hang out there. Ben, Will, and Charles. And, of course, Dan. You guys should stop out sometime."

They're nodding, obviously aware of my guys. "Dan doesn't want us to come around," one of them says.

"Well, I'm the new owner. Maybe we can start over."

"You own the place now?"

"Yep. Pretty recently. Enjoying it, though."

"Well, we come in here for our Bible study," one of them tells me.

"Bible study, huh?" I say, acting as if I have no idea what they're talking about. "Every day? You've all been around a while, haven't you covered that book front to back by now?"

One of them chuckles. "Sure. But it's always good to review."

"Okay," I say, with a little shrug. "Just if that ever gets boring, the guys at Dick's have probably heard it all a number of times too so you don't need to tell them all about it. You could just sit around and talk about other things."

One of the men surprises me with a chuckle. "Charles and Will and I actually went to church camp together for four summers in a row."

Another nods. "I was in Sunday school every week with Will and Ben."

I smile. "Sounds like Will knows all the Bible stories pretty well."

"He should," one says with another chuckle. "Maybe we should stop out there and quiz him."

"Tell you what," I say. "I'll let you do a little Bible talk in the bar if you agree to also spend equal time doing arts and crafts with the kids."

"Arts and crafts? Like glitter and stuff?" the church camp aficionado asks.

"Yep. Play-Doh, fingerpaints, all kinds of fun. You do some of that stuff with your grandkids, don't you?"

"Sure. I guess that would be okay."

"Maybe we could convince those guys to come to church," one of them says to the others.

Another laughs. "You've known them as long as I have. We're not getting any of them to church."

"But—" The guy glances at the TV again. "Pastor probably doesn't know that. And all we can do is try."

"True," his friend agrees. "If we have a stubborn case, we'll just have to keep going out there to work on them."

Another guy nods. "Good point. If it's a guy we've known for a long time and we were friends with back in the day, makes sense we would want to do our best to bring him around."

"And not just anyone is going to want to go out to the

bar in the morning. That seems like something guys like us should do."

I'm grinning at all of them. "Why don't you just stop by tomorrow?" I ask. "We'll see how it goes. I'll make sure we have extra cinnamon rolls, just in case. Did I mention they're free?"

They all sit up straighter.

"They're having a special celebrity edition of *Name 'Em Frame 'Em*," one of them says of the game show that's on television as we speak. "Scarlett Johansson will be on. I love her."

"I'll want to hear that at full volume," another agrees

"We'll be there tomorrow," the first guy tells me. "And we probably don't need to bring the Bibles. Like you said, those guys have heard it all before."

Ruby barely waits for the coffee shop door to shut behind us before she starts to laugh and says, "I don't feel weak *at all* by how easily I fell for you and your charm and dropped my panties. I swear you can win *anyone* over."

I grin. "Not everyone, but I do have a pretty good track record." I've always been very confident, and hanging out with royalty for the past decade-plus has definitely rubbed off on me.

"But the cinnamon rolls are not free at Dick's, by the way."

I wave my hand. I'm feeling incredibly triumphant. "They are now."

"We give the money back to the women who bake for the ingredients," she tells me as we head back for my car.

"Ruby, of course I will still pay them." I'm offended she would think otherwise. "In fact, I'm going to triple whatever they usually get just because you insinuated that."

She's giggling as I open the door for her. I love that

sound so fucking much. Especially when our visit to the coffee shop started with a run-in with her father.

Speaking of that asshole, my phone hasn't stopped vibrating with texts, and I know they're all from Iris. But I also know they're not full of information about Ruby's dad. They are various forms of *if you don't call me back, I'll make you sorry.*

A thought occurs to me as I round the car and get in. "So Mandy bakes cinnamon rolls at home once a week, and then Will shows up at Dick's later that same morning, and there are cinnamon rolls. How has he not figured out that they're the same cinnamon rolls?"

I back out of the spot and head for the bar.

Ruby grins at me. "Oh, he has figured it out."

I look over at her. "He has? Mandy said I absolutely could not tell him."

"I know. I don't understand it, but it's this game where they all pretend they don't know what's going on. But the men know who's doing the baking. And I actually think that the women know the men know." She laughs. "They're happy, and I find them amusing, and that's enough for me."

"Well, I hope the guys aren't upset when these guys show up."

Ruby takes my hand. "I think it's sweet you want to get this group of friends back together."

"I do. I don't think it's right that our guys are relegated to a bar outside of town. And hell, it seems like maybe the church guys need a break."

She nods. "It really does."

"But honestly, I want these church guys to meet April and the kids, too."

"Really?"

"Definitely. Your father has convinced these people that

single mothers deserve to be cut off and ostracized and don't deserve support and resources. Because of his own prejudices, he's making an entire group of people turn their backs on a vulnerable part of their community. Their neighbors and people they pass on the streets every day. People who haven't done anything wrong but who might just need a little help once in a while. It's the antithesis of community and certainly of the things he's supposed to be teaching from the book those guys had lying on that coffee shop table.

I want these men to actually meet someone their pastor is telling them to reject. It is so much harder to say no to something when there is a face to it in your mind, when there's a person that is representing the issue. Very few humans can look directly at another human and say I'm going to do something to hurt you."

"I don't know. My father certainly did that to Scarlett," Ruby says.

"And my father did it to me. But our fathers are the exception to the rule. I really want to show you that."

"You're doing this for me?"

I look over at her. "In part. Of course. You're always on my mind, Ruby. Since I met you, with everything I do, I think about what would Ruby think of this or how would this make her feel?"

I can see the emotion in her eyes. "Wow. That's...something."

I squeeze her hand. "I'm also doing it for April. And Elliot. And all of the other women and kids like them. Those men might still decide to follow your father and reject helping the single parents, but I'm going to make them do it with full knowledge of what their decision means. I'm not going to make it easy on them."

"Yeah," she says softly. "I didn't stand a chance."

I glance from the road to her again. "A chance of what?"

"Keeping my panties on around you."

I grin at her wickedly. "You wear panties way too often as it is."

"Interesting that you would mention that," she says, sitting back in her seat.

"Oh? Why's that?"

"Because I decided to see what it would be like to go without today."

That sinks in, and I growl. Then, make a sharp right at the next corner. We need to make a not-so-quick stop at home before going out to Dick's, it turns out.

CHAPTER 21
HENRY

We do, eventually, make it out to Dick's.

Everyone is having lunch by that time, but no one seems to mind that we weren't around before now.

April is completely fine. Elliot too. They're making airplanes out of popsicle sticks, and he offers to make me one that I can keep.

I can't think of anything I want more at that moment and I tell him so.

But after checking in on him, I'm out of excuses for not returning Iris's call. And I really do want to know if she has any information about Ruby's dad.

I take a breath and dial her number.

"About fucking time," she answers.

"Good morning," I say, going for laid back. It's still morning for her on the West Coast.

"So you're in Ohio without Cian."

Okay, no small talk then.

I could come up with some excuse. Probably. I could even tell her that Cian asked me to come keep an eye on Ruby and the house. He'd cover for me.

But Iris isn't stupid. And frankly, I've already hidden my relationship with Ruby for far too long. I've been fighting these feelings and dealing with barriers to being together. The only person I'm really interested in dealing with now is Ruby.

"Yes, Ruby, Scarlett's sister needed my help," I answer honestly and simply.

"So that's how this is going to be?" Iris asks.

I frown. That's not the reaction I was expecting from her. "Me helping the sister of one of our princesses? Yes. Of course. Our protection extends to the entire family of anyone brought into the O'Grady circle."

That's not an actual policy. Then again, none of the O'Gradys brought anyone into their circle until a couple of years ago when Cian's sister, Fiona, fell in love with her now husband, Knox.

But would we all do anything for Knox? Of course. He's one of us now. And I believe if Knox's sibling needed help, we'd also show up for him or her.

Of course, I'm pulling all of this out of my ass. Still, it sounds good.

"Uh huh," is all Iris says.

Iris isn't just smart. She knows me very well. She's been the head of the bodyguards for nearly the entire time I've been with Cian. There was just over a year where Declan, Cian's oldest brother, had about nine bodyguards that he kept firing, until Iris came into the picture. Not that he didn't fire her. She just refused to leave.

Besides, she only pretended to report to Declan. Ultimately, she reported to Alfred.

Which Declan knew the entire time he pretended to be the boss of her.

That stubbornness was exactly what the eldest O'Grady

needed, and what prompted her promotion to HBIC—Head Bodyguard In Charge, officially. She prefers Bitch for the B, though.

"What's the problem?" I ask. "Cian is fine." I pause and take a breath. "I know you think I'm better than Jonah at the job, but you're not going to make that obvious to him, are you? That would hurt his feelings, and he's already sensitive about being the only one without a cool accent." Iris doesn't have an accent either, but 'we', the guys, love to tease Jonah about his boring American accent when we've all got Irish or British accents.

There, I'll play this light-hearted, laid-back…

"Well, Jonah actually turns in security plans to me when he's about to take a trip. I don't think you've *ever* turned in a plan. About anything."

"The plan is always: *provide security, don't let any royals get kidnapped, hurt, or killed,*" I say. "Seems like a waste of paper."

"I need itineraries, locations, threat assessments—" Iris breaks off. "Never mind."

I actually grin at that. She knows she's wasting her breath. Not only am I not going to do those security plans, ever, she also knows that I know she'll never fire me because of it.

The O'Grady royals are not in actual physical danger ninety-nine percent of the time.

Fiona is the exception, and that's not because she's a royal, but because she works in animal rescue and rehabilitation and tangles with people who illegally keep, sell, and transport exotic, endangered animals at times, as well as run-of-the-mill asshole animal abusers. On any given day, she could run into a dangerous dickhead person. Or a dangerous dickhead tiger.

The billionaire playboy, Declan, might also occasionally be at risk of someone wanting to harm him or possibly try to get some ransom for his life. But honestly, he's pretty fucking charitable, so he's not angering anyone who might want to retaliate for some terrible environmental harm or anything.

Another billionaire who gets annoyed with Declan making him look bad, a celebrity who loses a girlfriend to Declan, or a politician who doesn't get a big enough check could all have reason to want to hurt Declan, I suppose. But as for kidnapping him, Declan's an intimidating son-of-a-bitch, and anyone wanting to keep him captive is going to have to be willing to put up with his broody, asshole, I'm-better-than-you-and-we-both-know-it attitude for an extended period of time. It would take real fortitude to kidnap *that*.

"What's going to happen the *next* time Ruby needs something, Henry?" Iris asks.

I shift uncomfortably, not so much because of the question but because of the sudden softness in Iris's voice. What the hell?

"I don't know what you mean. I'll help her if I can. As I said, she's Princess Scarlett's sister."

Iris sighs. "Knock it off. This isn't a group call or a group text. You're in love with her. You know that's okay, right?"

This softer tone of voice from Iris is making me itchy. She's a ball-buster, and God knows we need it. She manages us like an older sister. An older sister who pretty much resents all of us being born.

"It's going to be fine. I can handle it all."

Iris laughs. "You just abandoned your protectee to fly thousands of miles to be with her the moment you found out she *might* be *slightly* at risk."

I frown. "Jonah's report sounds like it was unnecessarily wordy."

"I got all of that when I called him about something else, and Cian answered his phone."

Oh, boy. Iris doesn't like when people other than the bodyguards answer their phones. Which Cian knows.

"Look, Ruby is..." I blow out a breath. "She takes care of people. She doesn't think about herself." The truth of those words hit me in the center of my chest. "She just needs someone to have *her* back once in a while. I knew everyone else was fine."

"And what happens next time?"

"I'll...assess the situation and make a decision." I can't promise I won't leave Cian to go to Ruby. That realization is startling. Though it probably shouldn't be. But this is the first time in more than a decade that I would have even allowed the *thought* of something or someone else being a priority before Cian.

"That sounds exhausting," Iris says.

Not the reaction I expected. "Maybe. Don't worry about me."

She laughs. "My entire job boils down to worrying about you. All of you."

I open my mouth to say something glib and sarcastic but find I can't. She's right, I suppose. We drive Iris crazy, and she doesn't hesitate to let us know that, but she's always been there for us, bailing us out, giving us resources, advice, direction, whatever we need, whenever we need it. Even kicks in the ass if that's what we need. And yes, we do need those. Often.

"Ruby is moving to New Orleans. Soon. I'll be able to be here fully for Cian, don't worry." Goddammit, those words taste awful in my mouth.

"Why is she going to New Orleans?"

"Law school."

"Ah." Iris sounds very interested in that. "Why New Orleans?"

"She got in at Loyola two years ago. She's been deferring her admission to be here for Scarlett. But now, because of Cian and everything, she feels like she can leave."

"Ah."

I just wait. Iris is thinking. She'll tell me if she wants me to know those thoughts.

Finally, she says, "We can get her in at Ohio State."

Yeah, that was my first thought, too. "No. It needs to be Loyola."

"It does?"

It does. I already knew that, but hearing Iris say so matter-of-factly that Ohio State is an option makes me even more certain.

Ruby has stayed with Scarlett through thick and thin. Even when Scarlett made the choice to try to reconcile with people who didn't deserve her. Twice. Ruby was there for her, supporting her, loving her unconditionally. Ruby was determined to stay as long as Scarlett and Mariah needed her.

She put her dreams and plans on hold for *years*.

Now that she finally has some freedom, her choice is to pursue a career where she can help even more people.

But she put moving to New Orleans for that on hold until everyone here is settled. Including April and Elliot, two people who just suddenly needed her. A co-worker. A friend, but not someone she's known for years and years.

And here I am, wanting to convince her to change all of her plans for me. I don't even need her *help*.

I just need...her.

I selfishly want her here because she makes me happy.

I clear my throat. "Ruby is going to New Orleans. That's what she wants."

"And what happens if she needs you when she's there?"

I blow out a breath. "Ruby doesn't ask for help. She gives the help. So that probably won't happen very often."

I want to give her all the support. The money, the encouragement, my presence. I want to be the one to support Ruby being Ruby.

She's been Scarlett and Mariah's main support all these years, pinching pennies, worrying, pulling extra shifts, moving around, dealing with whatever came up on her own. And putting off school.

But now she's got me.

She doesn't have to do any of that now.

She's not alone, and she never has to worry about anything again.

"What if you just miss her?"

"That's...not enough for me to leave the people who *need* me. I know that, don't worry."

Bloody hell. I *will* miss her. It will be miserable without her. But my life is amazing. I have to be grateful for what I have and not pine for what I don't.

Finally, Iris asks, "You're okay with that? Really?"

I take a deep breath. Only King Diarmuid, Alfred, Iris, and now Ruby know my *whole* story. Cian doesn't even know everything about my father or how Alfred pulled me out of school and put me into specialized training. Cian knows my mom died when I was a kid and that my father died a few years ago. He knows Alfred hired me. He knows I consider the O'Gradys my family. Those are the important things.

Alfred brought me in as Cian's companion. He told me

the young prince needed me, but Alfred was honest from the very first minute and told me he knew I needed Cian too.

And he was right.

Alfred saved me and I will never forget that.

"I'm okay with everything. She's got plans. And I'm going to help her make those happen." That is how I can best love Ruby. I can help make all of her dreams come true.

Watching her face, seeing her emotion around my plans for Ruby's Way here in Emerald, brought that home for me.

I want this woman to be happy.

Whatever that means, I will make it happen.

I will change this fucking world for her.

"So when Cian comes back to Ohio, you're staying there," Iris clarifies.

"Right."

"Without Ruby."

I swallow hard. "Yes."

"Henry—"

"It's fine," I cut her off. "I made a promise to Alfred, and I won't forget it. Cian's happiness is my first priority."

Iris doesn't answer for several seconds, but then says, "Okay."

"Why are you being so nice to me?" I ask. "It's creeping me out."

"Because you're in *Ohio*. On purpose. That feels like a cry for help."

I laugh. I can't help it. "Ohio is fine. Maybe you should come for a visit." I don't mean that. I *really* don't mean that. Iris would scare the hell out of these nice small-town folk.

Then again, some of them are real assholes. Maybe a dose of Iris is what a few of them need.

"I'll pass," she says. "But..."

Iris Lee is a direct, bluntly honest person. She doesn't tiptoe around anyone's feelings, least of any of ours.

"What?" I ask.

"Alfred never meant for you to sacrifice *your* happiness, Henry. He loved you, too."

My heart gives a hard thump. "Alfred was focused on the big picture. The O'Gradys and Olsens need to be secure, safe, and fully supported."

"Alfred wanted *everyone* to be secure, safe, and fully supported," she says.

"Right."

"You're part of 'everyone', Henry."

I let that just hang in the air between us for a moment. My chest feels tight.

"You're part of the family, too," she says. "You matter, too."

I have to actually swallow hard when she says that. If someone asked me if I felt like part of the O'Grady family, I would have said yes. I've always been included. I've always known they love me and have my back.

But no, I've never thought that it would be okay to choose myself over them. "Iris…"

"And besides," she goes on. "They're all good. The O'Gradys and Olsens are *finally* settled and good. The plan is in place."

I frown. "Wait, what? The plan? The thing that has been going off the rails for years?"

She laughs.

And my eyes widen.

I have worked for Iris Lee for years. She is smart, tough, loyal, driven, scary organized. She's also a whole bunch of other adjectives. But easy-going is not one of them. And I have never ever heard her laugh on a business phone call with one or more of us.

In fact, while I'm sure I have heard her laugh, I can't think of a time right off the top of my head.

"Everything is great. Torin is on the throne. Linnea is advising the palace, and so much more. Fiona is settled and happy doing her advocacy work. Saoirse is growing into an amazing young woman. And she now has an amazing cousin to share being a teenaged royal princess with."

I smile thinking of how quickly the bond formed between Saoirse and Mariah.

"Cian has finally found a true purpose, and it's *such* a good one. And Declan..." She trails off. "He's the one who's united the families and who will be the father of the O'Grady-Olsen heir. I mean...that's pretty amazing."

Her voice has softened. There's a note of, for lack of a better word, affection there.

"You sound happy about all of that."

She laughs again, and yeah, I don't think I've heard her like this, ever.

"I am happy. Everyone is not only doing meaningful things that will fulfill them and make the world better, but they're in love and happy! Including *you!*"

"None of this is according to plan," I say again.

"I know. And that definitely stressed me out when it was happening," she admits. "But now that it's all over and done, it's so great."

"So Declan and Astrid are good?" That wedding came out of the blue, and I got the impression it was mostly for show for Diarmuid.

"Well..." Iris hesitates. "They will be."

"You're sure?"

"Let's put it this way: they're both incredibly intelligent, and divorcing the other person would be very stupid. So that won't happen."

That does *not* sound like they're madly in love.

"And we've got the added bonus of Colin, Jonah, and you falling in love, too," she says.

Yes, she does sound genuinely happy.

That's... weird.

"I guess we just need you and Miles to fall in love," I say of Astrid's best friend and trainer, who is also her bodyguard, though no one knows that.

"What are you talking about?" Iris asks, her tone suddenly sharp.

"Just... you're the only two people in our group left, the only bodyguards not in love," I say with a frown.

"Oh." She pauses. "Yeah. I guess. Well, that doesn't matter."

Now she sounds strange. "Are you okay?"

"What? Yes, of course. I need to go," she says quickly. "Do you need me to get Ruby in at Ohio State? Have her admission to Loyola rescinded?"

"God, no!" I say emphatically.

"Okay, fine. As for her father, I haven't found anything specifically illegal. Unfortunately being an immoral asshole isn't illegal," Iris says. "But we do have a contact in the Governor's office who is willing to make a big deal out of Emerald being the only town to turn down the grant. We also have some news outlets—TV, newspapers, pods—that will run the story if we ask them to. We also have some big religious leaders in the state who will denounce this and draw attention to the state grant and to Ruby's Way."

I'm nodding. "That's all great. Not as great as a criminal indictment maybe..."

She laughs. "Maybe not, but embarrassing him, calling

his bigotry out publicly, shaming him in front of the town and his congregation? That's not nothing."

"True. Maybe we can even peel off a few members of his church."

"Or maybe more than a few," Iris says. "He seems most interested in power. The more people he can influence, the happier he is. So, we can maybe reduce that number, take some of his power away."

Make him *unhappy*. That would be great.

"You should devise a way for the other churches in town to be involved with Ruby's Way. You don't need their financial support, of course, but they should make a big deal out of approving the group's mission and work. They could show the town the alternatives to that church."

"Other people should show their support for the work we're doing, too," I agree. "Anyone in town who believes it's a good idea should say so. We could have some kind of event to kick things off. Simply to show that the bigots are outnumbered. And maybe people going to that church will start to look at who they are associating with. And who else in town they could be associating with instead."

"Take it down brick by brick," Iris agrees. "I know the O'Gradys—well, Declan anyway—are more into smashing things down in one fell blow, but dismantling things can happen in lots of ways."

"A slow bleed might drive the good pastor even crazier," I say, my mind turning. "And it would only take removing a few really key bricks. People who have been solid members, people who are well-known, liked, and respected in town. If they take a look at what that church is doing and decide they don't agree and leave, others will take a hard look at it too."

"We've seen it in major corporations," Iris agrees. "We

get the right VP to second-guess something or resign, and lots of others follow."

"And in this town, it's even more effective," I say. "The people here are connected. They have history. They have real relationships with one another."

"Great. If you want to ruin that church, I think you can do it. And it would be a service, honestly. What I looked into wasn't illegal, but it sure wasn't nice."

I chuckle. "No kidding."

"You should advertise about Ruby's Way, put together packets, all of that, and hint at being supported by 'most' of the groups in town. Just be careful not to get into anything they could yell defamation about."

"Oh, I don't have to worry at all," I tell her. "I don't need packets or ads. I just need a person. Someone who has a history here, who can talk to people with straight-forward facts and passion about what we're doing."

"A spokesperson," Iris says. "Even better. You?"

"Oh, no. There are dozens of better options."

"Better than the most charming person I know who *almost* always gets his way?"

I grin. "Believe it or not, yes."

"Okay, well, let me know if you need anything else from me."

"Of course."

"Talk soon."

We disconnect and I immediately round the bar to where April is working. "Does Cecelia go to Ruby's dad's church?"

April snorts. "No way."

"And is she well-liked in town?"

April thinks about that for a second. "She's well *known* in town. And I think people know that she's honest and no bullshit. Some people like that, and some don't." She shrugs. "I've learned that most of these people have been here long enough that they all have a few that don't like them. But that's normal, right? None of us are perfect."

I nod. "That's right. And totally normal." I grin. "You don't happen to have Cecelia's number, do you?"

"I do," she says. "She doesn't bake, but she's always said I can call her if I ever need anything else."

Of course, she did.

I don't know Cecelia well, but the little bit I did see of her makes me think that she might really get into taking down a manipulative mega-church human brick by human brick.

And as I've already learned during my time in Emerald, Ohio, I probably don't even need to give her a plan. She'll come up with something even better if I give her five minutes.

And maybe some cinnamon rolls.

CHAPTER 22
RUBY

"What do you think?"

I turn and look at Henry.

What do I think?

Is he kidding?

This is unbelievable.

Last night, I told him I felt like things were going well in Emerald and that I had done everything I needed to for April and Elliot. He agreed.

Then I told him I needed to prepare for my move to New Orleans and that I thought it would be better to get everything in place before Scarlett and Cian returned to Emerald. I need to get out of their way sooner versus later so they can settle into their new married-couple routine. He said he understood.

Then, in typical Henry fashion, he arranged for us to use the O'Grady's private jet, and less than twenty-four hours later, I'm standing in the middle of the living room of a luxury four-bedroom, four-bath apartment in the warehouse district of New Orleans.

"Do you like it?" he asks when I haven't answered after several seconds.

Of course he wasn't going to let me find my own apartment. Of course he took over. Of course he's going to insist on approving wherever I live.

And the guy has impeccable taste.

If you're a member of the royal fucking family of Cara.

The apartment is breathtaking.

We're on the top floor of the building in a corner unit. The ceiling soars at least sixteen feet above us. Two of the apartment's walls are exposed brick. The floor is Brazilian hardwood—I wouldn't have known that if the listing didn't say that— and the living room area is covered with a gorgeous, multicolored woven rug.

Natural light spills into the apartment through floor-to-ceiling windows that are covered by gauzy white curtains. The same windows are replicated in the master bedroom. There are also French doors off the kitchen that open onto a private balcony that overlooks the center courtyard that boasts a gorgeous stone fountain and a plethora of plants and flowers around the stone patio with adorable round wrought iron tables and chairs.

The whole apartment comes furnished, from the bisque-colored, four-piece sectional sofa to the I-don't-even-know-how-many–inches-large flatscreen television mounted on the wall to the chef's kitchen with stone countertops, stainless steel appliances, dishes, pots, and pans, and even dish towels, that are more plush than the nicest bath towel I've ever owned.

The enormous four-poster bed in the master suite is the type of bed I imagined celebrities were sleeping on in the high-end hotels in downtown New Orleans when they visited.

Each bedroom has an ensuite bathroom. The master has both a glass-encased rainfall shower and a clawfoot soaker tub that's deep enough that I feel I might need to buy a snorkel.

"It's gorgeous. Absolutely," I tell him.

He nods as if that was exactly the answer he was expecting. "I'm glad you think so."

"It's also over the top," I add. "Of course."

Henry found this place. Or had some highly paid real estate agent who only deals with people who have seven figures or more in their bank account find this place.

Henry has also informed me that he's going to be paying for this place.

I get it. I'm leaving Emerald, leaving him, I'm going to be out of reach, he's not going to be able to just bop down to the coffee shop and make sure everyone is treating me well.

But this is too much.

I do really love it, though.

"It's exactly the kind of place I want to picture you in," he tells me. "I would love it if you would turn one of the bedrooms into an office. A place where you can study."

I spread my arms and turn a three-sixty. "There are so many places I can study. The gorgeous dining table," I say, pointing to the huge cherrywood table that seats eight, for fuck's sake. "The breakfast bar. The couch. The balcony. My bedroom. I could easily put a desk in there."

"So you do intend to fill the bedrooms up with adoptees at the first chance you get."

I grin. I was surprised when he showed me a place with four bedrooms. "You think I'll find roommates?"

"No, I think you'll find people that need some help and you'll let them move in for free."

He knows me so well. "I promise to do background checks."

"Yes," he says firmly. "You will."

"And I'll make one a guestroom for when you visit."

He takes the three steps that separate us and looms over me. I know he thinks that's supposed to be intimidating, but I find it adorable. And hot.

"I intend to tie your wrists and ankles to that four-poster bed the second I walk in here and not untie you until I need to leave."

"Is that your way of saying you *don't* need turn-down service in the guest room?" I asked as lust swirls through me, imagining that scenario.

It's going to suck only seeing him on occasion, and I'm not sure I'm long-distance relationship material. In fact, I'm pretty sure I'm not. I like to be right on top of the people I love, up in their business, seeing them, hugging them, taking care of them every single day.

He is too.

But I'm willing to try this with Henry.

"That's my way of saying that if you think I'm going to be anywhere but glued to your pretty side when I'm in the city, you're a little nuttier than I thought."

"This place is great," I tell him. "But I want to show you the place I found. It's closer to school."

I would love to live in this place. But the warehouse district is not walkable to Loyola. I could bike or take the street car but that's at least a thirty-minute trip. I could drive, but I don't want to deal with parking. Getting a place closer to school and being able to walk makes the most sense. And I happen to know just the place.

"You can move into this place today," he says. He dangles the keys. "It's ready for you."

That is tempting. The apartment literally has everything I need. I'd need to have Scarlett and Mariah ship my things—clothes, books, a few personal items—from home, but I can replace my toiletries here, and I obviously not bringing anything large, like furniture, from Ohio. I keep thinking the sooner I get moved, the easier everything will be.

"Just let me show you the other place."

He sighs and gestures toward the door, but says as he follows me out, "Getting you to and from class is obviously not a problem. That's what Sammy is for. In part."

I stop, and he literally bumps into me. I turn. "Sammy? The guy who's driving us around today?"

I wasn't surprised that Henry had hired a town car driver for us today. He definitely seems like the type to have other people drive him around when possible. And it has been nice. Sammy is a fifty-eight-year-old white man with a wife and six grandkids, who has lived in New Orleans his whole life, has a delightful Louisiana accent, can make a pot of grits that will change my life, and knows the city like the back of his hand.

He picked us up from the airport, dropped us off at lunch and waited for us, then brought us over here. My understanding was that Henry has hired him for the entire day. Possibly for the whole time we're in town.

"Yes. But he's more than a driver. He'll be your... assistant."

"What do I need an assistant for?" I ask.

"Well, transportation for one," Henry says. "He'll also be taking care of the apartment, shopping, cooking, running whatever errands you have. Generally, just taking care of everything you need so that you can focus on studying."

"You hired me a butler?" I say.

"I hired you someone to help you out," Henry says.

"That is…" I shake my head. "Henry, we need to have a talk about your over-the-top spending habits."

He pushes the button to call the elevator and says, "Do we?"

"We absolutely do."

The elevator arrives quickly, probably because there are only eight units in this building. Henry ushers me into the car. "Can you give me an example? Something I bought that was completely ridiculous, with no worth at all?"

"Sammy," I say.

"Sammy is a Marine Corps veteran who worked as private security for a prominent family here in town, but he's been out of full-time work for a couple of years because of a back surgery that didn't go as expected. He's been doing some driving and we've hired him a couple of times when we've been in town. I asked him about the other services, and he was excited. He'll take good care of you. You're going to need the extra help so that you can focus on school. I am helping you out, taking care of you, which you know is very important to me, and I'm giving Sammy a job."

I blow out a breath. Okay, so that one is *borderline* ridiculous, but it has some merit. "What about just buying Dan's bar? You didn't need to do that."

"It gave Dan more money than he ever would've earned with that bar, allows me to help everyone in the bar out, including April, and I've really enjoyed it." He lifts a brow. "It's okay that I enjoy the things I spend my own money on, Ruby." His tone sounds mildly offended.

I roll my eyes. "Obviously."

"What else?" he asks as we step off the elevator and

cross the small lobby. "When I bought all of those things for April and Elliot the first night at your house?"

I sigh and shake my head. "No, that was very nice."

"How about the renovation I'm going to do on the bar? Where I'm expanding and making the kids' area bigger and nicer?"

Ugh, he's so frustrating. Because he's right and knows it. "No, not that either."

"Oh, probably the private jet we flew here on, right?"

I lift a shoulder as Sammy pulls up at the curb, and Henry opens the door for me. "Well, that probably was more than we needed."

"But you really liked it," Henry says as I slide into the back of the long black car. "Especially how soft and wide that bench seat is at the back."

My cheeks heat as I think about how Henry fucked me on that bench seat on the way here.

He's making me a bigger fan of not wearing panties, that's for sure.

"So, you're okay with the private plane?" he asks.

Instead of answering, I ask, "How about this?" as Sammy pulls away from the curb and heads toward the address I gave him earlier. "You know about swear jars? Every time someone says a bad word, they have to put money in the jar?"

He nods.

"Every time you spend money on something over the top, you have to donate money to a charity."

Henry laughs. "Okay, how much?"

"Ten thousand dollars," I toss out.

He nods. "Deal. And you're the judge of when something is over the top?"

I grin and nod.

"Fine. But I have a better idea. I'll just put the ten k into an account in your name. Then you can do the donating. Any charity, whenever you want."

I actually feel a little thrill at that.

He leans in, reading me well as always. "Do you like that idea?"

"I've always wanted to just write a big-ass check to some amazing charity I love."

Obvious pleasure crosses his face. "We can make that happen."

We pull up in front of the apartment building that I want Henry to see, but before I even open the door, Henry says, "No."

"You haven't even looked at it."

"It's a dump. And there's no security. You're not living here."

I turn on the seat. "This is where Scarlett and I lived when we lived in New Orleans."

He stares at me, then looks back at the building. "No, you didn't. You're messing with me."

"Swear to God. I can show you photos. Or I can get Scarlett on the phone."

"Jesus," he growls. Then he shakes his head. "No. You are not living here. You deserve better."

"You know that people actually do live here, right?"

"Fine." He pulls his phone out and starts typing.

"What are you doing?"

"I'm buying the building. And renovating it."

I stare at him and then realize that, yes, of course, he's serious. "Henry! These people can't afford an increase in rent!"

He frowns at me. "Bloody hell, Ruby, I'm not going to raise their rent. But I can make that place nicer to live in."

"How long will that take? Can I move in before the renovations are finished?"

His eyes narrow. "You're going to live in that gorgeous apartment in the warehouse district and let Sammy drive you to and from class."

"I could walk to class from here. I looked it up. It's a thirteen-minute walk. I probably even walk faster than average."

He sighs as if I am the bane of his existence. "What about when it's raining?"

"I'll use an umbrella. Like *everyone* does."

"What about when you're studying late and it's dark and you're alone?"

"I'll call an Uber, or I'll carry pepper spray, or I'll—"

"No. You are dating a multimillionaire who works for a prince. You are going to live in a gorgeous apartment and have a driver who also helps you out with normal everyday activities. If that's over the top, I will put ten thousand dollars a *week* into that account for you to donate to charity."

I open my mouth to object. But then close it again.

He's right. He has the money. He wants to do this for me. This is his way of taking care of me, which is as important to Henry as almost anything. I know how that feels. And if I had the kind of money Henry has, I would absolutely insist on spending it on Scarlett and Mariah and April and my mother and everyone else who is important to me. Even Henry.

Plus, he's not wrong about me walking around at night. I will almost certainly be studying late sometimes.

And that apartment is gorgeous and Sammy needs a job. And there are a ton of charities I would love to donate money to.

Finally, I just lean across the seat, brace my hand next to his thigh, and kiss him.

He cups the back of my head and, of course, deepens the kiss, turning it hot along with sweet.

When I lean back, I say, "Okay."

He studies my face for a long moment, then he says simply, "Thank you."

This man is thanking me for letting him spend crazy amounts of money on me.

But I get it.

I get him.

"So that settled," he says. "There's someplace I want to take you. Where I'd like us to go to dinner and stay overnight."

"I'm up for whatever."

"It's in Autre."

Autre. The tiny little town along the bayou where Henry and Cian lived before Cian came to Emerald. It's where Cian's sister Fiona and her daughter Saoirse live now. Scarlett visited once with Cian and told me all about it.

I know this town and these people mean a lot to Henry. "I'd love to go to Autre with you, Henry."

"Sammy, do you know how to get to Autre?" Henry asks.

"You bet. I hear there's some damn good gumbo down there."

"You can consider it all you can eat," Henry tells him.

"This gig just keeps getting better and better," Sammy says.

And I have to agree. This gig is better than anything I've ever dreamed of.

CHAPTER 23

HENRY

Thank God we got the apartment thing taken care of.

Ruby really has to live somewhere that I know is secure *and* where she will feel pampered and not at all stressed about anything. I need her life in New Orleans to be as easy as I can make it. This time.

I wasn't able to make the first thirty-six years of her life the happy, easy life she deserved to have. But I can do my best to make up for it now.

And I so appreciate that she understands me well enough to let me do that.

With some very Ruby-esque parameters.

When we are about ten miles away from Autre, we start seeing the signs for Boys of the Bayou Swamp Boat and Fishing Tours, as well as the signs for Boys of the Bayou Gone Wild, the petting zoo and animal park. The Landry family owns and runs both.

"That's the animal park that Princess Fiona works at, right?" Ruby asks.

I'm sure she's aware of it because the podcast out of Cara has extensively covered Fiona's rescue and rehabilitation efforts with exotic wild animals, particularly endangered species, and the fact that the tiny bayou town in Louisiana has giraffes, penguins, tigers, and lemurs, as well as the standard horses, alpacas, and goats.

"Yes. Though saying she works there is odd. She's such a huge part of it. And I don't think she takes a salary." I should ask about that. "It would be odd if she did. In fact, she probably gives a ton of money to the park."

"Well, if she's anything like the rest of you, I'm sure she does."

"The endangered species preserve on Cara is because of her," I comment.

"Oh, I know. I went to see it while I was there."

"I'm glad. It's impressive."

Ruby sighs happily. "Impressive is a good word for most things about the royal family."

For the most part, I agree.

We pull into town, and I immediately feel happier. The town and its people have a typical southern Louisiana laid-back, charming style. But the town is also full of people I adore and we've made a lot of good memories even in the short time we've been here.

I'm especially excited to share this place and these people with Ruby.

And her with them.

She is such a huge part of my life now and they have become so important to me that it has felt strange for the last several months that they don't know one another.

"Right here?" Sammy asks, slowing down by the nondescript building with the gravel parking lot.

I know I will find several people I know at Ellie's bar, but for now I say, "No, just keep going. Let's go to the petting zoo first."

"Have you been out on swamp tours?" Ruby asks as we drive past the swamp boat tour company's office and the boat ramps.

"Of course. It's required," I say with a chuckle.

"Are they as fun as they advertise?"

"The tour I went on is a bit different than the ones they give the paying guests," I say with a short laugh. "My first tour was to Leo Landry's old fishing cabin. Leo is the grandfather to the whole Landry clan." I frown. "Well, most of them. Not all, I guess. Anyway, his fishing cabin is extremely... rustic. It's deep in the bayou, and I promise it has seen some things."

"They don't take just anyone there?"

"No. It takes a bit to get to and you would be convinced that you were in the middle of a crime documentary about halfway there."

She laughs. "You are so dramatic."

"That's funny, that's what they said."

She shakes her head. "You consider Hilton hotels rustic, Henry. I can only imagine the horror on your face riding an airboat down the Louisiana bayou toward a 'rustic' fishing cabin."

"There wasn't a bottle of sparkling water or a crumpet to be found for miles," I say, playing right into the stereotype she's painting.

Which isn't that far off.

The fishing cabin did, in fact, horrify me.

"What is a crumpet anyway?" she asks. "Are those real?"

"Very real. And delicious."

We pull up in front of the building that houses the offices for the petting zoo and animal park. I don't have to wonder how I'm going to find someone or who it will be because there is a small crowd gathered right near the entrance to the goat barn.

"You can head over to the bar," I tell Sammy. "We'll meet you there in a little bit."

"Sounds good. I'll be the big guy face-first in a bowl of gumbo."

I laugh. "You won't be the only one. I'll look for the guy in the green shirt."

He chuckles. "Perfect."

I help Ruby out of the car, and we approach the group.

I only recognize some of them. Griffin Foster, who is one of the veterinarians for the animal park; his wife Charlie, who handles PR and marketing; Zander Landry, Autre's cop; and Knox, the longtime town manager who was a write-in for mayor once and now continues to win every election via write-in.

I'm already grinning as we approach because they're standing near the goat pen and Griffin is surrounded.

"What's going on?" Ruby asks.

"Looks like goat shenanigans," I say.

"You say that as if it's a regular occurrence."

"Oh, it is," I tell her. "One of the goats, Stan, can open any gate they put on any pen. This leads to the goats getting out, which leads to them roaming the town. It's such a regular occurrence that they have a goat phone that is manned twenty-four-seven. When people see the goats anywhere they're not supposed to be, they simply call the goat hotline, and someone from the animal park comes and rounds them up."

"The goats hate the petting zoo so much that they're always trying to escape?"

"Nope. Sugar, the one with the big pink bow around her neck, is in love with Griffin, the grumpy-looking one there with the dark hair. If she hasn't seen him for more than about twelve hours, she gets separation anxiety. Then Stan breaks them all out and she goes looking for him. The rest go with her for...moral support?" I grin. "Or just for the adventure of it. I don't know."

Ruby looks at me for a moment, realizes I'm not joking, and laughs. "Do we really want to know what's going on over there?"

I nod. "Very much."

"I'm just saying," the man I don't recognize says as we approach. "She was our sheep first."

"You didn't even care where she was until you noticed her on our website," Griffin says.

"You didn't even ask around if anyone was missing a lamb?" the woman I don't recognize says.

"What did you want me to do? Draw missing goat posters? The goats got out. They came back with a lamb. The poor thing was starving, and her front leg was injured. Obviously, whoever she belonged to didn't give a shit. We took her in and took care of her." Griffin is glaring at the two people.

"What is it that you want exactly, Brandon?" Charlie asks the man. "You think this is your lamb, but you can't really prove it."

"Y'all found a lamb. We're missing a lamb," Brandon says.

"You want it back?" Charlie asks.

"No," Griffin says immediately. "You left that lamb out in the pasture. That's the only way the goats would have found her. The only way she could have followed them home. You didn't have her in a barn the way you should have. She was starving. Clearly not being cared for by her mother or you. You can't have her back."

"We didn't know the mother had rejected her," the woman with Brandon, who I assume is his wife, protests.

"You're just proving my point, Jackie," Griffin says. "If you didn't even notice that, you shouldn't have animals in your care."

"And," Charlie interjects. "If you take her back, people are going to wonder what happened to the lamb and why she's not here, with her friends, who saved her, where she clearly wants to be." She holds up her hands. "And we'll have to tell them the truth. We'll have to add to her story on the website. I'm just putting that out there."

"You'll make us the bad guys?" Jackie asks.

"You're already the bad guys!" Griffin exclaims.

"Fine," Brandon says. "You can keep her. But we want some of the money you're making off her."

"Excuse me?" Griffin asks, stepping toward the man.

Zander starts to shift, but Charlie puts her hand on Griffin's arm.

She tips her head. "What money, Brandon? We're a petting zoo. We have people coming here to see animals every day. Goats, alpacas, rabbits, pigs. Now there's a lamb. But there's no way to prove that people are coming specifically because of her."

Jackie snorts. "Except that you have her up on the website with the story of how the goats 'adopted' her. And you've got stuffed lambs in your gift shop now. And the T-shirts that say *I want to be a goat at Boys of the Bayou Gone Wild too* with the cartoon lamb and goats on it?"

Griffin rolls his eyes.

Zander looks at Charlie, "You've got all of that?"

She shrugs. "Yeah. It's a great story and people love it."

"Do I need to be here for this?" Knox asks Zander.

Zander grins. "Probably not."

"So why did you call me and tell me to come?"

"I just wanted you here."

Knox sighs. "Do *you* need to be here?"

"Not sure yet."

"Can't you arrest them? Or at least make them give me the money I deserve?" Brandon asks.

"Arrest them for what?" Zander asks.

"Stealing my lamb!"

"It sounds like your lamb left you," Zander says. He looks at Griffin. "Have you ever touched that lamb outside of the Boys of the Bayou Gone Wild property?"

"No." Griffin sounds perturbed. "Of course not. We already have so many animals around here, why would I steal another one?"

"Well, you would if you thought it was being mistreated," Charlie says, patting her husband's arm.

"That's not really helpful," Zander mutters to her.

"I didn't know it was being mistreated until it showed up here," Griffin says.

"It wasn't being mistreated!" Brandon protests.

"Neglect is mistreatment," Griffin snaps.

"And when the lamb showed up here with the goats, Griffin didn't really have a choice," Knox says. "He simply did the right thing by taking care of an animal in need. As everyone would expect him to do." Knox looks at Griffin. "You're a veterinarian. It's probably in some ethical code for you to take care of the lamb, right? Do you have Hippocratic oath?"

"It's not called that, but there's something like it," Griffin says.

Knox looks at Brandon. "Seems to me he *had* to take the lamb in."

"I could...sue the petting zoo for letting the goats out,"

Brandon says. "If they weren't out roaming all over, they wouldn't have kidnapped my lamb."

"Kidnapped!" Charlie laughs. She looks at everyone. "Get it? Baby goats are called kids? The goats might have thought she was a goat so 'kidnapped' her?"

Griffin actually cracks a smile. Ruby giggles. I grin.

Brandon doesn't. "So you admit that *your goats* stole my lamb!"

"Well, that won't matter," Knox says. "The town passed a declaration about a year ago that no one could hold the Boys of the Bayou Gone Wild responsible for anything the goats do while they were out around town."

"*What?*" Brandon demands.

Knox shrugs. "I was surprised, too. It's ridiculous. But the town knows the animal park brings a lot of money into town, so they let them get away with a lot. And the only other option was to get rid of the goats. No one wanted that. They find the goats entertaining. Besides, the Boys of the Bayou Gone Wild is great about rebuilding fences, replanting gardens, and cleaning up after the goats, so no one really cares that they get out. In fact, a few people *want* the goats to dig up their flower beds because the replanted flower beds are always gorgeous. Anyway, you're not going to be able to hold the business responsible."

"Huh," Zander says. "Maybe you do need to be here."

Knox shrugs.

"So they just get to make money off a lamb that belongs to *us*?" Brandon asks.

"They get to make money off a lamb that they rescued from a terrible situation," Zander says. "And you get to avoid being prosecuted for animal neglect and cruelty. I also won't come check out your farm to be sure no other animals are at risk."

"Are you sure you shouldn't do that?" Griffin asks.

"How about this?" Charlie asks. "You *let* Zander and Griffin come look around your farm and—"

"No fucking way," Brandon says.

"Ooh, not a great way to seem totally innocent," Knox says.

"As I was saying," Charlie goes on. "You *let* them come look around, you leave Splenda here and—"

"Splenda?" Knox asks.

Charlie points at the goat with the pink bow. "Sugar." She points to the lamb. "Thinks she's a goat like Sugar. So... Splenda. The sweet, white stuff that's kind of like sugar, but not really."

Ruby giggles again, and I hug her against my side. I knew she'd love this place.

"*Anyway*," Charlie says. "You do that, reassure the guys that you messed up this *one* time and never will again, then we'll do a joint interview with the news station out of New Orleans that loves to cover the animal park. We'll tell them that Splenda is from your farm. We'll leave out the part about you neglecting her. We'll just let you link your name to the feel-good story and you can even plug your...what do you make again, Jackie?"

"Candles."

"Your candles," Charlie says. "Maybe you can name a new scent Sugar and Splenda. Make it white. Put a little lamb and a goat on the label. I'll bet people will buy that."

Jackie actually smiles at that. "That's a good idea."

Charlie nods. "I know."

"What's it going to smell like? A barnyard?" Brandon asks.

Charlie gives him a disappointed look. "Oh, Brandon.

That is *not* a good idea. I think you need to let me and Jackie handle this joint effort."

Brandon opens his mouth to reply, but Charlie steps forward, links her arm with Jackie's, and pulls Jackie away, walking toward the barn.

The men watch them go.

Then Brandon says, "I want to be on the news."

Griffin shrugs. "Then you'd better get back on Charlie's good side."

"Is that hard to do?"

"It sure can be," Griffin says. "And the methods I use are *absolutely not* available to you. So...good luck." Then he follows his wife with a huge grin on his face.

Zander looks at Brandon. "You should go home."

"But...Jackie."

"She'll find a ride home," Zander tells him.

"But she..."

"There's cappuccino, and probably gumbo, and a lot of animal visiting, and *a lot* of people visiting in her immediate future. It will be a while. But she'll come home happy, so...you're welcome." Zander turns him and walks him toward his truck.

Brandon doesn't seem to know what else to do, so he gets in his truck and drives off.

Finally, Zander and Knox notice me and Ruby.

"Henry!"

They come over with smiles. Well, Zander does. But Knox doesn't frown, which is basically like smiling for him.

"Hi, guys. Ruby, Zander Landry, and Knox. Fiona's husband."

She extends her hand. "Hi, Zander." She shakes his hand, then Knox's. "We met at Cian and Scarlett's wedding.

I keep meaning to ask someone, is Knox your first or last name?"

"You can just call me Knox," he says, taking her hand.

"Ohhkay."

"It's nice to see you again," Knox says. He looks at me. "You're taking her to meet Ellie?"

"Yes."

"So she's the one."

Well...yes, she is. I nod. "Yes."

Ruby looks at me. I meet her eyes and repeat, "Yes."

She smiles. "Let's go meet Ellie."

CHAPTER 24

RUBY

I've never seen Henry this laid-back. All of our time together has been spent in Emerald or in Cara. Both places where there has been more than a little chaos surrounding Cian. And more recently, chaos surrounding me. Here in Autre, Henry seems lighter, happier. It's obvious he's completely comfortable here, and I love this.

We walk up the dirt road past the Boys of the Bayou buildings and across to the building on the other side. There are several cars and trucks in the gravel-covered parking lot, but there are no signs indicating what this place is until we get closer to the door.

Then there is a simple sidewalk sign that says *Menu Today: whatever Ellie feels like making (and gumbo, of course)*.

"Okay, so who is Ellie?" I ask.

Henry grins as he reaches for the door. "That is actually a hard question to answer," he says. "The easy answer is the owner of the bar. And the grandmother to most of the Landrys I know."

"So what makes the question hard?"

"She's just so much more than that," he says. He nudges me through the door. "I think you'll see what I mean."

It takes me a minute for my eyes to adjust from the bright sunlight to the darker interior of the bar. My nose is actually the first thing to adjust. The air is scented with a tantalizing combination of spices, beer, and old wood.

Henry leads me toward the enormous bar that runs the length of one side of the building, which really just appears to be one big room.

As I take in the details, I note that none of the chairs and tables seem to match and the hodge-podge of styles and colors extends to the stools that line the bar. The eclectic mix of ages and styles also seems to extend to the clientele.

There's a big man leaning on the bar as we approach and when he sees Henry, he straightens with a huge grin. I realize immediately he is Zander's identical twin brother. I feel even more at home here.

"Henry, holy shit. What are you doing here?" the man asks, extending his hand for a shake.

Henry takes his hand, but they move in for a bro-hug.

"Just a quick visit. Came to New Orleans to find Ruby a new apartment and couldn't stay there when you all are right down the road," Henry tells him.

The man's gaze lands on me. "Damn right. I'm Zeke." He sticks his enormous hand out toward me.

I take it. "Ruby."

"You look familiar. Have you been here before?"

"This is Scarlett's sister," a woman's voice says.

I look across the bar to find an older woman with long gray hair lying in a braid over one shoulder. She's in a T-shirt that reads *No Is A Complete Sentence* and she's wiping her hands on a towel.

"Ruby, this is Ellie," Henry says." Ellie, you've already

figured out who this is. Didn't think for even a second it was Scarlett?"

"I've been around my share of twins," she tells him, her gaze going to Zeke and then back to Henry. "Zeke and Zander and then, of course, his baby girls. Twins might look alike, but they feel different."

Henry looks at me and grins. "They *feel* different?"

"Of course. They're two different people. They take up space differently, move through the world differently," Ellie says.

"Thank you," I tell her. "A lot of people don't really understand that. Twins get lumped together a lot. A lot of people assume that Scarlett and I like the same foods, the same music, the same books." I look up at Henry. "The same men."

"A lot of people are jackasses," Ellie says matter-of-factly.

I can't argue with that.

"Do you like gumbo?" she asks.

I decide Ellie Landry is not only someone I don't want to lie to, but she's someone who can tell if I do. "It's okay. I've had some that's good, but it's often too spicy for me. I prefer jambalaya," I say. "My favorite New Orleans staple is red beans and rice, actually."

She studies me. "With sausage?"

"Definitely."

"Okay then."

I smile. I feel like I passed some test.

"Ellie makes excellent gumbo," Henry says.

"Oh, Brit," Ellie says with a laugh. "I know you've been strugglin' with my gumbo since you first set foot in here."

He looks alarmed. "I...do like it."

"It's a bit much for you, admit it." She plants a hand on her hip.

I was right. Ellie Landry would rather hear the truth that is slightly insulting than a compliment that's a lie.

"Fine. It's a bit much for me," Henry says. "But I've been building up my tolerance."

"Eating it as fast as you can and then diving headfirst into a dish of bread pudding isn't building up a tolerance," Ellie informs him.

Henry puts a hand on his heart. "I would eat vats of spicy gumbo if I had to in order to get to eat your bread pudding, Ellie."

She scoffs, but she's smiling. "Mine's not even *spicy* gumbo."

Henry gives her a horrified look. Probably the same one he wore when he visited Leo's fishing cabin.

I giggle. I might have to find more things to put that look on his face. Henry Dean has moved through this world far too in charge and comfortable for the past several years, I think.

"It was the British accent that did it for you, wasn't it?" Ellie asks me.

I grin and nod. "At first, that was a big part of it, yeah."

She shakes her head. "You've gotta watch the accents. These Cajun boys have been using them for evil for decades. And these Irishmen...whew."

I laugh. "Yes, I've met one of those Irishmen. He definitely gets away with a lot."

"Ruby's moving back to New Orleans soon," Henry says. "I brought her here so that she'd have some people around in case she needs anything. But I think maybe I'll just introduce her to Naomi. She's sweet. Or Jordan. Jordan is really nice. And she already knows Fiona. You can just steer clear of Ellie."

Ellie waves her hand as if to say, "don't listen to him". "Everything those girls know, they learned from me," she says. "You might as well come straight to the top if you need something."

I already feel like Ellie could make just about anything better. It's not exactly a "motherly" vibe. It's more of a *I've got a shovel and I don't need the details, let's just get rid of the body before it starts to smell* vibe. Sometimes you need *that* on your side more than you need chicken soup or a hug.

Then again, Ellie Landry could probably bury a body, feed you the best soup you've ever had, and give you a hug to end all hugs, all in the same thirty-minute period.

I think I'm going to have to try her gumbo. Maybe I've just had the wrong gumbo all this time.

"Here's what you can come down here for," Ellie tells me, leaning onto her bar. "Great food. Shenanigans. A few laughs. A cute animal fix. To kill time. Book recs. An alibi. To borrow tools, cooking implements, any kind of vehicle, or any type of clothing. To learn to do anything from deep fry something to fixing a transmission. Just bein' around people who will accept you however you are. People who will listen to you rant and then say 'those assholes' about whoever you're mad at. Or just to flirt with some good-lookin' boys who will treat you like gentlemen should." She pauses, then winks. "Unless you don't want them to."

I literally snort at that last one.

"Um, no," Henry says. "Not that last bit. Not at all."

Ellie gives him an *oh really?* look. "Of course she can come here for that. I'll keep the assholes and the married ones away from her."

"She's with *me*."

"Well, then it's up to *you* to keep her from needin' that, isn't it?" She gives me another wink. "If you show up wantin' that, I'm not asking questions."

I giggle.

"I thought we were friends, El," Henry tells her.

"We were, until you did something to my friend Ruby to make her come flirtin' with the bayou boys."

With that, Henry steers me away from the bar and toward the big table at the back of the room where there is a huge group gathered.

"Nice to meet you, Ruby!" Ellie calls after us, laughing. "See you whenever!"

"Thanks, Ellie!" I call back.

"I've changed my mind," Henry says. "You can't come back here."

I laugh. "Oh, I want to come here all the time now."

"You'll hate it. The gumbo is terrible. Way too spicy. And there are no other British accents."

"I'll be okay. She said I can eat red beans and rice. And the Louisiana accent is also very—"

He stops, turns, and cups my face, bringing me in for a long, deep kiss.

When he lets me go, everyone at the back table is watching.

He points at them.

"All of *those* bayou boys are married," Henry says. "Now they know you're mine, and they *will* keep an eye on you, so your sweet smiles and flirty eyes and panty-less ass are for *me*, and only *me*. Got it?"

God, I love when he gets possessive.

I love that he's bringing me into this world that means so much to him.

I love these people already because of how happy they make him.

I love *him*.

I nod. "Only yours," I say softly.

He was expecting a sassy, teasing retort, and he blinks at me in surprise for a moment. Then he smiles. "That's right. Mine."

I'm going to miss him so damned much.

At least now I have a whole assed bar to come hang out in and drown my sorrows.

And bread pudding.

It won't fix my lonely heart, but bread pudding never made anything worse.

CHAPTER 25
HENRY

Ruby, of course, charmed everyone. I hadn't been worried. Well, until Ellie started talking about setting her up with Autre boys.

The Landrys and their friends are an easy group to get along with, and Ruby attracts people naturally. It's the way she sees people for who they are and accepts them as is. That will be what makes her fit in with this group perfectly. I suspect it won't take long before she comes to Autre on a regular basis and, not because she really needs anything, but simply because she enjoys it.

They're a rowdier bunch than she's used to, but they're all big-hearted and definitely subscribe to the idea that you don't have to be blood to be family.

As we pull up to the big house where Cian and I lived during our time in Autre, I feel the need to tell her, "I've never brought a woman to this house."

"You're not trying to tell me you were celibate during the time you lived in Autre, are you?" she says, giving me a *yeah right* look.

"Not bringing women here and being celibate are two

different, unrelated things," I say, not wanting to get into it any further than that.

She gets out of the car and meets me at the front bumper. She looks up at the house.

"When we first moved here, this was a typical two-story house with three bedrooms and two baths," I tell her.

"You're kidding."

"Nope. There aren't a lot of houses for sale in Autre, and we didn't want to build from the ground up, so we decided to remodel. Fiona liked the location because it's close to the animal park." I point. "She could see the giraffes from her balcony."

Ruby shakes her head. "That's incredible."

I grin. "Because Fiona, Saoirse, Torin, and Cian were all going to live here along with Colin, Jonah, and me—and not just the royals were used to nicer accommodations and quite a bit more space—" I say with a self-deprecating grin. "The house was *heavily* renovated.

"There are actually two 'wings' in the house. Fiona, Saoirse, and Colin were in the east and the rest of us were in the west. Each room has a large bedroom that includes a sitting area and an ensuite bathroom. We all love each other and get along great, but it was important that we all have our own space too.

"Additionally, the house has a full gym in the basement and a huge living room, family room, and enormous kitchen on the first floor."

"So why never bring a woman here?"

"There's just something about this house, and this town," I tell her. "This was sort of a haven. This felt more like home than anything had before. I think when we lived in Florida, Cian and I were younger, and things were a little more superficial. We were in college. We did a lot more partying and a lot more traveling. When we came here to Autre, we were more mature… at least I'd like to think so. Life seemed a little more serious. We were a little more settled. The house didn't feel like a big frat house like it had in Florida.

"And something about Autre felt more like coming back to our hometown, even though I lived here less time than anywhere else." I finally shrug. "I can't explain it. We went to New Orleans plenty, and partied and yes, met women. But nobody ever came back to this house with me."

Ruby is looking up at me with a mixture of emotions. She seems slightly amused, but there's also love there. "You sure you want to bring me here? We can go back to New Orleans."

I turn to her swiftly and crowd close. "I want you in this town, in this house, in my room, in my bed. I want to make love to you in this house. And every time I come visit you, I am going to fuck you in that very fancy apartment I got for you. But I also want to bring you down here, hang out with the Landrys, and love you in this house."

Her smile has died, and she's watching me with wide eyes. But she slowly nods. "Okay."

That's all she says, but that's all she has to say.

I lead her into the house and give her a quick tour of the first floor, but we're both eager to climb the stairs. She doesn't need to see anyone else's bedroom. I sent Sammy back to New Orleans to his family after he had dinner at Ellie's, so right now, we have the whole place to ourselves.

"How about you save the 'wows' and 'holy crap, that's huge' until we get into the bedroom, and I have my clothes off?" I ask as she says the words for the fifth time since coming through the front doors.

She giggles, and I can't help myself, I bend and sweep

her up into my arms, carrying her the rest of the way to my bedroom.

I stride through the sitting room area to the huge bed and toss her onto it.

"Show me I was right about the panties," I tell her.

We both strip off our own clothes, eyes glued to one another.

"Oh yes, you look very good on this bed," I tell her, leaning over to brace my hands on the mattress and then climbing up. She scoots up until her head is on the pillow, and I am looming over her.

"This room is easily as nice as any of the hotel rooms we could've stayed in," she says.

"Maybe," I agree. "But another perk of this room, is I can get a stripper pole installed in here."

She laughs. "That will cost you ten thousand dollars."

I lean down and say against her mouth, "I expect you to make that worth every penny." Then I kiss her.

As always, the heat flares between us quickly, the need climbing rapidly. But it also feels sweet. I want to savor this. Ruby is in Autre. Two of my favorite things are combined. I want to take my time.

My palms glide down her side, absorbing the silky feel of her skin and the way she shivers under my touch. I linger at her breasts, teasing the already stiff points. When I get to her hips, I squeeze, and she arches up closer to me.

Our tongues are hungry against one another, and we're moaning and gasping as her hands also travel down my back to my ass and then up my sides.

I settle all my weight more fully between her thighs and she opens them completely. I feel the heat of her pussy against my cock, and I rub against her clit.

"Wrap your legs around me," I tell her gruffly.

She does, her heels pressing into my ass.

I shift my hips back until the head of my cock nudges her hot, wet entrance.

"Yes, Henry," she pleads.

"You're already ready for me?" I ask.

"I've been ready for you since you bought that old building I used to live in and said you'd remodel it."

I move, sliding just the head of my cock into her pussy. "The building you gave me a hard time about buying?"

"It's so hot when you're making the world better, Henry Dean."

I slide in another inch. "So you've been walking around with wet panties ever since you met me," I say, making sure I sound arrogant rather than like she's wrapped a fist around my heart and is squeezing.

She giggles against my neck, and I give her another inch just for that happy sound.

"I pretty much have," she admits. "It really was the British accent at first. And then you turned out to be the best man I've ever met."

For that, I reach down and grasp her thigh, bringing it up and hooking her leg over my shoulder.

She gasps.

"We're perfect for each other," I tell her huskily, looking into her eyes. "Because you are the best person I've ever known." I slide in another inch. "And I know a fucking king." Then I thrust hard and bury myself fully in the pussy I will never get over.

Her moan is everything. Then her body clamps around me as if never wanting to let me go, and when I pull back to give her another long, hard stroke, the heat and friction is exquisite.

I pull back and thrust, pull back and thrust, and we

don't need any more words. We move together, making love to one another, making yet another memory that I will never be able to shake, and ingraining her even further into my mind and heart.

It doesn't last long enough. Our bodies need each other like we need water and oxygen. Soon we're both barreling toward our climaxes.

As we lie together in one of my favorite rooms in the world, I hold her close.

And for the first time ever, I wish I was a bartender, a veterinarian, a small-town cop, or even a town manager who got written in for Mayor over and over again. Anything that would allow me to stay next to this woman in bed every night for the rest of my life.

Anything but the bodyguard to a prince who would always have to eventually get on a plane and leave.

CHAPTER 26

HENRY

Breakfast at Ellie's is a fun, boisterous event with the Landry family. Or at least most of them. Getting them *all* in one place at the same time is a feat even Ellie accomplishes only a couple of times a year.

But Ruby eats quickly, and I wonder if she even tastes the praline-stuffed French toast once Fiona asks if she'd like to have a behind-the-scenes tour of the giraffe barn.

Now we're walking between the pens inside the enormous building that houses Fiona's gentle giants.

Fiona and Ruby are in front of Knox and me. We're hanging back, just letting Fiona show off her babies to a new enchanted fan.

I've been around giraffes as long as I've known Fiona, but they still amaze me. Still, watching Ruby experience this makes me realize how many incredible experiences I've had that I now want her to have. I want to take her to every country, every city, and every village I've visited and loved. I want to eat with her in every bistro, dive bar, five-star restaurant, and tavern I've enjoyed. I want to show her the

Northern Lights, the pyramids, the Himalayas, the Great Barrier Reef, and so much more.

I also just want to watch her enjoy a funny story told by one of my favorite people while eating the *best* bread pudding ever made.

I want to make her life as incredible as it can possibly be.

"Oh my *God*," Ruby says, looking up as one of the giraffes peers over the top of the wall at her. "This is amazing."

Fiona is delighted by her delight. "Let's go out here. Speir will let you pet her."

Ruby looks like a little kid as Fiona leads her into the outdoor yard where four giraffes are hanging out.

When they see Fiona, they start in her direction.

Ruby laughs. "Do they think it's feeding time?"

"They just love her," Knox says, referring to his wife, an affectionate note in his voice as he watches the animals approach. "They don't need treats to come to her. The rest of us? Definitely."

"They're so gorgeous," Ruby says, awe in her voice as one giraffe reaches where Fiona is standing and bows its head so she can rub his nose.

"I don't know why people get so enamored with them. They're really just tall cows," Knox says. "They make a *huge* mess, take up a ton of space, and are expensive as hell to keep."

Fiona laughs. "You're just grumpy because the inspector is coming tomorrow."

"The inspector is coming *again* tomorrow. She was just here," he grouses. "There's so much paperwork when she shows up."

"You love paperwork," Fiona reminds him. "Helping run this animal park should be your idea of heaven."

"Helping run this animal park while also helping run this town has gotten me *over* my love of paperwork," Knox says.

Fiona gasps. "Say it isn't so." She grins at Ruby. "He's lying. It's not the paperwork he doesn't like when the inspector comes. It's that he has to pretend not to notice her flirting but still be nice and polite while turning down all her advances." She gives her husband a grin. "Nice and polite are a little tough for Knox when people are being…"

"Irritating. Annoying. Rude. Audacious," he fills in.

Fiona laughs. "Those things."

Three of the giraffes are vying for Fiona's attention, and Ruby is able to rub their noses and necks. The look on her face is absolutely gorgeous. I love seeing her free from pressure and having joyful experiences that require no work or worry from her.

I *am* going to make more things like this happen for her. I know she'll be consumed by school for the next few years, but after that, I'll take her around the world.

The fourth giraffe lumbers over and is clearly headed directly for Knox. It grabs his hat in its teeth, tossing it to the ground, then nuzzling its snout into Knox's hair.

Knox laughs, pushing it back, but stroking the animal's nose. "I'm married with two kids," he says, still clearly talking about the flirty inspector. "I shouldn't have to turn down any advances from anyone."

"Being an amazing dad just makes you hotter," Fiona says, clearly unbothered by this other woman's flirting. "It's not her fault."

"Oh my God," Knox mutters.

It seems they've had this conversation before.

"What about my hot, kickass wife?" Knox asks. "Shouldn't this woman worry about messing with the husband of a woman who knows how to wrangle tigers?"

Fiona laughs. "I think she's holding out for a threesome."

Knox stops and turns toward his wife. "*What?*"

Fiona shrugs. "I flirt with her too."

"I repeat, *what?*" Knox says.

"I want good inspections! This animal park has a lot going on and we need to stay on her good side!" Fiona tosses her hair. "I think she's into me too."

"So you're making her think we're going to *sleep with her?*" Knox demands.

Ruby and I exchange a look. She's trying not to laugh. I'm not surprised by this exchange. I *am* surprised that Knox still hasn't completely figured out when Fiona is screwing with him, though. I've always found the way our princess keeps the big, grumpy guy on his toes entertaining.

"I've never *said* that," Fiona is telling Knox. "I've just never *didn't* say that."

Ruby comes to stand next to me and says quietly, "She's messing with him, right?"

I look at her in surprise. "You already figured that out?"

She laughs. "The more outraged he gets, the more outrageous she gets."

Of course, Ruby has figured them out. She sees people. I fucking love her so much.

"Fiona will still be doing that to Knox when he's ninety," I say. "And he'll still be falling for it."

"I'm not going to live to be ninety," Knox says with a sigh, overhearing. Apparently, he just figured out his wife was only trying to provoke him. "She's going to drive me to an early grave." He's watching his wife with a mixture of love and exasperation that I've seen a million times, but I never fully understood until Ruby came into my life.

"You're catching on to her faster than you used to," I tell him with a chuckle. "That's progress."

"He's just so easy to rile," Fiona says, sliding her arms around her husband's waist to hug him. She's so petite, and he's so tall that she only comes up to his chest.

"Does this mean you're going to tell the inspector to back off?" he asks, wrapping his arms around her and kissing the top of her head.

"Oh no," Fiona says. "I love how flustered you get when she flirts, and you have to figure out a way to turn her down without resorting to being your usual grumpy fuck-off self."

I'd love to be a spectator for that, but before I can get details about when the inspector will be here, my phone rings.

I pull it out and see that it's Cian. I show the screen to Ruby, then lift it to my ear.

"Hey."

"Hey," he greets. "So, don't be mad and don't freak out."

I frown. "We've talked about you starting conversations that way," I tell him. I turn and walk to the edge of the pen. "What's going on?"

"Everyone is fine," he says.

"Okay."

"I want you to repeat that back to me so I know it sunk in."

"What the fuck is going on?" I demand.

Ruby notices and comes over. "What's wrong?" she asks.

"I'm not sure yet."

"Everyone is fine," Cian says. "Repeat it."

"Everyone is fine," I say shortly. "What happened?"

"Scarlett, Mariah, and I are on our way back to Emerald."

"I thought you were going to New York for another community opening first."

"We were. But…" He trails off.

I brace myself.

"There was a car accident."

"*What?*"

"Everyone. Is. Fine," Cian repeats, slowly and firmly. "There was a car accident. Someone hit us at an intersection. It was just me and Scarlett. We did go to the hospital but were released after Scarlett's arm was cast."

"Her—" I cut myself off, not wanting to panic Ruby.

"She broke her arm. One of the bones in her forearm. It's not a big deal, except that it's her right arm, so she's going to need some help for a while and won't be able to work at the shop. But we're heading home, and we're still planning to go open the moms' community in Omaha in two weeks."

I blow out a breath.

He sounds fine. It's a broken arm. Both Cian and I have had broken bones and we're fine.

If this was more serious, Cian wouldn't be the one calling me. And I'm sure Jonah and Iris will both be checking in with me soon.

Everyone. Is. Fine.

"Okay," I say. "Ruby and I are in Louisiana, so, I'll meet you in Emerald."

"You're in Louisiana?" he asks. "Are you in Autre?"

I can hear the smile in his voice.

"We are."

"That's great! Hey, you don't have to rush back. We're okay."

Except that April and Elliot haven't fully moved out, and…

Cian and Scarlett were in a car accident. And in the hospital. And I wasn't there.

Suddenly, my stomach knots and my lungs refuse to inflate. Jesus. They were in a *car accident*. They could have been seriously injured. They could have…died.

I squeeze my eyes shut.

I absolutely cannot imagine a world that doesn't have Cian O'Grady in it.

I hate even picturing Cian hurt or in pain.

I've seen him banged up and even with broken bones.

And I've fucking hated it.

Something worse is impossible to even conceive.

And while that was happening, I was thousands of miles away.

A part of my mind, the rational part, understands that I couldn't have necessarily prevented the accident even if I'd been there. But my rational mind isn't always in charge when it comes to the people I love.

I need to be there *now*. I need to see for myself that they're fine. And take care of whatever they need to have taken care of.

I respect that Cian is Scarlett's husband now, but he's not exactly an expert in caregiving. He's been the recipient of most care. I just need to be sure everything really is okay.

It's my bloody job.

"I'll be there as soon as I can," I tell him.

"Okay. We're getting on the plane in about an hour."

I do a quick calculation. "Okay. See you soon."

We disconnect, and I meet Ruby's gaze.

"Is everything okay?" she asks, clearly concerned.

"Well—"

Her phone starts to ring.

I'm one hundred percent certain it's her sister. "Talk to Scarlett. I'm going to get us a plane."

"Henry," she says, her eyes wide.

"Everyone is fine," I tell her.

She takes a breath and nods. Then answers her phone. "Scarlett, what's going on?"

My phone rings as I'm scrolling through my contacts for our airport contact. "Jonah," I answer. "What the fuck happened?"

"Everyone is fine," my friend and fellow O'Grady protector says.

"People really need to stop saying that to me."

"The guy ran a red light, but he was going pretty slow. Cian had just pulled out. They were in the car alone. We were right behind them and saw the whole thing. They were hit on Scarlett's side. She broke her right arm. Clean break. They were able to set and cast it. She'll make a full recovery."

I appreciate that he just gets to the point and gives me all the information I would ask for before I have to.

"She and Cian both also have mild concussions, but they've been cleared to fly. Mariah is flying home with them, and they don't feel that they need Linnea and me with them, so we're going to stay here in Portland for a couple more days, then head home. If you need anything, I can be on a plane to Ohio in less than an hour."

That all actually sounds good. It's nothing major. Nothing to panic about.

I glance at Ruby. She's frowning slightly but nodding. She doesn't look too upset, just mildly worried.

She meets my gaze but doesn't give me much indication of what she's feeling or thinking.

"Thanks, Jonah."

"I can be with them in Omaha in a couple of weeks," he says.

I shake my head. "No need. I'll be there."

"Okay. Let me know if you need anything else." He pauses. "Are *you* okay?"

"Yeah." I blow out a breath. "I'm great. Nothing broken. Head's fine."

"I mean…" Jonah pauses again. "You know what I mean."

Jonah has been Torin's bodyguard and, more importantly, friend, as long as I've been with Cian. Their relationship is as close as mine and Cian's is.

I know exactly what he means.

"Cian's never been in the hospital when I haven't been there. He was never in the hospital as a kid after he was born. He didn't even have his tonsils out until he was twenty-two. And he still has his appendix." I sigh. "It just feels weird."

"I get it," Jonah says. "But for what it's worth, he's doing a fantastic job."

"A fantastic job of being in the hospital?"

"Well, he's fine, physically. But he's shaken up seeing Scarlett hurt. Still, he held it together, was calm, asked all the right questions, and hasn't left her side. He's taking amazing care of her."

I think about that.

And how Scarlett has changed my best friend in so many great ways.

"I'm glad to hear that."

"I'm just saying, you don't have to worry," Jonah says. "They're good."

"They were in a car accident. That could have been really bad." In fact, I can't even let myself go there fully. I can't let myself imagine what *could have* happened. I don't know what I would do.

"It could have been," Jonah agrees. "But it wasn't. That's what you have to focus on. Any time any of us leaves the house, something bad could happen. That's the problem."

"The problem with us not always driving them everywhere they go?" I ask.

And for the first time in my life, I'm actually annoyed at the thought that I might not be able to ever let Cian travel without me.

Dammit.

I don't want us to be joined at the hip for the rest of our lives.

Friends? Of course. In constant contact? Definitely. In each other's business all the time? Sure. But physically together every damned day? Not really.

"What? No." Jonah laughs. "You have *no way* of knowing that accident wouldn't have happened if you'd been driving. What I meant is that's the problem with loving our protectees like family. And, well, it's too late to change that, so we're just going to have to deal with it."

I frown. "You're really that nonchalant about the idea of something bad happening to Torin?"

"Nonchalant?" Jonah asks. "Fuck no. But the realization that something bad could happen makes me want him to have as many amazing experiences and happy times as possible. It's how I feel about Linnea. My parents. Everyone I love." He pauses. "Even you."

I pause at that. Then smile. "I love you too, Jonah."

He chuckles. "Thanks. Talk to you later."

"Thanks for covering me in Portland."

"It was great. Any time."

We disconnect, and I take the few steps to where Ruby is saying, "I love you too. So much. We'll talk soon."

She disconnects and looks up at me.

"We should go pack," I tell her.

She looks down at her phone, then up at me. "Yeah. Um, I'm not going back to Emerald."

I frown. "What?"

"I'm not going back. Not right now. I'm going to stay in New Orleans. In the new apartment. Mariah is going to pack up my room and send what I need."

I stare down at her, not fully understanding what she's saying. "Did Scarlett tell you about the accident?"

Ruby nods. "Yes. And her arm."

"You don't want to check on her?"

She wiggles her phone. "I just did."

"That's enough?"

"Yes." She straightens. "She and Cian are fine. She said he's been great, that they have a plan, that she's a little sore, of course, but her meds are working." She stops, then says, "She doesn't need me, Henry."

I shake my head. "Come on, Gem. You know that's not true. Let's go home. You'll see."

But she just smiles. "I'm not saying that in an 'I'm so sad she doesn't need me anymore' way. I'm glad. I'm... relieved. She sounds great. The fact that she's letting Cian take care of her is huge. Scarlett doesn't do that. I'm the only one she's ever leaned on. This is big for them."

"You will *not* be in the way. It's not like she won't be glad to see you," I say, guessing at her feelings now.

"That's not it." Ruby reaches out and squeezes my arm. "This is *good*. I'll admit that I was a little worried about what it would be like once I started school. Would there be a time when something happened, and Scarlett or Mariah would want me to come home to help out? It's how it's *always* been, Henry. We're a unit. A team. And we're amazing. But now I don't have to worry." She smiles, and it seems completely genuine. "I can go to school and not worry. I can fully focus and not wonder if I'm going to feel the need to go back to Emerald. Cian's there, stepping up, and Scarlett is letting him. It's awesome."

What feels like a ribbon of panic sneaks through my gut.

I'm not ready to leave her. I'm not ready for goodbye.

"Don't you want to pack your own stuff? Say goodbye? Have a going away party at the bar?"

She laughs. "No way."

"What? Really? But these are your people. Your community."

"I know. And I'm going to miss them like hell. Saying goodbye to them will suck no matter how I do it. This way it feels kind of less official and big and sad. This feels like I'm just away on a trip and I'll see them soon when I come home. It'll just be a visit, but by then we'll have all adjusted to the new normal."

"It's a long time until classes start." I feel like I'm grasping at straws.

I'm also reeling a bit from her not wanting to go back. From being *able* to not go back.

"I know, but I can get settled and enjoy New Orleans and feel really ready by then. I've never done full-time classes. Once they start, it will be intense. I need time to prepare."

I try to think of another excuse, something else to convince her. *Anything* else to say.

"I'm not ready to say goodbye," I finally tell her. Might as well be completely honest.

That makes her smile fade. She swallows, and nods. "I know. Me either. But I'm never going to be. It's not going to be any easier if I go back and then leave. In fact, it will be harder."

She's right. I know she is. But I still don't want this.

"I'm disappointed," I tell her. "I thought you'd want to check in on them, make sure they're really okay, and that April and Elliot get moved, and that you'd want to see what happens with the church guys and the free cinnamon rolls."

"I'm sorry you're disappointed." She frowns as if she really doesn't like that word. "But none of that needs me. It will all be okay whether I go back or not."

"Yes, because I'm going to go back and take care of it."

Now *she* looks disappointed. "All of that will be okay without you, too. You could sta—"

"Stop." I cut her off before she can finish that sentence. "Don't make me say no, Gem," I say, my tone pleading. "Please."

She presses her lips together.

"I need to get to the airport," I tell her. "I can drop you off at the apartment."

She shakes her head. "Why don't you just send Sammy down here after he takes you to the airport?"

"You're going to stay here?"

"Yeah." She looks around. "It's really nice to step into a strong, fully formed, happy community. One that takes you in instead of..."

"Being the one that puts it together?" I ask.

"Yeah." She smiles up at me, a little sadly. "I expect I'll put one together eventually. But I like this one."

"You'll probably put more than one together."

She just lifts a shoulder, not bothering to argue.

"This is what I wanted for you," I tell her. "I wanted *you* to be taken care of for a change. I wanted you to feel what you do for everyone else."

Her eyes get a little shiny. "Then you don't have to worry about me, Henry. I'm in a great place."

Yeah. She is. I can leave her here, and she will be fine.

Without me.

I lean in and kiss her. She fists the front of my shirt and kisses me back.

Then I turn and leave.

To go back to the job that has meant more to me than anything else in my life.

Until now.

CHAPTER 27

HENRY

It took far too long for me to set up a charter flight between New Orleans and Columbus, and by the time I make the drive to Emerald and walk through the back door of the house, Cian, Scarlett, and Mariah are already home.

The smoke detector is squealing, the kitchen is filled with gray smoke, and I nearly trip over the five grocery bags sitting just inside the door.

"What the hell?" I yell.

"Oh my God!"

The sound of glass hitting tile and shattering barely registers over the squealing alarm.

Scarlett spins to face me and opens her mouth, but just then, Cian storms into the room.

"What the hell!" he bellows. He grabs the broom from where it rests in the corner near the fridge, strides to the smoke detector, and bangs the handle against the plastic disk until it falls to the floor, now silent.

"I leave you alone for five minutes so I can unpack our bags and you're burning the place down?" he asks Scarlett.

"I was just preheating the oven for Diane's casserole!"

she exclaims. "Something must have spilled on the bottom of the oven sometime."

"You should have waited for me," Cian says. "I would have heated the oven."

"I was just *heating the oven*!" Scarlett says. "My God, I wasn't drywalling the room or rearranging the furniture."

"Then why is the casserole on the floor in a broken pan?" Cian asks.

Scarlett looks down, then over at me. "Henry scared me, and I dropped it."

Cian notices me for the first time. "Oh, hey!"

"Sorry to scare you," I say, pushing the back door open to air out the room, then picking my way over the grocery bags, but catching my toe on one and tripping. "Dammit."

"Sorry, the place is kind of chaotic," Scarlett says. "We got home only a couple of hours ago. People have been bringing stuff over. Diane brought a few casseroles, Mandy and Ada brought cinnamon rolls and pecan rolls, Amber went to the store and brought..." She gestures at the bags. "A bunch of stuff."

I can't help but smile. Of course, all those people brought stuff over. Scarlett's been helping all of them since the day she moved back to town. I'm sure they're thrilled to have the chance to pay her back a bit.

"Then April and Elliot stopped by and brought more groceries and picked up their stuff."

Dammit, April doesn't need to be spending money on other people. Especially a man with unlimited funds. Still, I know it was her way of supporting Scarlett and saying thanks more than anything.

"I was going to help them get their things gathered up," I say, crossing to open the window over the sink, then surveying the casserole mess to decide how to best clean that up.

"It was no problem. I told them they should stay," Scarlett says.

"They said they're staying at Mandy and Will's, though," Cian adds.

I nod. "Recent development, but yes."

"Will drove them over. We loaded everything up quickly."

Scarlett grabs the roll of paper towels and starts to kneel next to the broken casserole dish. Cian swears and scoops her up, throwing her over his shoulder.

"Cian!"

"You are supposed to rest," he tells her. He smacks her ass. "You know I'm just getting the hang of all of this. Give me a fucking break, okay?"

She grins at me. "He's doing great, actually."

I take in her appearance now. She's got a bright red cast on her right forearm, and her long dark hair is wet and in a braid.

I'm guessing Cian had to wash and braid her hair. Scarlett is right-handed, so many activities will be impossible for her while that cast is on, but doing her hair—or probably showering alone in any case—will be difficult regardless.

And just now he was upstairs unpacking?

"You're going to the couch," Cian says, starting for the living room with his wife over his shoulder. "And you will *stay there* while I put another casserole in the oven and finish upstairs. Understand?"

I can still hear them from the kitchen as I start cleaning up the mess.

"I can put a pan in the oven with one hand," Scarlett tells him.

"Obviously not without it turning into an ordeal," Cian says.

"That was Henry's fault!"

"I can and *will* spank your ass, arm cast or not, little witch," he tells her.

"I'm not an invalid."

She mutters it, but I still hear.

"Glinda," Cian says, his voice gentle as he uses his nickname for her. "Let me take care of you. Please. I'll do a good job."

There's a pause, and I imagine they're kissing. And this is exactly why living with them now that they're married could be a problem.

Well, one of the reasons.

"Of course you will," she finally says. She sighs. "Okay. I'll just sit here and watch TV or read."

"Good girl."

There's another pause, and I focus on picking up the jagged pieces of the glass casserole pan, praying that they're not doing *more* than kissing.

"Oh, hey, you don't have to clean that up."

I look up as Cian walks back into the kitchen. I frown as I dump the broken glass into the trashcan. "It's fine."

"I just didn't mean for you to walk in the door and need to start cleaning up." He chuckles. "I didn't mean for there to be things for you to clean up."

"It's what I'm here for," I tell him. Then internally wince. That sounded kind of dickish. I do not just clean up messes for Cian.

I make sure he's safe and happy, yes, but I love being

around him. I love my life with the O'Gradys very much. I've never wanted anything else.

Not until I left my heart in Louisiana.

"You okay?" he asks, studying me from where he's kneeling on the floor, wiping up what looks like rice in some kind of sauce.

"I'm..." I sigh. "Not really," I tell him honestly.

He sits back on his heels. "Ruby?"

"Yeah."

"You weren't able to work things out?"

I look at him, confused. "What do you mean?"

He stretches to his feet, carrying the messy paper towels to the trash. "I thought maybe having some time just the two of you back here in Emerald would help you work through things. Then, when you said you were in Autre together, I was sure you were back together. I'm sorry that didn't happen."

"We...did work through things," I say. "We're madly in love."

He looks surprised, then grins. "That's great! But..." He frowns. "She's staying in New Orleans, though, right? Scarlett told me about law school, that you found her a great apartment, and that she's basically already moved in."

I nod. "Yeah, she starts in the fall."

"So..." Cian gives me a puzzled look.

"So what?"

"So what the fuck are you doing *here*?"

Seriously? I stare at him. "Um, *you're* here. My *job* is here."

Cian laughs. Then sobers when he realizes I'm not joking. "What? Henry... what? You're here instead of with Ruby because of *me*?"

I love this man. I really do. But sometimes I really want to punch him. Like now.

"*Of course*, I'm here because of you. What the hell did you think was going to happen?"

"Well, I thought that you and Ruby were going to get back together and we were all going to live here in Emerald together," Cian admits. "But when I found out Ruby was staying in New Orleans, I assume that meant you weren't back together. But if you are...I expect you to be with her."

My chest feels hot and tight, and I struggle to keep my voice calm. "Instead of with you?"

"Well...yeah." He glances toward the living room. "Henry, fuck..." He looks back at me. "If you feel for Ruby what I feel for Scarlett, then yeah, you should be with her instead of me. Definitely."

"You're not just my best friend," I remind him. "I'm not just here to hang out and shoot the shit and play video games and plan our next vacation. It's my *job* to be with you."

"Are you worried about money?" he asks, clearly surprised by that idea. "Because I'm sure—"

"No," I cut him off. "It's not about money."

It hasn't been about money in a long time. Maybe ever, actually. I didn't take the job for the money. I took the job because it was exciting and because it filled the hole in my heart that my father had carved out when he made me feel at fault for not taking care of two of the most important people in my life.

The money was nice, for sure, but I'd stayed with the job because these people are my family now.

I've invested most of the money the O'Gradys have paid me, and it has grown very nicely over the years. My father's will, surprisingly, left both my brother and me impressive sums and a substantial amount of property in England. Then Alfred had shocked me by leaving me not only an enormous amount of money but also his shares in a few of the companies he'd invested in, including a few of Declan's.

So, I'm doing just fine financially.

I'm not here because of any of that.

I'm here to take care of Cian.

But as I study him now, I can't stop the thought that goes through my mind.

Take care of what, exactly?

No one wants to kill this man. No one wants to hurt him. Kidnap him? Maybe. But if that attempt was made, he knows what to do. He's well-trained in self-defense and highly skilled with a number of weapons. I know because I've trained him myself. He also has a vast network of people to call for any kind of help, of which I am only one person.

Scarlett and Mariah have also been trained in the protocol for what to do if Cian is ever threatened or doesn't show up somewhere he's supposed to. I know that because I did that training as well.

And really, it's always been more about making sure he's happy and supported and empowered than about his physical safety.

And he's clearly all of that. In large part because of Scarlett. And Mariah. And our extended group of family and friends.

That's not just on me, either.

"Then what's it about?" he asks. "Because I'm good. Really good. I'm so fucking happy." He meets my gaze. "Are you?"

I nod. "Yeah. Of course."

"But could you be *happier*?"

This man is like a brother to me. I believe he wants me to be happy. So I nod again, "Yeah, I could be happier."

"In New Orleans, with Ruby," he says.

"Yeah."

"Then you should go, don't you think?"

"I...don't know." I swallow. "This...job." It's always felt strange calling Cian a job. All of this has always been so much more. "This, with you, has been my entire life for so long. The thought of not doing this feels strange."

He grins. "The thought of living in a small town in Ohio and substitute teaching at the high school and being a stepdad to a teenager and being *married*, and..." He glances toward the living room and lowers his voice, "...being responsible and mature and stuff feels strange to me."

I laugh despite everything.

His grin grows and he's clearly pleased that he could make me laugh. "But I'm doing it, and it turns out, just because it feels weird doesn't mean it's bad. It's just new. And you and I have always been up for an adventure."

I look at him for a long moment. He already seems more mature.

"You know what I need?" he asks. "And it is your job to get me what I need, right?" he adds.

I narrow my eyes, but nod. "Yes."

"I need my best friend in the entire world to be happy." His tone is serious now. "I want you to have what Scarlett and I have. If you have even a *chance* of that with Ruby, you have to go to New Orleans."

My heart is now pounding, and I feel pressure in my chest that I swear must be hope trying to grow. "Alfred made me promise to keep you safe and happy."

"He made me promise the same thing about you."

My heart kicks. I shake my head. "What?"

"Yeah. He talked to me when his dementia was getting bad. He told me that he knew you were my bodyguard, but from the beginning, he knew we'd be best friends, and he said that I've been exactly what you needed. He made me promise that I'd always make sure you were safe and happy."

That tightness in my chest isn't just hope now. It's the stabbing pain of loss that I often get when I think of Alfred Olsen, the man who changed my life. The man who *saved* my life. It's also a love that is so intense and so big that I have a hard time taking a breath. Love for Alfred, love for Cian, love for Ruby. Love for the life that's brought all of these people to me.

"Bloody hell," is all I manage as I rub a hand over my face.

"And it's not like I'll never see you. This is Scarlett and Ruby. We're probably going to be coming down there to visit like twice a month. Plus, all the holidays and birthdays and stuff."

"You think so?" I'd love to think I'll see him regularly.

Of course, we can make that happen with some effort. But unlike Jonah, who is married to Linnea, an Olsen and a woman who is very much a part of the royal family, I won't necessarily have the same level of automatic inclusion that he does.

"And it's only two years until Mariah graduates. At that point, we can look at moving. She'll maybe even look at college in New Orleans. She loved living there."

I feel the hope build, pushing out the pain of loss. "You guys would consider moving back?"

"Of course. We're okay here, but we don't need to stay

here in Emerald. Scarlett loved New Orleans and we'd love to be closer to Autre, my sister and Saoirse, and you guys."

Now the hope is big and real. "I guess that's true."

"You didn't think we'd never see each other, did you?" Cian laughs. "Brother, you've literally traveled the world for me. I think it's time you determine where we go for a change, don't you?"

My throat tightens, and I swallow thickly. "Yeah. Okay. I think New Orleans would be great for all of us."

Cian laughs. "This is *so* great! We're going to be married to *sisters*, Henry. Twins. You think you and I can't be apart for long? I give it a week before Scarlett wants to fly down there. And hey," he says as a thought occurs. "We'll be even more like brothers! Did you know that our kids will be half-siblings?"

My eyes widen. "*What?*"

"Seriously. Mariah was telling us about it. If Scarlett and I have a baby and you and Ruby have a baby, those babies will legally be cousins, but genetically, they'll be half-siblings because of the identical twin thing. Isn't that wild?"

I let that sink in. Then I start laughing. "So you and I would be dads to half-siblings." I shake my head. "Why does that seem..."

"Fitting?" Cian asks. "Complicated and kind of hard to explain, but also awesome?"

I nod. "Like so many things about us."

He's smiling as he nods, too. "Exactly. We're family. In all kinds of funny, tangled, perfect ways."

"Alfred never meant for you to sacrifice your happiness, Henry. He loved you, too."

Iris's words from the other day come back to me.

"Alfred wanted everyone to be secure, safe, and fully supported. You're part of 'everyone', Henry. You're part of the family, too. You matter, too."

"You really think you can survive without me?" I ask Cian.

"I think that Scarlett is going to have her hands full," he says with a grin. "But I think she's up for it."

I laugh. "I'm sure she—"

Suddenly, I hear a squeaky grunting noise and look down.

Into the face of a little pig.

An actual, live little pig.

It's looking up at me expectantly and grunts.

I sigh. "You didn't." But I know he did.

I'm not even surprised.

Cian leans over and scoops the animal up. "I told you I was going to. This is Pete."

"I sent you a whole bunch of reasons not to," I say, studying Pete. He is pretty cute. And there appears to be only one of him. For now, anyway.

"No, you sent me a whole bunch of reasons to think it through. Which I did."

Yeah, he's going to get more pigs.

I look from the pig to Cian and back. "You know what?"

"What?"

"I think me going to New Orleans is a great idea."

I do not want to live with a drove of pigs inside the house. Yes, I looked up the word for a group of pigs.

He grins as he nuzzles the pig's side. "You're going to miss me."

I roll my eyes but say, "Yes. But less if you come with pigs. So thank you for that."

He just laughs.

"Good thing you've got a private jet."

Cian nods. "And a good thing *I* can't lose my job."

"Or even quit it, really. You tried after all, and it didn't stick."

"True. Thank God. I think that maybe I'm not so bad at being the spare to the spare heir of Cara."

I clap him on the shoulder. "You're actually doing a fantastic job. At all of it."

And I really mean that as I watch him carry the not-going-to-be-tiny-forever pig into the love of his life who is resting, as ordered, on the couch, then returns to clean up the kitchen, starts a new casserole baking, and then heads upstairs to deal with their laundry.

All I do is put away a few groceries.

And then make a plan for tomorrow.

And then send my boss a text telling her that I'll be relocating to New Orleans and will be available to travel with Cian and Scarlett on trips in the US, but that Jonah should accompany them internationally.

It only takes three minutes for her to reply.

Fine. I assume I still won't be getting security plans for the US trips? Or does being in love make you more responsible?

Me: *I'll send it now. Security plan: provide security, don't let any royals get kidnapped, hurt, or killed.*

I stop, scroll back, delete 'hurt' since, as I've learned, things like car accidents can happen, are difficult to prevent, and can still be...okay.

I send the revised plan.

Iris: <middle finger emoji>

Me: <kissy face emoji>

Iris: *It's all going to be great. I'm happy for you.*

The middle finger, I expected. The nice response still

throws me a little. Iris being more laid-back and happier is going to take some getting used to.

Me: *Still feel like everything is on track? I'm not fucking this up?*

Iris: *It's even more on track. Alfred would be so pleased that you're in love.*

Iris: *Alfred would have really liked Ruby.*

He definitely would have.

Iris: *I'm also really pleased, in case you care.*

She might be surprised to know that I do care.

Iris: *Just be happy, Henry, you deserve it.*

That chokes me up unexpectedly, and I have to think about how to respond. I don't have a glib or sarcastic retort, so I simply ask, *I'm not fired then?*

I prepare for her to say something like *let's just say you're on probation* or something similarly sassy.

Instead, she says, *You can't fire family.*

I take a deep breath.

Fuck, things feel good.

This is all going to work out.

I think about heading back to the airport right now. I could be with Ruby by bedtime. But there are some things at Big Dick's I want to tie up tomorrow before I leave.

I think about texting Ruby and telling her I'm coming back. But I decide I want to surprise her.

Instead I simply send, *I love you.*

She replies quickly. *I love you, too.*

Then I look around. I'm not sure what to do now until tomorrow morning.

Suddenly, I hear squealing from the living room, then Scarlett laughing, then something crashing to the floor, then Scarlett yelling, "Cian!", then footsteps on the stairs.

"Good lord, you all are a lot of work!" my best friend,

Prince of Cara, the 'a lot of work' in my life for the past twelve years, exclaims.

And all I do is grin, cross to the fridge, pull out a soda, then perch on a stool at the breakfast bar to wait for dinner.

I'm not going to do a thing about any of that.

I told him not to get a pig.

CHAPTER 28
HENRY

Bright and early on Monday morning, I walk into Big Dick's with a huge smile.

Then stop short and frown.

What the *hell*?

Christopher is coming toward me.

"What are you—"

But April steps up next to him. "Hey, Henry."

I turn my frown from Christopher to her. "What's going on?"

"It's okay."

"It's not."

"It really is. We're just talking about a plan," she insists.

"I don't like him being here."

"I'm leaving," Christopher says shortly.

"Good. *Don't* come back," I say firmly.

He looks at April.

"I'll talk to him," she assures him.

"You are *not* welcome here," I tell Christopher.

He nods. "I know. I just stopped by because I want to work something out."

"You are *not* going to harass April here. Or anywhere," I add. "But this place is absolutely off limits."

"So I've been told," Christopher says. He glances over his shoulder.

I follow his gaze to the table in the middle of the room where our regulars are sitting. But today there are three newcomers with them.

I know those new guys. Those are three of the men from the coffee shop. The churchgoing, "live right" guys. The ones I invited here.

"I'll think about what you said," April tells Christopher.

"Fine." He nods once, then pushes through the door and leaves.

"What are they doing here?" I ask April, inclining my head toward the table of older men drinking coffee and eating cinnamon rolls.

"They said you invited them here to watch game shows and talk about church."

"I did *not* say they could talk about church." I swear to God, if they brought Christopher here, heads are going to roll.

"All they did was ask Will if he remembers church camp. He said yes, Paul asked if he remembered the verse about just a few people gathering in God's name. Will said yes and that he also knows the one about removing the plank from your own eye before worrying about the speck in someone else's." She shrugs. "I don't really know those verses, but they were all nodding, then shook hands and all sat down together."

That all sounds like some strange religious forgiveness ceremony.

I study the group. They seem happy. They're talking,

even chuckling. As I suspected, there are new stories to be told and new gossip to be shared.

Will, Charles, Ben, and Michael are smiling. Even Dan is there and isn't scowling.

That's good enough for me. "By the way, their cinnamon rolls are free."

She smiles. "They told me that too. *Anyway*," April continues. "Christopher showed up this morning, asking if he can come out here to have lunch with Elliot a few times a week. He found out from the church guys that they're going to be coming here, and he thought maybe I'd agree if they were here to supervise." She points. "Randy—that's the guy in the gray shirt next to Charles—is Christopher's dad's best friend. He said he would personally ensure that Christopher is on his best behavior. Or he said I could choose one of our guys to supervise. Randy also said if I didn't want Chris here, he'd throw him out himself."

I open my mouth to reply, but she's not done.

"Randy said they're not trying to convince me to take him back. They just want Chris to have some time with Elliot a couple of days a week. But they also want Chris to know that his behavior is unacceptable and because of that, he can only see us in public."

I blow out a breath. "I don't like that they're using this opportunity out here to help Christopher get close to Elliot again."

She nods. "I called Cecelia to see what she thought of it."

"You did?" That surprises me. "Not Mandy?"

"Mandy's sweet. Kind. Generous. Cecelia is tougher and no bullshit." April smiles. "They're all amazing, but in different ways."

"What did Cecelia say?"

"That Chris can have lunch with Elliot, but *she* is going to come out and supervise."

I smile. I like that solution.

"But generally, she thought it would be okay," April goes on. "She said it would look good for me to be cooperating as much as I can when we go to court. And she likes the idea that all of these people are watching Christopher, and he knows it. And she was surprised, but happy, to know that the church guys were not just all on Christopher's side. She likes knowing that these men she's known all these years are who she hoped they were."

I look over at the table. The men are all visiting, and there isn't a Bible in sight. The game shows haven't started yet, but these guys showed up anyway. Maybe they really do want to see if some of these relationships can be repaired.

That's what I wanted.

I wanted my guys to see that they're not outcasts.

"Okay. I just don't want them to come in here and take over," I say.

April nods. "Me either. But our people are very protective of this place. I don't think that will happen. And I also heard that there are going to be fewer Live Right sessions in town this week."

"Really?"

"Yeah. These guys aren't having theirs at the coffee shop, and it sounds like they've talked to some other people and they've decided they're sick of it too. I know of at least three that are taking a break this week." April shrugs. "And Cecelia has been talking non-stop about the church and how they were part of turning that big grant down and saying that doesn't sound very much like Jesus to her. She's told her knitting club, her feral cat club, her wine club, and her origami club."

"Cecelia's in a lot of clubs," I comment. She was the perfect choice to bring into my take-down-the-megachurch plan.

"She is." April laughs. "People find her to be...a lot. But you can't help but overhear her and, I don't know, she plants seeds, you know?"

I definitely know.

"Those seem like small things, but it's amazing how just one person can take a little action that starts a ripple that grows, isn't it?" April asks.

Those words hit me harder than she intended, I'm sure.

It is amazing.

Over and over again, I've witnessed one person do seemingly small things that change the course of everything.

"Hey, I need to tell you something," I say.

"Okay."

"I'm moving to New Orleans. With Ruby."

April's face falls. "Oh. When?"

"Today. Tonight. Ruby is already there. I'm leaving this afternoon."

April's eyes fill with tears. "Oh."

"I know you're going to miss her," I say quickly. "But she's going to law school. She's got a huge opportunity to do amazing things. She's going to be so great at that."

April nods. "For sure. That's perfect for her." She takes a shaky breath. "I'm just going to miss this place. And these people. Especially now that all of these things are coming together."

Oh, shit. I handled that badly. "I'm not shutting Dick's down," I tell her. "In fact, I want you to manage it for me."

April frowns. "Wait, what?"

"You know more about this place and these people than I do anyway," I tell her. "I'm going to make you the manager. Full benefits, big raise."

She wipes at her eyes. "Wh—what?"

"You'll be in charge of the day-to-day. In fact, if you want to, we can arrange a situation where part of your benefits is a slow buy-in over time. Eventually you can be a co-owner with me. Or maybe even someday buy me out. Or, if you don't want that and you've got your eyes set on something else, or somewhere else, that's fine too." I hand her the credit card I got in her name a few days ago. This was my plan even before I decided to move to New Orleans. It's ridiculous for her to *not* run the place. "But until then, I want you to run Big Dick's."

April stares down at the credit card. "But..." She looks up at me. "Really?"

"Really. You can do whatever you want. I want to do some expansion and renovation at the back, for the kids, but I'll show you all of that. If you don't like it, we can do something else."

Suddenly, she throws herself at me. I barely have enough time to react to spread my arms before she's hugging me around the waist, her face buried in my chest. "Oh my God!" she exclaims against my shirt. "Oh my *God!*"

I smile and pat her back.

After a few seconds, she pulls back. "Thank you, Henry. I promise I'll do a good job."

"I'm absolutely certain of that."

"Everything okay over here?"

I look over to see Will, Ben, Dan, Michael, and Charles

all watching us. They wear a combination of expressions from curious to protective.

That's exactly how I want them to look about April.

April spins to face them with a huge grin. "Henry just made me the manager of the bar!"

All of their faces relax into smiles.

"Of course he did, honey," Will says.

"Good for you, sweetheart," Ben says.

"Good call," Michael tells me.

"She'll do a good job," Dan says.

I nod. "I know she will. And you guys will be here to help, right?"

"Every day," Charles says.

"Can I ask you to look out for Cian and Scarlett and Mariah too?" I ask them. "Ruby and I are going to be in New Orleans for a couple of years while she goes to law school."

"Good for her," Will exclaims. "That girl is so smart and sassy. She'll be a great lawyer."

I grin and feel a surge of pride. I couldn't agree more. "She'll miss all of you."

Will waves that away. "She knows where to find us. She can come visit any time."

"You tell her she'd better," Ben adds.

"I will. And you'll look out for Cian and Scarlett?"

"Of course," Will says.

They all nod.

I chuckle. "Let me guess, you're first cousins with their late stepdad, right?"

Will laughs. "Nah. We don't have any family connection."

The other men shake their heads.

"We just really like Scarlett. And Ruby," Ben says.

"And Mariah," Dan says.

"And Cian," Michael adds.

Damn, I'm going to have to make their morning coffee free here too.

"Thank you. And I hope you all know that I'm only a phone call away if any of you ever need anything. I'll do whatever I can. And I have a lot of resources."

Will nods. "We appreciate that."

"I thought you said Ruby was already in New Orleans," April says.

"She is. We both were this weekend, but I came back to tie a few things up."

"Uh..." April points to something over my shoulder.

I turn. And my heart skips.

"Ruby?" I start toward her immediately.

She's standing just inside the door.

In flannel pajamas.

The set is light blue with little fat sheep all over them.

"You're wearing flannel pajamas. In August. In a bar," I say as I come to stand directly in front of her.

She nods. "It would have been fine if you'd been at the house in bed like I expected." She lifts her arms out to her sides, then lets them drop. "But I have to tell you, these didn't work worth a crap."

She looks bloody adorable. From the top of her gorgeous head with her hair pulled back in a ponytail to the tips of her toes that are currently hidden by fuzzy light blue slippers.

"What didn't?"

"I was sitting in that gorgeous apartment in a city I love, lonely and sad. So I ordered flannel pajamas. You said those would make me feel better. Comforted." She takes a breath. "But you know what happened when they showed up and I put them on? All they did was make me realize that I screwed up."

"You ordered the wrong ones?" I ask.

God, I love her so much. I know exactly what she's telling me here, but I want to let her say it.

"No. I realized that *you* are my flannel pajamas, Henry."

Okay, I didn't expect her to say it like *that*. My throat tightens and my heart feels like it swells in my chest. "I am?"

She nods. "*You* make me feel better. *You* comfort me. You make me a better person. You lift me up. When you were dropped off at school and could have used pajamas, it's because you had lost what comforted you and you couldn't get it back. When April and Elliot needed pajamas, it was because they had left the comfort of home and what was familiar, and couldn't go back. But then you found "pajamas"," she says, making air quotes with her fingers. "With Alfred, and then the O'Gradys, and then the Landrys. And you helped April and Elliot find "pajamas" by surrounding them with good, happy things, and the community here at Dick's rallied around them." She takes a deep breath and takes a tiny step forward. "The thing is...I don't need to leave what comforts me. I don't need pajamas to make me feel better. Because I have you. I just need to be with you." She takes a breath and blows it out. "And I can be."

She steps forward again until she's directly in front of me and tips her head back to meet my gaze. "I can be with you, so why would I *choose* to not be?"

I lift a hand and cup her face. "Because of law school. Because you want to do more. Because you *should* do more."

She shakes her head. "I want to be a lawyer so I can help people. I can get my law degree at Ohio State and help people. It's ridiculous to think I need to be in New Orleans."

"But—" I start.

She keeps going. "What am I trying to prove? That I *can* do it? Of course I can do it. I know that. You know that. Everyone who knows me knows I can do it. That I can be on my own? Sure, okay. What's that prove? I'm so fucking lucky to have so many people to love and who love me. Why do I want to be on my own?" She reaches up and grasps my wrist. "I don't want to be away from you. We can have it all...the jobs that matter to us and the people that matter to us and each other. I'm not going to give that up."

"Okay, that's it," I say.

I bend, cup her ass with both hands and pick her up. She wraps her arms and legs around me and buries her face in my neck.

I turn with her in my arms and realize we have an audience.

"We need a minute," I tell them.

I stride toward the small room behind the bar that's used as an office. I kick the door shut behind us, and sink into the office chair, with her legs straddling my thighs. I grasp both her thighs, squeezing gently.

"Okay, let's talk," I tell her.

She hugs me again, then pulls back. She smiles at me and lifts a hand to my cheek. "There's nothing more to talk about. I love you, Henry. I just want to be with you wherever you are."

"I love you too. And I just want to be with you. I was on my way to the airport from here. I said goodbye to Cian, Scarlett, and Mariah last night. I was going to be with you tonight." I squeeze her thighs. "For good."

She stares at me. "Really? For...good?"

"Do you really think you can get rid of me now?"

She smiles. "God, I hope not." She suddenly flings her arms around my neck again. "Oh God, Henry! I love you!" She pulls back just as suddenly. "But I'm not going to make you leave Cian."

"Well, we can stay here if you really want to but..."

She arches her brows. "But?"

"I think we're going to be bored here."

She laughs in surprise. "What?"

I nod, my grin growing. "We did too good of a job. They're all fine. They're taking care of each other. They don't need us."

She seems to think that over. "Oh. Well, that's good. But we could stay here and just... relax?"

I snort. She grins.

We are not the type to relax. Not for longer than maybe a week on a gorgeous private beach somewhere.

"We could," I say. "Or we could go to a new city and find some new people who need us."

Her eyes get a little shiny, but she nods. "Yeah. We could do that."

"I think we *should* do that."

"That sounds really good."

"Let's go to our new apartment, Gem. Right now. I want to fuck you in every single one of those rooms *tonight*."

I feel the little shiver that goes through her.

"Okay."

"Come on. Let's go get your stuff and leave. My bags are already in my car, and the plane is on standby."

"My stuff?" she asks.

"Your suitcase."

She spreads her arms. "I didn't bring a suitcase."

"What?" I laugh.

"I called Jonah and asked if he could get me here. He said yes, he could get me a charter, but I had to get to the airport right away. So I called Sammy and he came to get me. It was super early this morning. You know I'm not a morning person. I just got in the car and then got on the plane."

I love that she knew she could call Jonah. I love that he made this happen. I love that Jonah didn't tell me that she'd called him for help. Then again, it had to have been around three in the morning. "You went to the airport in your pajamas?" I asked.

"It's a private plane," she says with a shrug. "And I was coming straight to the house to see you." She laughs. "I didn't think I'd be in public."

"This bar with those people out there isn't really public."

She smiles at that.

I run my hands over the soft flannel. "I like them."

"They're cute," she agrees. "But they're really hot. I mean temperature hot. I'm sweating."

I laugh. This woman always makes me happy, lighter, better. "Let's go." I stretch to my feet and let her slide down my body. "I'll help you out of those pajamas on the plane."

"I don't know if that will help me cool off." She grins up at me. "I'm not wearing panties underneath them."

"Let's go say goodbye to your sister and niece," I say, practically dragging her out of the office.

"I thought you already said goodbye to them."

"I did. But don't you need to?"

She shakes her head. "They don't even know I'm here. I didn't see them. They were still asleep when I snuck into the house to find you, and I snuck back out when I realized where you were."

I stop and look at her. "You really want to just leave town? Not see Scarlett and Cian? Just leave them on their own?"

She grins. "Kind of? What about you?"

I think about it. Then nod. "Yeah. They'll be fine."

"I agree."

We stand just looking at each other. Then we look out at the bar.

Everyone is sitting around the tables, drinking coffee. The game shows have started, and no one is paying us any attention.

April is laughing with the ladies at the end of the bar.

I do not want to have to say goodbye to Elliot. I plan to send him cool postcards from New Orleans, including some with jets and old planes from the World War II Museum. He'll love that, and we can talk about them when I come back and visit him.

"We'll see them all later," Ruby finally says.

I smile. "Of course we will. They're our family."

"Exactly. And I know a guy with access to a private plane, so traveling back and forth is no big deal."

"He sounds amazing."

"He is. Best brother-in-law I've ever had."

She giggles as I sweep her up into my arms with a growl and stride for the door. "Shhh," I tell her. "They might notice us and need something."

"We wouldn't want that," she whispers with a softer giggle.

And, for the first time in either of our lives, we actually do sneak off without telling anyone where we're going or how to get ahold of us for the next several hours.

I even fuck her on the plane and in half the rooms of our new house before we turn our phones back on.

Which is a mistake that keeps me from fucking her in *every* room.

Still, we're both happy when we snuggle on our new sofa and look out at the view of New Orleans from our new apartment windows, with the AC turned way up so Ruby can wear her new pajamas, and answer dozens of texts and emails to all the other people we love most in the world, together.

EPILOGUE
RUBY

Six months later...

"I can't believe I was wrong about him being a criminal, though," Henry tells Iris.

I'm sitting in an armchair along the wall in his gym, waiting for him to finish up so we can grab dinner before going home.

On Fridays, I often get done early with class and go to a study group, but tonight, my group can't meet, so Henry wants to take me out to a romantic dinner.

We haven't had a nice dinner out, just the two of us, in months.

Law school is amazing but often feels all-consuming, and we, of course, have lots of things going on when we do have free time. We're in Autre a lot, and then, there are our roommates, the friend of the sister of one of my class-mates, and a young guy Henry met through one of the trainees he's working with. They both had very rocky childhoods, are no-contact with their parents, and are now enrolled in college thanks to a personal scholarship from

Henry Dean. They both need mentoring for sure, but they're doing great.

"Well, at least there's that," Henry tells Iris over the phone. "Thanks for letting me know." He pauses. "Okay, talk to you later."

He disconnects and sighs.

"They still haven't found anything my dad's been doing that's illegal?" I ask.

"No. That's simply impossible to believe," he says.

Henry and Cian would both love to see my father sitting in a prison cell. I'm just happy that his church is slowly failing.

"Attendance at church is down fifty percent, though," he says. "And contributions are down sixty-two percent. The youth group is also down to about ten kids."

I nod. "I actually like that better. It's one thing for people to turn their back on him if he's an actual criminal, but somehow it's kind of sweeter that they all just realize he's not a good guy and leave him because of that."

Henry drops into the chair next to me. "I guess."

I laugh. "Sorry my biological father isn't a hardened criminal."

Henry looks over at me and grins. "Me too."

He looks so good. He's been working out with Tabitha, Kai, and Sera, the new young adults who've been recruited as bodyguards into the O'Grady-Olsen circle.

He's training Tabby and Kai to accompany Mariah to college, and Sera will eventually be assigned to Saoirse. Saoirse will probably have at least one other as well, but Sera showed such promise that Iris, Miles, and Henry agreed they needed to bring her in early.

Tabby and Sera live in New Orleans full-time right now, but Kai only travels in on occasion. He's already been training as a bodyguard for about two years and spends most of his time in Emerald as an 'exchange student' from Hawaii. That helps explain why he's living there and going to school but has no parents with him. He keeps an eye on Mariah and also checks up on Cian and Scarlett whenever Henry needs a report.

"What time is our reservation?" I ask, sliding into Henry's lap, straddling his thighs, and slipping my hands into his hair.

He's a little sweaty, he hasn't shaved in about a week, and he's wearing athletic shorts and a black tank that stretches over his broad chest and flat stomach.

He looks so hot. I wiggle on his lap and feel the hard shaft of his cock between my legs.

He's also been teaching me self-defense whenever we have a chance and that gets *very* hot.

"Maybe we could have a session?" I say, pressing closer and rubbing against his erection.

He grasps my hips and holds me still. "As much as I'd love to have a session, fuck you on these mats, and then just order pizza like we did last time, we haven't been out on a really nice date where we can linger over dinner, and I can treat you and pamper you in a very long time."

He leans in and runs his stubbled jaw along my jaw, down my neck, and over my collarbone, making goosebumps break out everywhere.

"The money is just building up in my bank account. I don't know what to do."

I laugh. "Oh, no. I know how you get when you can't throw it around on ridiculous things."

He chuckles and the vibration against my neck causes my nipples to tighten.

"Let me pamper you tonight, Gem," he says huskily. "I'll

fuck you hard and sweaty and dirty another time." He nips my neck. "Lots of other times."

I tip my head back so he can kiss and lick and nip his way to the other side. "Well, gee, okay."

He squeezes my hips. "That's my girl."

"But you *will* fuck me tonight, right? Maybe slow and sweet? And dirty?" I already know the answer.

"If you're a good girl at dinner."

"And that entails…" I ask with an eyebrow up.

"Well, for one thing, when I slide my hand up your leg and beneath your skirt under the tablecloth, there better not be any panties in my way."

I moan. "That can be arranged."

"And—" He's cut off by his phone ringing. He sighs. "Hold that thought."

He reaches into his bag and withdraws his phone.

I see Cian's name on the screen.

"Hey," Henry answers, hitting the button to put Cian on speaker.

"Hey! We're ten minutes from your place!"

Henry stiffens, and our gazes meet. Our plans are about to get derailed.

"You're in New Orleans?" he asks.

"Yeah, we're on our way back to Ohio from the community opening in Dallas and thought we'd stop in. Surprise!"

Yes, Cian and my sister still manage to drop in even though they live a thousand miles away.

It's been a month since we've seen them. I text Scarlett every day, and we talk at least three times a week, but my schedule is crazy with school, and it's hard to connect more than that. She understands, of course, and is super supportive, so it's all fine. We do send selfies and photos and memes all the time. We text about the podcast after every episode. I made sure to send her a photo of the amazing muffuletta sandwich I had the other day—her favorite—and she and Mariah send photos of Pete the Pig almost daily. He's getting huge.

But we haven't *seen* them in a while. We miss them, of course, but time goes fast in-between visits. We're busy. They're busy. And they are doing so great.

What should I do? Henry mouths.

My phone dings with a text. I look at it.

Scarlett: *Hey! We're in town!! <heart eye emoji>*

Oh, man.

I don't know, I mouth to Henry.

"Hey, Cian, hang on. I'm at the gym. Just finished up a session with the kids. Give me a minute." He mutes the call. "Gem, we haven't had a lot of time, just you and me. I really want that tonight," he says.

I nod. "Me too."

"So..."

"So... we send Cian and Scarlett to Autre tonight and we see them tomorrow."

"Exactly what I was thinking."

That's fine. We shouldn't feel guilty about that. They'll love seeing everyone in Autre and we'll have the whole day tomorrow, maybe the whole weekend, together.

"Oh, I do have to study Sunday night, though," I say.

"We'll kick them out if they're not heading out by two," he says.

"Okay."

Henry unmutes the call, and I text my sister.

"Sorry about that," he tells Cian. "So, we've got plans tonight and won't be back until late. Do you think we can meet up with you in Autre tomorrow?"

Me: *Hey! I'm so excited to see you! We've got stuff going on tonight, but can we meet you in Autre tomorrow?*

"Oh, yeah," Cian says. "Sure. We should know better than to pop in. You guys are busy." He chuckles. "I'm *still* getting used to you not dropping everything for me every time."

Henry laughs. "I know."

Cian chuckles too. "Okay, okay. I'll go hang out with my sister and other people who love me and will be so excited to see me."

"And we'll be down there for breakfast," Henry says.

"Okay, see you then."

Scarlett: *Okay! I have BIG news and I want to tell you in person! But... don't blame me if other people get to hear it first...*

I gasp and show Henry the message. "She's the worst."

He shakes his head. "She's never going to tell other people something *really* big before she tells you. You're *you*."

I take a breath and blow it out. "Okay. You're right. Probably."

He kisses me, then says, "We can go to Autre tonight if you need to."

I shake my head. "No, I want to go on our date." I kiss him, making sure he feels my sincerity. I pull back. "Honestly. They're fine. They don't need us to rearrange everything when they waltz into town unexpectedly."

"Exactly." Henry nudges me off his lap, and we both stand. "Let's go get ready. Our reservation is at eight."

We walk out to the car, hand in hand. I'm looking forward to the evening. We haven't dressed up and gone out somewhere really nice in forever.

But I can't stop wondering what Scarlett's news is.

No, that's not true. My twin connection is tingling, and I think I know what it is.

"Ruby?"

I look up at Henry. He's got the car door open and is waiting for me to get in.

"Will that work?"

"Will what work?" I ask. Obviously, I missed his question.

"Can you get ready in time if I move the reservation up to seven?"

"Yes, but why would you do that?"

He grins. "Because I know you're going to be itching to go to Autre. We can have dinner and head down there tonight."

"But our evening…"

He leans in, brushes a kiss against my cheek, and then says in my ear, "I think we both know that I can do all the things I want to do to you tonight in the bed in Autre as easily as I can here."

That's very true.

"Are you sure that's okay?" I ask.

"You're already worrying about her news," he says with a smile.

"Well, if she blurts out that she's pregnant to someone before she tells me, I'm going to be so disappointed!"

Henry looks like I just told him Scarlett and Cian are actually aliens in human suits. "Wait. She's *pregnant*?"

"I'm ninety percent sure."

He's clearly stunned. "Cian…is going to be a dad?"

"He's already a dad to Mariah."

"Well, yes, but she was already…Mariah. He didn't start from scratch with her."

I laugh. "True."

It all seems to sink in, and Henry slowly smiles. It's a

smile full of love and pride. "Wow. They're going to be amazing parents."

I nod. "And we get to be an aunt and uncle. Again."

"That's awesome."

He looks so happy. I press my lips together, then say, "You know, I'm really proud of us putting ourselves first and going out tonight before seeing them and not just turning our plans upside down for them the way we both have for so many years."

He nods. "Yeah. That's good. It's important that we recognize that we're just as important, and our lives can be separate from theirs."

I nod. "Definitely. We're the main characters in our story."

"For sure."

We both pause.

Then we say, "But..." at the same time.

I grin. "We could go to Autre tonight and see them. That doesn't mean we're putting them first all the time. We have definitely put ourselves and our new life and our relationship at the center. But we love them. And there's something big going on. And we miss them. And that's all totally fine."

He leans over and kisses me deeply. "You are and always will be the most important person in my life, Gem."

"I know. And same."

"I know."

And an hour later, we're in Ellie's bar, celebrating that Scarlett and Cian are, indeed, expecting a baby.

Scarlett pulled me to the side to tell me before they announced it to the entire group, and I immediately burst into tears. Happy tears. It was so different from the last time she told me she was pregnant.

Most importantly, this time, she has an incredible amount of support and love around her.

I love that she gets to have this experience again, this time full of positivity and celebration. I could not be happier.

Henry hugs me against his side as we watch Cian and Scarlett shining at the center of one of our many beloved communities.

"You know what?" Henry asks.

"What?"

"We are really fucking good at this."

"This?"

He looks down at me. "Loving people."

I smile up at the best man I've ever met. "We really are."

"And I want to do it with you forever."

"Me too."

"So will you marry me?"

I pivot out from under his arm so quickly he nearly stumbles. I turn to face him. "Did you just propose to me?"

"I did."

"At Cian and Scarlett's pregnancy announcement?"

"Yes. Because that's *their* main focus. But *we* are *our* main focus. And I love you and want to marry you and I didn't want to wait to ask you any longer."

I think about that and...yes. Yes, to all of that.

"It doesn't take anything away from their moment," he says. "This is just between you and me right now. But I want you to be my wife, and this place and this moment felt like the right time to ask you."

It really does.

The two people we loved and took care of for so many years are now going to become the ultimate caregivers themselves.

They're so ready for it.

And the master of over-the-top and going overboard just casually proposed in the middle of this happy, wholesome, almost quiet—relatively—moment because it felt right.

"Yes," I say. "I will absolutely marry you, Henry."

His smile is wide and bright, and it makes my heart so full.

"I love you," he says as he lowers his head and kisses me deeply.

When he lifts his head, I look around. We've talked to everyone, hugged everyone, heard the amazing news, and told Cian and Scarlett how happy and proud we are.

And anyway, we'll see them all for breakfast.

They don't need us anymore tonight.

"Let's get out of here," I say, taking his hand and starting toward the door.

"Uh…" But he looks around and clearly comes to the same conclusion. He nods. "Yeah. We're done here."

"Well, for tonight," I say as we step out of Ellie's and start for the car.

"Right. Just done for tonight."

"Right." I stop by the car and take a deep, contented breath.

Henry and I will never be completely done taking care of people.

"By the way," he says as he opens the car door for me. "I'm going to be putting about fifty-thousand dollars in the charity account."

My mouth drops open. "*What*? Why?"

"Because I'm marrying my dream girl," he says. "A woman who is way too good for me but said yes anyway. So

I'm going to go *way* overboard on the ring, the wedding, the honeymoon...all of it."

I grin. "I don't need a big, gaudy, crazy ring."

"Too late," he says, and pulls something out of his pocket.

A big, *gorgeous*, crazy ring. That he's obviously been carrying around.

He slips it onto my finger, then lifts it to his lips and kisses it. "I'm going over the top for this. For us. Deal with it."

And dammit, what am I supposed to do? We've all heard of Prince Charming, but no one prepared me for Prince Charming's hot, bossy bodyguard with a heart of gold.

There's no resisting that.

So I just say, "Fifty-thousand or an amount equal to what we spend on the wedding, whichever is greater."

He leans in and growls. "I expect you to make it worth every penny."

I grin and say, "Ditto."

And I have no doubt everything will surpass my wildest dreams.

Thank you so much for reading *Recklessly Rogue!*
I hope you loved Henry and Ruby's story!

Declan, Astrid, Iris, and Miles are all coming soon!
Visit here if you want to get in on some gossip about them
from the podcast!

erinnicholas.com/wait-till-i-tell-ye-episode-908

And the best place to find out all the news about that (including title and cover reveal, release date, and more!) is right here:
bit.ly/Keep-In-Touch-Erin
(be sure you get those capital letters and dashes in there!)

And this is your personal invitation to my Facebook group, **Erin Nicholas's Super Fans** where you can get first looks, behind the scenes peeks, and daily fun with fellow romance lovers (including me!)!

Acknowledgments

Huge thank you to my team who is *always* there for me,
always says 'you can do this' and 'how can I help?' and 'yes
of course I'm available', and then always gives me your
best.
I don't know what I'd do without you, and honestly, I don't
plan on finding out!
Lindsey, Jen, Fedora, and Clare, you're the best.
xoxox

CONNECTED BOOKS FROM ERIN NICHOLAS

All of these can be read as stand-alones, even though they are part of interconnected series! Jump in anywhere and enjoy!

Want to know more about Torin's sister Fiona, his brother Cian, and their bodyguards, including Henry and Colin?

Check out **Kiss My Giraffe** (a grumpy-sunshine, princess-in-hiding, small town rom com!) and **Better Safe Than Safari** (a bodyguard-rockstar, curvy-girl, steamy rom com)**!**

Find all of these and so much more at www.ErinNicholas.com!

About Erin

Erin Nicholas is the New York Times and USA Today bestselling author of over sixty sexy contemporary romances. She's known for her blue-collar book boyfriends and big, boisterous found families in small towns. Her stories have been described as toe-curling, enchanting, steamy and fun. She loves to write about reluctant heroes, imperfect heroines and happily ever afters.

She lives in the Midwest with her husband who only wants to read the sex scenes in her books, her kids who will never read the sex scenes in her books, and family and friends who say they're shocked by the sex scenes in her books (yeah, right!).

Find her and all her books at
www.ErinNicholas.com

And find her on Facebook, BookBub, and Instagram!

Editor: Lindsey Faber

Cover design: Qamber Designs

Digital ISBN: 978-0-9973662-5-9

Paperback ISBN: 979-8-9908220-6-1

Special Edition ISBN: 978-1-952280-84-9